P9-DHJ-820

Praise for the novels of *New York Times* bestselling author
Erica Spindler

THE FIRST WIFE

"[A] heated romantic thriller . . . strong personalities make
for some wonderfully tense revelations."

—*Publishers Weekly*

"Spindler hooks readers into her latest . . . the mystery is
engaging." —*RT Book Reviews*

JUSTICE FOR SARA

"A spine-tingling romantic thriller . . . Spindler keeps the
reader guessing until the last page." —*Publishers Weekly*

"Spindler's chilling novels explore our deepest fear—that
danger is closer than we think. She is a master of addic-
tive suspense." —*New York Times* bestselling
author Lisa Gardner

WATCH ME DIE

"Guaranteed to chill your blood and set your teeth on
edge." —#1 *New York Times* bestselling author Lisa Jackson

"A gripping thriller [with] numerous twists and turns until
the startling conclusion." —*Publishers Weekly*

BLOOD VINES

"*Blood Vines* is as mysterious and delicious as a fine cabernet . . . TOP-NOTCH SUSPENSE."
—*New York Times* bestselling author Linda Castillo

"A fast-paced, intense story that's hard to put down."
—*RT Book Reviews* (4 stars)

BREAKNECK

"A gripping story that unfolds with breakneck speed, heart-quickening suspense, and characters you can't help but root for."
—Bookreporter.com

"Filled with well-developed, multidimensional characters, Spindler's latest boasts fast-paced action and emotional tension. . . . The intricately woven plot makes this novel a sure winner for readers who like to keep guessing all the way to the end."
—*RT Book Reviews* (Top Pick!)

Also by Erica Spindler

THE OTHER GIRL

ERICA SPINDLER

St. Martin's Paperbacks

NOTE: If you purchased this book without a cover you should be aware that this book is stolen property. It was reported as "unsold and destroyed" to the publisher, and neither the author nor the publisher has received any payment for this "stripped book."

This is a work of fiction. All of the characters, organizations, and events portrayed in this novel are either products of the author's imagination or are used fictitiously.

THE OTHER GIRL

Copyright © 2017 by Erica Spindler.

All rights reserved.

For information address St. Martin's Press, 175 Fifth Avenue, New York, NY 10010.

ISBN: 978-1-250-19105-2

Our books may be purchased in bulk for promotional, educational, or business use. Please contact your local bookseller or the Macmillan Corporate and Premium Sales Department at 1-800-221-7945, ext. 5442, or by e-mail at MacmillanSpecialMarkets@macmillan.com.

Printed in the United States of America

St. Martin's Press hardcover edition / August 2017
St. Martin's Paperbacks edition / October 2018

St. Martin's Paperbacks are published by St. Martin's Press, 175 Fifth Avenue, New York, NY 10010.

10 9 8 7 6 5 4 3 2 1

For my guys,
For being the men you are.
And loving me for who I am.

ACKNOWLEDGMENTS

Thanks to all of those who helped bring *The Other Girl* to life: my publisher, St. Martin's Press, and editor, Jennifer Weis; my agent, Scott Miller; friend and assistant, Peg Campos; writing retreat gal pals Hailey North and Robin Wells; and for once again sharing his immense knowledge, Captain George Bonnett, St. Tammany Parish Sheriff's Office.

And most of all, thanks to my family, for the support and unending love.

PROLOGUE

June 2002
Jasper, Louisiana

Jasper, Louisiana, in July was as hot as hell and as close as a tick on a retriever. But school was out for the summer, and as far as Randi Rader was concerned, that made up for it—and pretty much everything else, too. As far as she was concerned, school was a total waste of time.

"I'm goin' out!" she called from the double-wide's open screen door. Not waiting for a response, she darted into the buggy night. She ducked out of sight between two trailers as her mother's voice pierced the night.

"Damnation, girl, you get back here! Like, right now!"

Randi angled right, heading for the path that led to a shortcut to the main road. Her brothers had said they'd pick her up by the power station at eight sharp, warning her they wouldn't wait. Her brothers, she knew, meant it. If she were one minute late, she'd have to find herself another ride.

She checked her watch. It was gonna be tight, and she picked up her pace. The spot came into view; a truck was waiting. But not her brother's. A bright red, Ford F-150.

Only one truck like it in Jasper. Belonged to Billy

Boman, a friend of her brothers. She sidled up to the driver's side. He leaned his head out. "Hi'ya, sweet thing."

"Hey, Billy-Bo," she said, flashing him her best flirty smile. "What you doin' here?"

"Waiting on you."

"Me?"

"Your brothers told me to come pick you up."

Figured. But she asked anyway. "Why didn't they come?"

"You know Wes and Robby, they always got something going on. You gonna hop in, or what?"

Billy-Bo was irritating but harmless. She supposed the thing that turned her off about him was the way he sweated—a lot and all the time, no matter the weather.

She felt kind of sorry for him, 'cause he couldn't help it. She'd heard a couple teachers talking about it; they said it was a glandular problem.

Randi had big brown eyes and she knew how to angle them, just so, to get a reaction out of a guy, and she practiced on Billy-Bo. "I don't know if I should?"

"Aww, come on. I've got a cooler full of Dixie long necks. Maybe you want to party?"

"Sounds like a good time. Coming around, Billy."

Randi climbed in and he handed her a beer. "Opener's in the console," he said, pulling onto the road, spitting up gravel as he did. She reached for the opener and saw that wasn't the only thing stashed in there—he had a baggie of weed, not much but enough to get the both of them good and high.

This night was looking better and better. Randi popped the cap and took a long swallow; the ice-cold brew slid down her throat and she shivered.

"How you doin' tonight?" she asked.

"Can't complain. It's Saturday night."

"Hell yeah, it is."

"How about some tunes?" he asked and turned on the radio.

Toby Keith's new song roared through the speakers, and she sang along between swallows of beer.

Billy-Bo cut her an amused glance. "Robby told me you got into some trouble recently."

She drained her first beer and reached for another, then popped off the cap. "Yeah, asshole cops caught me drinking and raised all kinds of hell." She snorted. "Threatened to get me sent off to juvie."

"That blows."

"No shit. Mama's all over me like white on rice. I'm under—" she made quotation marks with her fingers, spilling some beer on her shirt in the process "—house arrest."

"So how'd you get out tonight?"

"Waited until Mama got in the bath. Besides, what's she gonna do, call the cops on me? I don't think so."

"Suppose not." He took a swallow of his beer. "Heard your daddy's back in jail."

She stiffened. Good ol' boy "Pops" Rader had gone on another bender and gotten himself incarcerated. Again.

"Yeah," she snapped. "What about it?"

"Not a thing, sugar. Just makin' conversation."

"Well, I don't want to talk about him or anything else that sucks." She downed her second beer, stuck the empty in the cooler, and grabbed another.

He eyed her. "Maybe you want to slow down?"

"Hell, no!" She raised her arms and hooted. "I like to go fast!"

He laughed and depressed the accelerator; the truck surged forward. Away from Jasper. Away from the crappy double-wide on the wrong side of the tracks, her beaten-down mother, and all those folks who thought they knew everything.

Randi took another long draw on the beer. Far, far away . . . that's where she wanted to go. Someplace nobody looked at her *that* way again. Like she was trash, a no-good girl from a no-good family and going nowhere damn fast.

California, she thought. Yes, ma'am, that's where she'd go, the minute she got the chance.

Another one of her favorite songs came on and she cranked it up and began to sing, loudly and off-key. The miles passed and the brew worked its magic. Lightheaded, she leaned her head against the seat back and gazed at the summer sky.

The music turned from rockin' to mellow, and Billy-Bo pulled onto a side road and stopped the truck. He cut the engine, but left the radio on. The mood in the truck's cab changed, and Randi figured she knew what was coming next.

She was right.

"Why're you way over there?" He patted the seat beside him. "Come on over, sweet thing."

Billy-Bo didn't do a thing for her but she *was* drinking his beer and riding in his truck, so she supposed she owed him a few kisses . . . maybe even a little tongue; it wouldn't kill her.

Randi slid across the bench seat and he started in, straight up. Pressing her back into the seat, mouth open, tongue writhing. He didn't taste too bad, she told herself, like a combination of Dixie and Juicy Fruit. She played along, acting like she was into it.

Until he stuck his hand under her shirt. At first she tried to be subtle, moving this way or that, letting him know without words she didn't want that, but he didn't get the message.

She grabbed his hand, and attempted move it. "Stop, Billy-Bo."

"Aw, baby, don't say that. You know you like it."

"No, I—"

"Don't be such a cocktease."

When she tugged on his hand again, he shoved his other up the leg of her short-shorts, finding her panties.

She jerked. "No, stop! Don't—"

"C'mon, Randi, you've been fucking since you were twelve."

Is that what he thought? She was too shocked to respond. She'd gone to third base this last year, but only that once.

He jammed his hand farther up and she felt his fingers pushing at her panties, then sinking into her. "I knew you liked it," he said against her ear, pressing her back against the seat, breath hot against her neck. "You're all ready for me, aren't you?"

It felt like he was trying to swallow her face with his mouth. His tongue lapped at hers and his giant hands were like lobster claws pinching at her breast and vulva.

His weight was suffocating. Panic rose up in her. She couldn't breathe, couldn't fight. Tears welled in her eyes. This wasn't right. She didn't want . . . her first time, like this? With Billy Boman forcing himself? He'd tell everyone they did it . . . that she'd liked it. That she begged for more.

Hell, no, it wasn't going down that way. "Stop," she managed again. "I'm gonna be sick, Billy-Bo! I can't breathe. I think I'm gonna throw up!"

He was off her in a flash. As she scooted over the open console, she had an idea. "Don't look!" she cried bringing her hand to her mouth.

He jerked his face the other way. "Just don't puke in my truck!"

Randi grabbed the bag of weed, threw the cab door open and leapt out. She slammed the door behind her, ran to the side of the road, but instead of throwing up, she spun to face him.

"No means no, you big, sweaty jerk!"

Surprise registered on his face, then fury. "What . . . you were faking it?"

"Not the part about being disgusted by you. But the part about being sick? Yeah, faking that."

He turned red. "You think you're so smart? How you going to get home, cocktease? Huh? Maybe you should have thought of that!"

She flipped him the bird. "Screw you, Billy Boman! You better watch out, my brothers are gonna kick your ass for this!"

He laughed and started up the F-150. "Stupid little bitch! Why d'you think they had me pick you up?"

"Liar!" she shouted as he drove away. She bent and scooped up a handful of gravel and hurled it after the truck. "Asshole!"

It wasn't until his taillights disappeared from sight that she realized he'd had a point. How was she going to get home now? No phone. No flashlight. And she didn't even know where the hell she was.

It didn't matter, she decided, starting to walk. She had his pot and he was gonna be so pissed when he realized it. She smiled and patted her shorts pocket. And anything was better than trapped in that truck being pawed by that freak.

Well, maybe not anything, she thought thirty minutes later. It was hot and buggy, and walking in her flimsy flip-flops was damn near impossible.

When headlights came around the curve up ahead, she jumped up and down, waving her arms.

Please stop . . . please . . . please . . .

For a moment, she thought they were going to fly on by her. Then the brake lights lit up and the car pulled to a stop at the side of the road.

Randi ran up to the car. The driver lowered his window; the smell of pot rushed over her in a cloud.

A young guy in a University of Alabama baseball cap. A girl riding shotgun.

"Need a ride?" the guy asked.

"Sure do."

"Your car break down?" the girl asked.

"I was riding around with one of my brothers' friends and he kicked me out, told me to walk home."

The driver tugged his ball cap a little lower. "Now why'd he go and do something like that?"

Billy's words—cocktease—played in her head. These two were obviously older and more experienced. The last thing she wanted was them thinking of her as a stupid little virgin. "We just had a disagreement over something, that's all."

"Where're you trying to get to?"

"Home. Jasper."

"Well, we'll be heading that way later," he said. "Right now we're heading to a spot I know to have ourselves a party. Want to join us?"

Randi looked at the other girl and she smiled. "The more the merrier."

"Hell yeah, I would."

"Hop on in, then."

Randi didn't have to be asked a second time. She yanked open the door and climbed in.

CHAPTER ONE

Harmony PD Detective Miranda Rader parked behind the two cruisers already at the scene. Their flashing blue lights violated the otherwise still, spring night, bouncing off the trees and surrounding homes, spinning and tilting like a carnival midway on crack.

She closed her eyes and for a moment she was fifteen again. Police lights bouncing off the trees. This knot in the pit of her gut, this sense that nothing was going to be the same, not ever again.

She let out a pent-up breath and flexed her fingers on the steering wheel. *Shake it off, Miranda. Focus.*

She grabbed the ponytail holder she kept in the car's front cubby and gathered up her shoulder-length brown hair. She couldn't work with her hair in her face and she sure as hell didn't want to leave any behind. She popped a piece of peppermint gum in her mouth and climbed out of her vehicle.

Victim was Richard Stark, an English professor at ULH, and even more important, the university president's son. In a college town like Harmony, that was as close to royalty as you could get.

Miranda breathed deeply, her gaze on the brick two-story and the crime-scene tape stretched across its entrance like a clown's freakish grin, beckoning: *Don't be afraid. . . . Come inside, see what thrills await.*

Miranda slammed the car door and started up the walk. Gerald LaRoux, fresh out of the academy, manned the door. Judging by his greenish pallor, this was young LaRoux's first murder.

He straightened as she approached. "Detective Rader," he said and held out the log.

She signed in, then met his eyes. "How're you doin' tonight, LaRoux?"

"Hangin' in there, Detective." He handed her Tyvek booties. "Chief said you'd need these."

That meant blood, blood spatter, or other biological evidence. No wonder LaRoux was green around the gills. "It'll get better," she said. "You get used to it."

"Yes, ma'am. That's what they say."

She took the booties. "Cap's with the vic?"

"Yeah. Master bedroom. Through the great room and to the right."

The chief met her at the bedroom door. Buddy Cadwell, a fireplug of a man, broad and thick but short, filled the doorway despite his lack of height. He exuded confidence and sheer strength of will.

So it had to be the lighting, because Miranda could have sworn the thirty-year veteran of the force looked shaken.

"What've we got?" she asked, bending to slip on the booties.

He cleared his throat. "Stark was stabbed several times in the chest, his throat was slit, and he was—"

He bit it back. She glanced up from the booties. "And what?"

He hesitated, as if searching for the right word. "Let's call it dismembered."

It took her a moment to find her voice. "You've got to be kidding me."

"That's all I'm going to say. I want to get your take, unvarnished."

"Gotcha." She fitted on her gloves. "What about Jake?" she asked, referring to her partner, Jake Billings. "Is he on his way?"

Buddy shook his head. "Just you and me for now."

"You and me?" She cocked an eyebrow. "What's up?"

"Jake has ties to the university community, because of his parents being professors. I think it's best if you and I handle the initial investigation."

She hesitated a moment, still finding it odd that he'd be here instead of one of the other detectives.

As if reading her thoughts, he added, "Ian Stark and I have known each other for a long time. I thought it should be me here first, as a courtesy."

He moved aside and she stepped into the room. The vic lay face up on the bed, naked and spread-eagled, hands and feet tied to the bed rails. As Buddy had described, Stark had been stabbed multiple times; the blood spatter decorating the floor and walls would have done abstract expressionist Jackson Pollack proud. And, as a sort of cherry on the top of this blood-fest sundae, the perp had cut off Stark's penis and stuffed it into his mouth.

It peeked out at her like some one-eyed alien creature and her stomach lurched to her throat. She forced the queasiness back. Getting weak-kneed was a luxury she couldn't afford. It wasn't just that she was a woman in a man's field, needing to prove herself every single day. It went deeper than that, to the essence of who she wanted to be, the person she had crafted her life around:

solid and dependable, good under pressure and cool in a crisis.

The person everyone trusted.

She focused, took in the scene; really took it in. The blood—on the ceiling, walls, and bedding. Stark's gaping throat, like an obscene second mouth.

Another wave of nausea threatened her and she forcefully tamped it back. This was a homicide, just like the many she'd worked before. Hell, just last week old Mrs. Tyson had whacked old Mr. Tyson on the head with an iron skillet. She hadn't meant to kill him, she'd tearfully told Miranda, she just couldn't take his criticism anymore. All it had taken was forty-two years of complaining and a chicken-fried steak dinner to cause a sweet old lady to snap.

That Miranda understood. But this bizarro kink-kill? No way. She stopped beside the bed. So, what had precipitated this perp's breaking point? Now, *that* was a question she could focus on.

Her gaze settled on the neckties that had been used to bind his wrists and ankles. Silk, from the look of them. Looked expensive. And judging by the bright splashes of color and bold patterns, Stark hadn't been the typical buttoned-down English professor. A peacock, she thought.

Miranda shifted her attention slightly. A sailor's knot. She bent, studied the knot. It was good and tight; the perp had known what he or she was doing. And Stark had struggled to get free. Raw skin on his wrists—and ankles, she saw a moment later—where the fabric had rubbed as he fought.

Miranda straightened. Most probably a woman, although they couldn't eliminate a man until they knew Stark's sexual orientation. Crime of passion. Enacted in a frenzy.

Problem. Miranda drew her eyebrows together. *Something missing.*

She moved her gaze over the scene again, slowly, absorbing. The passion in the crime, she realized. The frenzy in the frenzied act.

She looked toward the doorway, and Buddy waiting. "Where are the footprints? Whoever did this would've been dripping blood. Where's the trail?"

He nodded. "You tell me."

"This perp was mighty pissed off. No doubt it was personal. But being passionate about killing someone doesn't make a crime of passion."

"Go on."

"Our perp's a sailor. This is a bowline knot. Well executed, I might add," she said as the chief crossed to stand beside her. "The beauty with this knot: the harder Stark struggled, the tighter the knot became. He couldn't have escaped even if he'd managed to get, say, a hand free. This baby is impossible to undo when there's tension on it."

"Where'd you learn about sailing knots, Rader?"

"Old boyfriend. From my couple years in New Orleans." Another time in her life that she preferred to leave in the past. "My thinking is, if your bondage game's just for fun, a less serious knot will do. I'm going to call this strike one against the crime-of-passion scenario."

"With you so far," he said.

She motioned to the bed. "This is a king. Stark's in the middle. He's stabbed in the chest, his throat is slit. Perp's got to be on top of him."

Buddy agreed. "That'd be a long reach from the side of the bed, and even if our unsub could, the angle's wrong."

"Pattern of blood spatter seems to bear that out," she

said, pointing. "Bet the angle of the wounds will as well." She motioned to the vic again. "So, she's straddling him, all nice and cozy."

"Right. Naked."

"Undoubtedly."

"So, where was the knife?" he asked.

"She hid it beforehand. Maybe in her purse or with her clothes. She ties him up, nice and tight, then goes and gets it. He goes from hot and bothered to begging for his life."

Buddy pursed his lips. "Like you said, she's mighty pissed off. She wants him to be scared, to beg for his life, or cry like a little girl. That's part of the satisfaction for her."

"Strike two."

"Which brings us back to the footprints," he said.

"Exactly. So she does the deed, climbs off him, and heads to the bathroom to shower off the blood."

"And there, her clean clothes are waiting, no doubt neatly folded."

"Right. But she cleans up before she dresses." Miranda smiled grimly, visualizing the crime being carried out. "She's thorough, takes her time. It's the middle of the night and she's not worried about being interrupted."

Miranda made her way to the master bathroom, Buddy behind her. The bath was large and luxuriously appointed. The walk-in shower was big enough for two—or even three—people. Party central. On the floor in the corner nearest the door sat a heap of bloodied bath towels. On the counter by the sink stood a bottle of spray cleaner with bleach.

"Look at the bottle," Miranda said. "It's all but sparkling. She wiped everything."

"One problem—the towels. Why didn't she take them?"

"She didn't take *those* towels. My guess is the towel she dried herself with is long gone." Miranda crossed to the shower, peered in. "Quite the little housekeeper. I can see practically see myself in the fixtures, they're so shiny."

She looked over her shoulder at Buddy. "This was no crime of passion, Chief. It was a premeditated, thoroughly planned murder."

"Strike three," he murmured, the corners of his mouth lifting, the way a parent's would at a child's achievement. "We'll get her. No way she didn't leave something behind. A hair, a drop of blood, saliva. A missed fingerprint. No matter how careful she tried to be, trace gets left behind."

"What's next?" Miranda asked.

"You're lead on this. Billings assists. You good with that?"

"Why wouldn't I be?"

"Call him in now. And as much as I hate to admit it, this scene is way bigger than the HPD can handle. We're gonna need the Parish's crime-scene unit for the biological and trace collection."

She'd already come to the same conclusion. "You want to call?" she asked. "Or should I?"

"You do it," he said. "I want a report as soon as you and Jake wrap up here."

CHAPTER TWO

4:15 A.M.

Jake arrived moments after the crime-scene van. Miranda finished directing the evidence-collection techs and went to the door to meet him. "Billings," she said. "Welcome to the party."

He bent to fit on his booties. "I'd say thanks for the invite but I was in the middle of a pretty amazing dream."

"Sorry I screwed up your good time."

"Want to hear about it?" He glanced up at her, laughter in his eyes, "I'm happy to share. You may be surprised."

"It's a little early in the morning to plunder the depths of your perversions."

He straightened. "Heart. Broken. You're a coldhearted woman, Rader. Just sayin'."

She rolled her eyes. "Yeah, I've heard that before."

His warm brown eyes crinkled at the corners. "I'll bet."

"LaRoux said Chief Cadwell was here earlier."

She motioned him to follow her. "Yup."

"That's weird."

She looked over her shoulder at him. "Not so much. Victim's Richard Stark."

"You know him?"

"Nope. You?"

"Met him through my folks. Seemed like a good guy but not someone I'd hang with."

"Why's that?"

"Seemed like he was his favorite subject."

"Gotcha." She stopped at the door to Stark's study. "We called in the parish techs to collect biological and trace evidence. They just got started."

"I saw that. Doesn't seem like a call you or the chief would make. What's up?"

"Vic's in the master. Take a peek, then ask me that question."

She watched him head off, then turned to Stark's cluttered desk. Organized chaos; obviously, Stark spent a considerable amount of time here. Open laptop. What looked to be a manuscript in process. Notes and notebooks, papers being graded. Half-full can of Red Bull.

She flipped through the stack of mail; nothing of note jumped out and she moved on to the computer. She tapped the return button; the device sprang to life. He'd been on Facebook. The page of a woman named Rhonda Peale. Miranda checked her profile: she was a fellow professor at the university.

Jake returned. "I could've lived my whole life without seeing that. For a moment I thought I was going to puke."

She looked up at him. "You are a bit green."

"Poor bastard."

"Right. So why did our perp think he deserved that? That's what I want to know. Come take a look at this."

He crossed to stand behind her.

She indicated the monitor. "Time stamp suggests Stark was here at his desk, cruising around Facebook at midnight. Last thing he looked at was this profile."

"Attractive woman."

"Yes. And guess what—she's a psychology professor here at ULH."

"Abnormal psych, by any chance?"

"Funny." Miranda clicked on Stark's messages. "Bingo. He contacted her just before midnight. 'Free tonight,'" she read, "'Come on over.' Looks like we've got ourselves a suspect."

"Could be, but she didn't reply. Wouldn't she have?"

Miranda frowned in thought. "Maybe she saw the message and called him."

"Maybe. What if she wasn't the only woman he messaged last night?"

"Good point." She scrolled through. Messages were almost all to—and from—women. Girls, a lot of them. University students—asking about a lesson, complimenting him on a lecture. Some obviously flirting, but to his credit he kept his responses professional.

"The guy was obviously a player," she said, "but nope, the lovely professor's the only one. Via Facebook, anyway."

"It's a start. Have you collected his phone?"

"Haven't even seen it but haven't searched. Bedroom is my guess."

He made a face. "Lucky me. You going to finish with the desk?"

"Yeah," she said, turning back to it, carefully sliding open the desk's center drawer. "Keep me posted."

Pens. A pack of teeth-whitening gum, two thumb drives, a pad of Post-it notes, and several receipts, all from favorite hot spots around town. She bagged and labeled the items she felt could prove useful, then moved to the side drawers.

The first contained hanging files, each neatly labeled. Class schedules. Research. Expenses. Taxes. She stopped on the last. Passwords. That would come in handy, she thought.

She went to the opposite drawers. The top contained a mishmash of office supplies and, tucked way into the far corner, a bag of weed and a pipe. Recreational, obviously, and nothing to be killed over.

She moved on to the bottom drawer. Used yellow legal tablets, a dozen of them. She slipped out the first, thumbed through it. Notes, research for the novel he was writing. Character outlines.

Miranda flipped forward, skimming, and stopped on a character profile.

Ava Strong. Math teacher by day. Dominatrix by night.

Interesting, considering the way Stark's real-life story ended. She turned the pages. It seemed to be an intersecting story novel, each new character a client of Ava's. She wondered at the story's ending—would one of the clients end up dead?

"No phone."

Miranda looked over her shoulder at Jake. "Perp must have taken it." She indicated the legal pads. "Stark was writing a novel. Guess what the main character was? A dominatrix."

"Interesting. In a really creepy way."

She nodded. "I thought so, too."

"Research gone bad, maybe?"

"It's a possibility." She turned back to the legal tablets. "I'm going to bag them all. If nothing else, it'll be entertaining reading."

As she lifted them out, a yellowed news clipping fluttered to the floor. She retrieved it and her heart stopped. It was a short piece, not even a half a column, from the *Harmony Gazette*. About a teenager who'd sent the police on a wild-goose chase in an attempt to divert the authorities from her own infractions—possession of an illegal substance and underage drinking. The sixteen-year-old was charged in juvenile court and sentenced to six months in juvenile detention.

Not sixteen, Miranda thought. They got that wrong. Fifteen and scared out of her wits.

"What's up?"

Jake, she realized. Looking at her from across the room, eyebrows drawn together in question.

"Nothing."

"You made a sound."

Headlights slicing across the dark road. Pinning her.

He motioned toward the news page. "What's that you're reading?"

She glanced at it, then back up at him, meeting his gaze evenly. "An article about an out-of-control teenage girl. Someone I knew."

CHAPTER THREE

That night in June
2002

A horrible sound. High and shrill. Then . . . nothing. A devastating silence, as if whatever had cried out for its life had been forcibly silenced.

Randi moaned, eyes fluttering open. A foreign landscape of towering shadows. Another sound, a rhythmic *slap . . . slap . . . slap . . .*

The darkness overcame her once more.

Something. Biting her. Many somethings. Or pins poking and pricking. Her arms and legs, her back, head, and neck. Randi moaned and shifted. A sound followed. A crackling, like the crunch of dry leaves in the fall.

Her eyes popped open. Not in her small bedroom in the double-wide, not curled up in her narrow bed. Where?

She blinked and focused on the darkness. Trees. Lots of them. Underbrush, something rustling there.

She was on the ground. The smell of pine straw and rotting vegetation stung her nose. She whimpered. How'd she get here? She'd been in Billy-Bo's F-150 . . . no, walking. She'd hitched a ride. The guy in the 'Bama ball cap . . . the other girl—

Randi became aware of another sound. A broken

mewl, like a fretting baby. What was a baby doing out here?

Not a baby. The other girl. Randi searched her foggy brain for the girl's name. Carly? No . . . Cassie or—

Something dropped from a branch above her, landed on her arm, and scurried. With a cry she went to swat it away—and found that she couldn't.

Her wrists were bound.

So were her ankles.

Momentary disbelief was quickly followed by panic. Randi fought against the binding, but no matter how she tugged and twisted it didn't loosen. Her wrists and ankles burned, her head throbbed, and she flopped back, tears leaking from the corners of her eyes.

The soft sobbing from nearby had stopped. Randi craned her head in the direction from which it had come. "Are you there?"

"Yes."

"Where . . . is . . . he?" Her voice shook so badly, she could hardly get the words out.

"Gone. He went for food."

"Let me go," Randi begged. "Please come untie me."

Her request brought silence. It seemed to stretch on forever. When the other girl finally spoke, it was so softly Randi had to struggle to make out what she was saying.

"You think I . . . I'm tied up, too!" Her voice rose. "He raped me. He held me down and he—"

She started to cry, not softly. Wracking sounds of despair and hopelessness.

The sounds she'd heard earlier, Randi realized, the contents of her stomach lurching to her throat. She rolled as best she could onto her side and vomited. She retched until it felt her diaphragm might split clean apart.

"You're lucky," the other girl said. "That's why he didn't touch you. You did that earlier, too."

"I don't remember," Randi whispered, voice choked with tears. "What are we going to do?"

"We've got to try to get free." The other girl paused, the moment of silence foreboding. "He's coming back."

Coming back.

Randi's blood ran cold at the thought.

"Randi?"

"What?"

"Maybe you can get loose?"

"I can't. I tried."

"Stay calm . . . deep breath—"

Randi did as she suggested, sucking in one deep breath, then another.

"Are your hands behind your back?"

"No, in front."

"Look at the binding. What is it?"

Randi lifted her arms. "Tape. The wide kind. Clear."

"Tape," the other girl repeated, sounding surprised. "He used rope on me. Maybe you can break it?"

Using all her strength, Randi tried tugging her wrists apart. "I can't break it! It's seems like it only makes it— wait, I've got an idea. Maybe I can tear it with my teeth."

"Try it, Randi. Hurry! He'll be back soon."

For several minutes she tried without luck, gnawing at the edges of the tape, trying to find a vulnerable spot. Finally, at the point where her wrists were joined, she found one. Using her tongue and teeth, she worked it until it began to give, ripping millimeter by agonizing millimeter.

Her hands were free. Tears running down her cheeks, she frantically tore at the tape around her ankles.

With a cry she scrambled to her feet, hurrying to the

other girl. She reached her and started on her ropes, freezing at the sound of tires on the gravel road. Headlights, cutting across the trees.

"Don't stop! Hurry, before he gets back!

Randi tugged on the knot at the other girl's wrists, hands shaking so badly she couldn't control them.

"I can't loosen it."

"Keep trying! You can do it, you—"

The slam of a car door. The crinkle of a take-out bag. "He's coming. I've got to go."

"No! Don't leave me! Please—"

"I'll get help." Randi straightened, took a step away. "I promise—"

He was whistling some light, happy tune. It was getting louder. She took another step. "I have to get help. It's the only way. I'm sorry . . ."

"You can't leave me." Her voice rose. "No . . . no—"

Randi backed away, tears streaming down her face. "I'll get help. I promise."

With one last glance back, she turned and ran.

CHAPTER FOUR

They'd finished processing the scene and Miranda and Jake sat on the hoods of their cars, parked side by side at Irma's Coffee, Cakes & More. The "more" included breakfast sandwiches to die for. Or to die from, considering they consisted of egg, bacon, and cheese, all piled on a buttermilk biscuit.

"You want to talk about it?" Jake asked, then took a bite of his sandwich.

"About what?"

"About what you've not been talking about for the past couple of hours. Ever since I asked you about the news clipping."

She looked at him. "Oh, sure, now you go and get perceptive."

He laughed and took another bite. She followed suit, using the time to assemble her thoughts. She decided on the direct, short and sweet approach.

"That article was about me. I was that out-of-control teenager."

He snorted. "Did not see that coming. So much for perceptive."

"I was arrested for possession and sent to juvie for six months."

"Possession of pot? That seems harsh."

"Wasn't my first brush with the law. There'd been the shoplifting episodes, the drinking, the truancy. Oh, and let us not forget the defacing of public property."

"Let me guess, graffiti?"

"Yup."

"I'm surprised they didn't give you life."

He sounded so amused. He didn't get it. He couldn't. "You didn't grow up here. You didn't live in a trailer on the wrong side of the tracks or have a daddy who was a habitual loser and two older brothers following his example." She met his gaze. "Of course they threw the book at me, Jake. That's what the law does to folks like me."

He shook his head. "That's not who you are, Miranda."

"Not anymore." She turned her gaze to the horizon. "I was mad when I got sent away. And bitter. Real bitter."

"What about your mom?"

"I was more trouble than I was worth to her. Truth was, I think she was happy to see me go."

"I'm sorry. That does pretty much suck."

She stuffed the last of her sandwich into the paper bag it came in and slid off the hood of the car. "I'm glad it happened. It forced me to think about where I was going and what I wanted out of life."

For a moment he didn't respond, just stared at the horizon. "How long have we been partners, Rader?"

"A couple years. Why?"

"Two and a half," he corrected. "And we're friends?"

"We are."

"And you trust me?" She nodded and he went on. "So why haven't you mentioned any of this before today?"

She crossed to the trash and dropped in the bag. "It's complicated."

"No it's not. We're friends, you trust me. Or we're not and you don't."

"It's not about you or our partnership, Jake. It's about me. That girl I told you about—she doesn't exist anymore. I left her behind."

"You left her behind?" he repeated. "How do you do that?"

"You just do."

"You can't run away from your past. It always catches up to you."

She cocked an eyebrow. "Isn't that a bit too philosophical for your pay grade, Billings? Besides, I didn't run away from my past. I just moved on."

"Okay." He climbed off the car, tossed his trash in the receptacle. "Got a question."

"Shoot."

"Why'd Stark have that clipping?"

It was a good question. One that was nagging at her. "I'm wondering that myself, Billings. It's got to be a coincidence, but it just doesn't feel right."

CHAPTER FIVE

Chief Cadwell looked anxious. He didn't smile as he waved them in, didn't share his usual good ol' boy anecdotes or laid-back, small town pleasantries.

Life in Harmony was different this morning.

He folded his hands on the desk in front of him. "You have an update?"

"Better than that," Miranda said. "We've got a lead on a possible suspect. Around midnight, Stark messaged a woman on Facebook and invited her to come over."

Jake jumped in. "She's a fellow ULH professor. Name is—" he looked at his notes "—Rhonda Peale."

"Hot damn," Buddy said, thumping his fist on his desk. "That's what I wanted to hear."

"We're going to question her as soon as we notify Stark's family."

"Already done. Did it myself."

Miranda couldn't hide her surprise. "Without me or Jake?"

"Considering Ian Stark's contribution to this community, I thought it should come from me. Alone."

She understood. Although the two weren't close

friends, as two of Harmony's most influential men they shared a kind of bond of responsibility to the community and each other.

"They were devastated." His voice shook slightly. "It was one of the hardest things I've ever had to do."

"We'll still need to talk to them," she said softly.

"I told them you would," he went on. "Of course, they assured me that they would do everything in their power to help find their boy's killer."

Miranda glanced at Jake. "I say we interview Rhonda Peale as soon as possible."

"Agreed."

She turned back to Buddy. "This could be a case of a woman with an ax to grind. From what I saw online, Stark was quite the player."

Chief Cadwell's gaze seemed to sharpen. "Anything there that's going to make the university look bad in the press?"

"From what I saw online, no. But we've only begun digging."

"President Stark was quite anxious to protect the school's reputation. Keep me apprised of everything you uncover, and I mean *everything*."

Miranda found it odd that Richard Stark's father was so concerned with the school's image at a time like this, but maybe that went with the job. "Looks like Stark was writing a novel," she said. "Found notebooks with characters and plot points in a desk drawer."

"Main character's a dominatrix," Jake offered. "Maybe he was doing a little research when he got himself whacked. It'd explain the kinky situation we found him in."

The chief retrieved a roll of antacids from his desk

drawer and popped a couple into his mouth. "You got his phone?"

"Not at the scene," Miranda replied. "Which means either he didn't have one or our perp took it—the most probable explanation."

Cadwell agreed. "Let's get subpoena paperwork to Judge Jackson. I want Stark's call logs and text records ASAP."

She looked at Jake. "You want to get it started? I need to speak to the chief privately."

Jake frowned slightly but started for the door. "I'm on it."

Miranda watched him go, then turned back to her boss. "One last thing. In Stark's desk, I found an old newspaper clipping. From that summer."

He knew exactly what summer she was talking about. It'd been his first year as HPD chief; he had been involved.

He sank back to his chair. "What the hell?"

"That's pretty much the way I felt."

"Why'd Stark have it?"

"I have no idea."

"Did you know him?"

"No."

"Your families, did they—"

"God, no."

He frowned. "Had you ever met him?"

"Not that I recall. It's got to be some strange coincidence. I don't know why else he'd have it. I collected it for the sake of transparency."

"You're sure you never met him?"

"Positive."

"And this won't interfere with the investigation in any way?"

She held his gaze. "Why would it?"

"Good. Thanks for bringing it to my attention." He waved her toward the door. "The press is going to be all over this—and us. I want something solid to share with them as soon as possible."

CHAPTER SIX

9:00 A.M.

Rhonda Peale lived in a charming bungalow in the university area. Small, with a wide front porch and gabled roof, this house—like the others in this neighborhood—reflected the style of the post–World War II housing boom.

Miranda parked in the driveway, directly behind a compact white SUV. She and Jake climbed out, slamming their doors in unison and falling into step together. They crossed the porch and rang the bell.

And attractive dark-haired woman answered the door. Miranda held up her shield. "Professor Peale?"

"Yes?"

"Police. Harmony PD. We need to ask you a few questions. May we come in?"

"What kind of questions?"

"Do you know Richard Stark?"

"I do."

"How are you two acquainted?"

"We're both professors over at the university. But I suspect you already knew that. What's this about?"

Jake stepped in. "So, your relationship with Richard Stark is strictly professional?"

She hesitated a moment, then shook her head. "We've gone out a few times."

"A few times," Miranda repeated. "You weren't a couple?"

"Definitely not." She drew her dramatically arched eyebrows together. "Again, what's this about?"

"Where were you last night?"

"Here. Grading—" She bit off the last, frowned, and moved her gaze between them. "Has something happened to Rich?"

"He's dead," Jake said softly.

For a split second she stared blankly at him, then turned and walked into the house.

Miranda and Jake followed her, closing the door behind them.

They found her in her living room, slumped on the couch, face in her hands.

"Professor Peale," Miranda said quietly, "can I get you something? Or call someone?"

She shook her head, but didn't look up. When she finally did, her eyes were wet. Miranda wondered if the tears were real or if she had covered her face to have the time to manufacture them.

"Do his parents know?" she asked.

Odd first question, Miranda thought. "Yes."

"How did he . . . what happened?"

"He was murdered."

Her already pale face became ashen. "That's not . . . possible."

"Why not, Professor Peale?"

"Everybody loved him."

"Did they?"

"Yes. His students . . . the other faculty."

"Especially women," Jake said. "Isn't that right?"

She looked at him, gaze sharpening. "Everyone liked him, including women."

"He have any enemies that you know of?"

"No." She shook her head, said it again. "No."

"What about a recent breakup?"

"Not that I know of."

"He mention any relationship that had gone bad, a crazy ex-girlfriend or anything like that?"

"No, not that I—" She bit back the last and frowned, moving her gaze between them. "You think a woman may have killed him?"

"Actually, we *know* a woman killed him," Jake said.

Miranda stepped in. "Where did you say you were last night?"

"I was here. Grading papers . . ." Her words trailed off, her eyes turned glassy. "If I'd . . . maybe . . ."

"If you what?" Jake prodded.

She looked away. "If I'd gone to see him, maybe he'd still be . . . you know, alive."

Miranda wasn't convinced. "We know he invited you over. Why didn't you go?"

"How did you—of course, Facebook. That's why you're here." She brought a hand to her mouth; Miranda saw that it trembled. "I wasn't about to run over there like some besotted teenager. So I didn't answer."

"But you saw the message?"

"Yes." She cleared her throat. "I posted grades at one. Or a little after."

"Was it unusual for him to contact you that way?"

"He usually calls or texts."

"And you usually go?"

She looked at her lap. "Yes."

"Why not last night?"

Without lifting her gaze, she shook her head.

"You said you didn't want to look like a besotted teenager. What did you mean by that?"

"Isn't it obvious?"

"I don't like to put words into other people's mouths, Professor Peale."

"I have some pride. And I'm not desperate."

"You're a beautiful woman," Jake said. "Obviously smart and accomplished. Why would he think of you as desperate for taking him up on his offer?"

She looked at them. "Because I knew I wasn't the only woman he makes those kind of offers to."

Miranda worked to hide her excitement. Rhonda Peale had opportunity and now, admitted motive. "He cheated on you?"

She laughed, the sound tight. "How can it be cheating if there's no commitment to begin with?"

"Is that what he told you?"

"Yes." She curved her arms around her middle. "And then he messages me that he's free. Bastard."

"You were in love with him."

"I didn't say that."

"But you were," Miranda coaxed. "Handsome, charming, smart, seems to me it'd be hard not to fall in love with him."

"He seemed perfect," she said, voice small and vulnerable. "Until that night when I realized—"

She bit it back. Miranda pressed her. "When you realized what?"

She hesitated a moment, then said simply, "That he wasn't."

Jake stepped in again. "Before last night, when was the last time you saw Richard?"

"Sunday night. I surprised him by stopping by."

Miranda glanced at Jake and could see he was

thinking the same thing as she. "He was with someone else, wasn't he?"

Color flooded her cheeks. "Yes. I was completely humiliated."

"Who was he with?"

"I don't know. I didn't see her." Her voice thickened and she cleared her throat. "I didn't get past the front door."

"I'm sorry that happened to you," Jake said. "You didn't deserve that."

Her eyes flooded with tears. "No, I didn't."

"That's when he gave you the commitment speech," Miranda said. "Am I right?"

She nodded. "Yes."

"Was there a vehicle you didn't recognize in the driveway or out front?"

Peale thought a moment then shook her head. "I parked in the drive. And I didn't take note of other vehicles." She stood. "Do you mind if we cut this short, detectives? I'm not feeling so well."

"Of course not." Miranda got to her feet; Jake followed. "One last question. Were you aware that Richard Stark was writing a novel?"

"Of course. He talked about it often."

"You know what it was about?"

Her mouth thinned. "A dominatrix and the lives of her clients."

"Are you into that sort of thing, Professor Peale?"

"Excuse me? What could that possibly have to do with—" She stopped short, eyes widening. "You're not saying—"

"It was just a question."

"No," she said stiffly, "I'm not."

"Was he?"

"A novel is fiction, detectives. Make-believe."

"I'm aware," Miranda said lightly. "But that doesn't answer my question."

"No, as far as I know, he wasn't. And certainly with me he wasn't."

She walked them to the door.

When they reached it, Jake handed her a card. "My number's on there. Call me or Detective Rader if you think of anything else."

She agreed she would and they stepped out into the burgeoning day.

Miranda stopped her. "One more thing, Professor. You asked if we'd told Richard's parents. In fact, it was your first question. Why?"

Her face went blank; she looked at Jake. "I did?"

"Yeah," he agreed, "you did."

"I don't know," she said.

"You must have had a reason," Miranda went on. "You must admit, it's a little odd, learning your boyfriend's been murdered and the very first thing out of your mouth is a question about his parents."

Peale reached up and nervously smoothed her hair. "They were very close. Rich and his parents, I mean."

"Closer than parents and their grown children usually are?"

"I don't know." Her voice rose slightly. "Why does it matter? Obviously they didn't kill him!"

"Of course they didn't," Miranda said softly. "Thank you for your time, Professor."

CHAPTER SEVEN

9:50 A.M.

Neither Miranda nor Jake spoke until after they'd buckled in and she'd started the car. Miranda pulled away from the curb. "What do you think? Is she our perp?"

"She fits the profile. They were lovers, she caught him cheating. And they communicated right before the murder."

"And no alibi."

"Right." He angled in his seat to look at her. "But?"

Miranda eased to a stop at the sign, then rolled through. "But it can't be that easy."

"Why not? I like easy."

"I do, too, but—" She thought a moment. "It doesn't feel like an easy one. There's something more going on here than a pissed-off girlfriend. Too much . . . fury there."

He snorted. "I dated one of those fatal-attraction types."

"No kidding?"

"When I was living in Austin. I met her in the library—"

"You're making this up."

He laughed. "I'm not, honest. Before it was all over,

she'd keyed my car, conned her way into my apartment when I wasn't there, slashed my clothes and her wrists. Not enough to actually kill herself, just enough to smear blood over everything."

Miranda turned onto University Avenue. "Tasty."

"We'd dated three weeks. All that craziness for a guy she'd known three weeks."

"How'd it end?"

"She was arrested, charged, and found guilty. Turned out I wasn't the first guy she'd done that to." He fell silent a moment. "So all that fury doesn't have to be bigger than one woman with a psychological disorder."

Miranda nodded. "You're right, it could be our lovely and very normal-seeming Professor Peale. By the way, what did your girlfriend get?"

"Three months, time served. Court-ordered psychiatric evaluation and treatment. And I got a restraining order."

"Smart move, Billings." She turned onto President's Drive. "Let's do some background work on Peale, see if any boyfriend issues pop up. And a database search might turn up some possibles as well."

Miranda pulled to a stop in front of the university president's residence, a large, southern-style home, incongruous with the university's original Art Deco buildings. Miranda and Jake climbed out of the car and headed up the azalea-lined walk.

Ian Stark opened the door before they rang the bell. Miranda had expected some outward sign of grief; instead, he looked furious. Wordlessly, he moved aside so they could enter.

Miranda stepped into the large foyer. Directly ahead stood an ornate table decorated with a spray of fresh flowers. The arrangement included lilies, she noted. She couldn't stand the smell of them. A chandelier hung over the table; to the right a curved staircase led up to what was, no doubt, an equally over-the-top second level.

"President Stark," Jake said, "we're so very sorry for your loss."

"We are, too," he said gruffly and motioned they should follow him.

He led them to a sunny parlor where Catherine Stark waited. She sat erect, hair perfectly coiffed, pearls in place, ankles neatly crossed. Like a figure from a wax museum, frozen in time. Even so, despair emanated from her in waves. She was a woman whose world had crumbled out from under her.

"Mrs. Stark," Miranda said, "our deepest condolences. I can't even imagine how difficult this must be for you."

"No," she whispered, "you can't."

"We promise we'll do our best to find your son's killer."

The woman opened her mouth to respond, but her husband cut her off. "I'm sure you will," he said. "But what I want is your promise of an arrest."

She held his gaze. "I can't promise that. However, I can promise we will move heaven and earth to find your son's killer."

That seemed to mollify him. "Let's sit. I want to hear what you have so far."

Miranda took a seat on the couch. She noted several framed photographs on the side table to her left. An adorable little boy was pictured in each; no doubt a very young Richard Stark. She wondered why there were no photos of him as a teen or young man.

Instead of sitting himself, Ian Stark went to stand behind his wife, hands on her shoulders. He looked at

Jake. "We've met before. You're Theo and Sarah's youngest, yes?"

"I am."

"The university lost two talented academicians when they retired. How are they?"

"Very well. Enjoying retirement more than I thought they would."

"I'm glad to know you're on our team. I understand you have a suspect. Tell me about her."

"Excuse me, President Stark," Miranda said. "How did you know we had a suspect?"

He glanced at her almost dismissively. "Buddy called. Is she in custody?"

Miranda worked to hide her shock. Buddy called and shared information of an ongoing investigation? With the victim's family? What the hell?

"Buddy told us Rich was murdered . . . in the act. We can't allow those details to get out. How would that look? It'd be all anyone could talk about."

Catherine Stark whimpered. Miranda saw Stark squeeze her shoulders, but whether in reassurance or warning, she didn't know. Either way, Miranda was having a hard time feeling sympathetic for the man. So she kept her gaze on Mrs. Stark.

"We're not here to discuss our investigation with you, President Stark. I'm sorry if you got that idea. We're here to see if you might know something that would lead us to your son's killer.

"The woman we questioned communicated with your son via social media shortly before his death. At this time, we have nothing else to link her to the crime, but that may change."

"What's her name?"

"I'm sorry, we can't divulge that information.

However, if an arrest becomes imminent, you won't be taken by surprise."

Color flooded his face. "You know who I am, obviously?"

"Yes," she said softly. "I know who you are and how important you are. But I also know homicide investigations, and the less you know, the better. Sharing too much about the investigation jeopardizes it."

He frowned slightly, as if wanting to argue, then shook his head. "How can I help you?"

"Did your son do a lot of dating?"

"He was handsome, single, and successful. He liked women and they liked him."

"Which doesn't really answer my question, President Stark."

"Define *a lot*."

Jake jumped in. "Was there anyone he was serious with?"

"Not that we knew of."

"Ever? A bitter breakup? A past engagement?"

"No." Catherine lifted her head. "I longed for a grandchild but he . . . wasn't ready. Now I'll never—" She choked the rest back, eyes flooding with fresh tears. "Forgive me . . . I just . . . I can't—"

"You shouldn't have to," Miranda said softly. "This is an awful situation, one no mother should have to face."

Jake stepped in. "Tell us about your son."

She looked helplessly up at her husband. He nodded and began, "We were very proud of him." He paused, as if collecting his thoughts. "Richard could have gone anywhere—he had offers from other schools, but he came back to Harmony. He was beloved by the students, absolutely adored." Stark looked at Jake. "And the fellow faculty respected him. You know that's true."

Jake inclined his head. "My parents spoke highly of him, that I do know."

Stark looked back at her in challenge. "Everyone liked him, Detective. Everyone."

"Obviously not everyone, President Stark. His murder was an act of hatred and rage."

"A freak did this. Buddy told me—" his voice shook "—what she did. How she . . . disfigured him. She'd have to be some sort of . . . aberration."

"We're working that angle," Jake said. "It's extremely viable."

Miranda shot Jake a warning glance and took over. "We certainly understand your feelings, President Stark. But you have to know, this wasn't a random crime. And it was personal."

"Of course it was personal!" He stared her down. "But that doesn't mean she wasn't a psychopath!"

"Ian—" Catherine reached up and covered his hands with hers.

At her touch, he seemed to deflate. As if all the bluster that had held him up just . . . evaporated.

He suddenly looked old. And defeated.

"Ask anyone," he said, voice raspy. "Go over to campus. Go to city hall. Everyone will say the same thing. He was a great guy and an outstanding man."

"I'm sure he was," Jake said softly and stood, sending her a warning glance. He handed Stark his card. "If you think of anything . . . anyone we should question, call me."

Stark stared at the card a moment, then looked back up at Jake. "There's a vigil tonight. Ask anyone. He was . . . beloved."

CHAPTER EIGHT

4:20 P.M.

The young woman sitting across from her had a broad, earnest-looking face. Her blue eyes were bloodshot from crying, and she clenched a sodden tissue in her right hand.

She'd been one of Richard Stark's creative writing students. The head of the English department had given Miranda and Jake a list of Stark's students' names. The list was long, so they'd decided to divide it, with her questioning the females and he the males. Luckily, the department head had also arranged with the students to meet them here in the humanities building, and had provided an empty classroom for them each to conduct interviews.

"Ashley," Miranda said softly, coaxing, "tell me about Professor Stark."

"Tell you about him?"

"Yes."

Tears flooded her eyes. "He was . . . awesome."

Miranda made a note of her response. "How so?"

"He cared about his students . . . in a way most of the instructors don't."

"Could you give me an example, Ashley?"

She nodded. "He recognized something in my

writing and encouraged me. He—" She paused a moment as if to compile her thoughts. "—offered real guidance. Like he was able to put his finger on just what my work needed to make it better."

"You're a senior, right?" She nodded. "Did Professor Stark ever act inappropriately toward you?"

"What? No!" She shook her head and her curly hair bounced against her shoulders. "Never."

"To any other female student?"

Her cheeks flooded with color. "No. Why are you asking me this? He's dead and you're what—suggesting he was to blame?"

"Not at all," Miranda said, keeping her voice low and soothing. "My job is to find who murdered Professor Stark. To do that I have to look at this case from every possible angle. That's all."

Her tears spilled over and Miranda held out a box of tissues. Ashley grabbed one and blew her nose. "Yeah, I guess."

"Would you say you had a special relationship with Professor Stark? Because of your writing?"

She nodded. "I think so."

"Were there any of the other seniors who knew him well or interacted with him a lot?"

"We all did. He'd come hang out with us sometimes."

"Where?"

"P.J.'s Coffee, State Street Station, even The Metro."

"The Metro? The dance club?"

"A couple times. No big deal."

No big deal? It seemed to Miranda that a single male professor hanging out in clubs with his female students was, at the very least, borderline inappropriate.

Miranda shut her notebook, stood, and held out her hand. "Thanks, Ashley. I really appreciate your help."

She took it. "Sure. I'd do anything to help."

She started to walk away.

"Hey, Ashley?" The girl stopped, looked back. "Did you know Professor Stark was writing a novel?"

"Sure. Everybody did."

"Did you know what it was about?"

She shook her head. "Only that it was a character-ensemble story. Why?"

"No reason. Why wouldn't he talk about it?"

"Sometimes if you talk too much about your stories you don't write them."

"I don't understand."

"Writing is a creative impulse. If you talk about it too much, it's like you've already told the story and the impulse goes away. He taught me that."

"Makes sense, sort of."

Ashley started off, then stopped and looked back. "He might have talked more in depth about his novel to Jessie and Belinda."

Miranda glanced at the list. Neither a Jessie nor Belinda was on it. "Why might he have talked to them?"

"They're his graduate assistants. They help him with grading papers, teaching, research, and stuff."

"Gotcha. Thanks again, Ashley." She handed her a card. "My number's on it. If you think of anything else, call me."

The next student said almost the same things about Stark, as did the three after that.

Miranda and Jake had arranged to meet in the student union and grab a sandwich before the candlelight vigil began. They took their food and headed for a table in the corner.

"Well?" Jake asked, unwrapping his sandwich. "Anything interesting?"

"When President Stark said his son was beloved by his students, he was right. At least that's the way it's playing out for me so far. What about you?"

"Ditto." While he chewed, he checked his notes. "Heck of a guy," he read. "Fair. Liked to party."

She stopped him on the last. "Apparently he'd hang out with his students. Not all the time, but more than just occasionally."

"Yup." He dipped a fry in catsup. "One of the guys mentioned, 'the girls liked him too much.' It irritated the crap out of him sometimes, because they were always, 'Professor Stark this, Professor Stark that.'"

"Interesting." She snagged one of his fries. "I asked the girls if he ever acted inappropriately with them, they all denied that he had. I don't know, to my thinking going out partying with them is borderline."

Jake arched his eyebrows. "These aren't high-schoolers, they're adults. I don't think it's a big deal."

She took a bite of her burger and opened her notebook. "All but two of the women I interviewed knew Stark was writing a novel. None knew what it was about."

"Same here. Said he talked about the process a lot. About his progress. But no content details."

She snitched another fry. "Did any of them mention Jessie or Belinda?"

He skimmed his notes, then shook his head. "Nope. And neither's on the list."

"They're both graduate students. Research assistants, among other duties. The first person I interviewed suggested they might know more about the book."

"And the research."

"Exactly." Miranda finished her burger and washed it down with the last of her drink. "Let's see if we can locate them before the vigil begins."

CHAPTER NINE

The sun had begun to set. Small clutches of students stood huddled together, talking in hushed tones. Some softly sobbed. Violence had touched them, some for the very first time in their young lives.

One group sat in a circle around votive candles arranged in the shape of a heart. Another group had brought books and were taking turns reading passages. Miranda moved her gaze around that circle and beyond, pausing on each face. Was Stark's killer here? Secretly gloating. Proud of herself. Probably. Unless she was long gone.

They ran into Ashley, who pointed out Belinda. The dark-haired girl sat at the center fountain handing out candles. A guy with bleached blond, short, spiky hair sat with her.

"Hi, Belinda," Miranda said, and held up her shield. "I'm Detective Rader and this is Detective Billings. Could we have a few moments of your time?"

Her expression became immediately guarded. "What for?"

"We're trying to find Professor Stark's killer. We hope you might be able to help us."

She nodded and glanced at her friend. "I'll be right back."

They found a place away from others and Miranda wasted no time. "What did you think of Professor Stark?"

"He was a great guy. A good teacher. I respected him." She moved her gaze between them. "What else am I supposed to say?"

"I don't know. What else do you want to say?"

"He was demanding to work for. But I respected him for that, too."

"You're a research assistant."

"Now I am." She stopped, a strange look coming over her face. "Actually, I guess now I'm out of work. That sucks."

"What did you mean by 'now' you're a research assistant?"

"That was Jess's job. I was his teaching assistant. Then she up and dropped out of the program about a month ago. Left me to do it all until the fall. It really messed up my schedule."

"Why'd she drop out?" Jake asked.

"She said some family emergency, but I think it was because he rebuffed her."

Bingo. "Rebuffed her?" Miranda repeated. "As in rejected her advances?"

"Oh, yeah. She had a huge crush on him. Huge. Everybody knew it."

"Did Professor Stark know it?"

"Sure. But he always kept it super-professional."

"He always keep it super-professional with you?"

She looked surprised. "Yeah. That's who he was."

"Anybody else have a crush on him?"

She snorted. "I'm not sure you've got enough paper

in that notebook. Even some of the guys had a crush on him. He had it all—looks, smarts, and heart."

"How about you? You have a thing for him?"

"Nope. See the dark-haired woman over there? Red shirt?" She pointed. "That's my girlfriend."

"Gotcha." Miranda glanced at her notes. "By any chance, do you know where Jessie lives or have her number?"

"Yeah, sure. I tried calling her a couple times today, but she didn't pick up. Sent a text. Got no response." She frowned. "Wondered if she'd heard. I was sort of worried about how she'd take it."

"You haven't seen her tonight?"

She said she hadn't and moments later Miranda and Jake walked away with Jessie's contact information.

"What do you think?" Jake asked. "Pay this Jessie a visit?"

"Absolutely.

"Randi? Is that you?"

She stopped and looked back. A woman she recognized from high school had separated from a group of faculty and started for her. They hadn't been friends—totally different sides of the track—but she was smiling as if she'd found her long-lost BFF.

"Randi," she said again, smile widening, "that is you."

"Miranda now," she corrected, meeting her. "How are you, Paula?"

"Good, until this happened. It's so awful."

Miranda agreed. "You're on the faculty here?"

"Started in January. Mathematics."

"Props to you. But then I seem to remember you being good at math."

"And I remember you being not so good at it."

"Thanks for that description of my skill with numbers. It was generous."

She laughed. "You work here at the university?"

Miranda shook her head. "I'm a cop."

"*You're* a cop?"

At her incredulous expression, Miranda laughed. "Hard to believe, isn't it? This is my partner, Jake Billings. Jake, this is an old schoolmate, Paula Gleason."

Paula shook his hand. "So, you two are here in an official capacity?"

"We are," Jake said. "Did you know Richard Stark?"

She looked away, shook her head. "Not really. I'm just getting to know the people in my own department." She returned her gaze to his. "I came to show my support."

"You never even met him?" Miranda asked.

She shifted, looking uncomfortable. "I didn't say that. I met him but I didn't really know him."

Miranda handed her a card. "If you think of anything else or hear any rumors about Stark, call me."

Paula looked at the card, eyebrows drawn together in thought. "What do you mean, rumors?"

"Relationships he was in, hearts he may have broken, someone who had an ax to grind. That kind of stuff."

"Oh. Okay." She looked at Jake. "Good to meet you."

Miranda watched her hurry back to the group of faculty, frowning in thought. That'd been weird. Definitely. But had it been so because of their own history? Or because she hadn't been honest about her familiarity with Stark?

"What the hell, Miranda?"

She looked back at Jake, surprised. "What?"

"Rumors? Hearts he may have broken?"

"What's wrong with asking that?"

"It's leading, that what's wrong with it."

Her cheeks heated. "I'm looking for a motive."

"More like trying to create one. And at the expense of Stark's reputation."

"That's bullshit. Stark was brutally murdered by a sexual partner. And I don't think it happened because he was such a 'great guy.'" She made quotation marks with her fingers.

"You're case lead, but I'd be careful if I were you."

"Why's that?"

"You ask the wrong person things like that, you might find yourself in a world of hurt."

CHAPTER TEN

8:25 A.M.

Chief Cadwell looked like he hadn't slept well. Miranda's last check in the mirror confirmed he wasn't the only one. Jake was on his way; he'd stopped to get them both coffees.

They'd been up late, trying to chase down Jessie Lund. She hadn't been at her home; her neighbor on the other side of the duplex had claimed he hadn't seen her in a couple days. They'd learned her family lived in Metairie, near the New Orleans airport. They'd made the drive—and come up empty.

Jake arrived. "Sorry I'm late." He handed her a large cup and a paper bag.

"Bless you," she said, nearly swooning at the aroma wafting up from the cup.

"Close the door," Chief Cadwell said, "and take a seat." He folded his hands on the desk in front of him. "The Stark case. Update me."

"We've made progress. We interviewed Rhonda Peale, the psychology professor to whom Stark sent a message just before his death. She insists she didn't respond to Stark's message."

"But she saw it?"

"Yes."

"Alibi?"

"Nope. She was home alone the entire evening. Grading papers and posting grades online."

"And, obviously, checking Facebook."

"Yup. She offered up a motive for being a suspect, right then and there. Apparently, she stopped by his place Friday and found him shacking up with somebody else."

"Who?"

"She didn't see them or ask a name. He offered the information up as the reason she couldn't come inside. Didn't see his sleeping around as an issue because they hadn't made a commitment to each other."

"Pretty cold. And classic woman-scorned motive."

Jake jumped in. "Which is why she didn't respond to his invitation the night of his death. She said she had her pride."

"Meaning she wanted to go."

"I asked if she was in love with him. She didn't answer directly, though she implied she was."

Chief Cadwell nodded. "She seems like a really good suspect to me."

"She is," Miranda agreed. "There's just . . ."

"What?"

"No twitching. No thrumming fingers or jumpy gaze."

"You mean she didn't act guilty? That means squat, Rader. You know that."

"Yeah, I know. But I bought her story. Either way, we probably have enough to subpoena phone and Internet search records."

"Do it."

"We've got another good lead," Jake offered. "Jessie Lund, Stark's former graduate assistant. She up and quit a month ago. Dropped out of school, the whole bit. Supposedly a family emergency."

Miranda took over. "Her fellow assistant didn't buy it. Said Lund had a major crush on Richard Stark and figured Stark had rebuffed her advances. We're still trying to locate her."

"She hasn't been seen in a couple days. We even travelled to Jefferson Parish to her parents. They said they haven't heard from her."

"You believe that?" Cadwell asked.

Jake shook his head. Miranda seconded it. "They were too calm. Your daughter's unaccounted for and you're not worried? No way. Otherwise, we've got one glowing testimonial after another. The man all but walked on water."

The crime scene filled her head. The rage of it. Someone had felt differently. Someone had hated Richard Stark—even if only for those minutes with the knife.

"'Beloved' was his father's description," Jake said. "And that pretty much played out."

Chief Cadwell settled his gaze on her. "How did that interview go?"

"With President and Mrs. Stark?" He nodded and she went on. "As well as could be expected."

"Meaning?"

Something in his tone sounded off. She frowned slightly. "They'd both suffered a major loss and weren't particularly . . . receptive to our questions. In fact, Ian Stark was particularly accusatory toward me."

"I find that hard to believe."

For a moment she was shocked silent. "Excuse me?"

"Why would he act accusingly toward you?"

"Your guess is as good as mine."

He looked at Jake. "You read it the same way?"

Jake hesitated a moment before answering. "Pretty much," he answered cautiously. "He was a bit hostile toward us . . . but, as Miranda said, they'd both suffered a shocking loss. Every person reacts differently to grief."

The chief shifted his attention back to her. She suddenly had the sense that something was wrong. That he was looking at her in a way that was different from the way he usually did.

"What's going on, Chief?" she asked.

"Ian, President Stark, he said you were impertinent toward him."

"What!" The word exploded out of her. "Me? I was impertinent?"

"Yes."

"That's not true. I know how to handle myself and I was completely professional." She looked at Jake. "Wasn't I?"

"Absolutely," Jake replied.

"Have you ever met President Stark before?"

"No, never."

"What about his son, Richard?"

"You mean the victim? No, I told you that before."

"President Stark wondered if you had."

She glanced at Jake. He had a look on his face she couldn't interpret. She turned back to her superior officer. "Why?"

"Because, in his opinion, you acted like you had an ax to grind with him. Or Richard."

"Are you calling me a liar?" She hated that she sounded as hurt as she felt, but she couldn't quite wrap her mind around what was happening here. This was Buddy, mentor and friend, asking her.

"I'm just following up on a complaint."

"Maybe the problem was that I didn't kiss his ass."

"That's enough, Miranda."

"No, maybe it's not. I wonder if you're the one who's—"

"So, you never met Richard Stark?"

"For the third time, no. Never."

"What did you know about him?"

"Before the murder?" She thought a moment, then shook her head. "I didn't know he existed. I knew the Starks had a son, I guess . . . but that's it. Chief, Buddy, I treated Ian Stark the same as I would anyone in that position. Did I get a little frustrated? Yeah, I suppose. I tried not to let that show, but maybe it slipped through. If so, I apologize. But you weren't there. Frankly, he acted like a dick."

"Jake," Chief Cadwell turned his way, "you second Miranda's version of events?"

"Wait a minute," she said. "My version of events? This is feeling, and sounding, a lot like an interrogation. What the hell's going on?"

"Your fingerprints were found at the scene."

That stopped her cold. She knew she must look shocked, because she was. Completely. "That's not possible."

"They were." He opened a folder, extracted a piece of paper, and slid it across the desk. It was a printout of the computer match.

She studied it a moment, then looked back up at Buddy. "This makes no sense at all. I had scene gloves on and there's no other way my prints could have been at the scene."

Buddy nodded. "You had them on when I was there earlier."

"Of course I did." She was obsessed with following orders, procedure, protocol. That's who she was, the kind of cop she'd made herself.

This was wrong. Impossible. She didn't know Stark, had never met him.

Yet, they had found her prints at the scene. And the news clipping about her.

Someone was setting her up. What other explanation could there be?

"Miranda?"

She refocused on Buddy.

"So, how'd your prints end up at Stark's place?"

She blinked, opened her mouth to tell him she had no clue—and lied instead. "I took my gloves off. To call Jake. My phone's touch screen doesn't respond when I've got them on."

The ease with which the lie spilled off her tongue shocked her. Years ago, lying had been a way of life. To her parents, her teachers, the law. Whatever she needed to say to save her own skin or get what she wanted.

But she wasn't that person anymore. Her hands in her lap began to shake and she curled them into fists. She'd left that girl behind.

Apparently not, Randi. Looks like you're the same, no-good, lyin' trailer trash you were back then.

Buddy didn't believe her. She saw it in his eyes as he gazed at her. It wasn't too late. She could still retract. Tell she was mistaken. Tell him—

"That's right, Chief," Jake said. "They were still off when I got there."

Chief Cadwell shifted his gaze to Jake. "You're just remembering that now, Billings?"

Jake didn't react to the sarcasm. "Worst scene I ever worked. Having to remind Miranda to put her gloves on isn't what stands out."

Miranda looked at him, torn between gratitude and dismay. He'd stuck up for her, literally put his own career on the line for her. No one had ever done that for her, not even her family. They'd been more the every-man-for-himself kind of folks. But with dismay because now he was in it with her. She went down, he went down. She couldn't even recant without implicating her partner.

A couple seconds ticked past. They seemed like hours. It felt as if both men were staring, waiting. Her heartbeat boomed in her head and sweat pooled under her arms.

"Yeah, that's right." She sounded easy, like a carefree teen. "That's the way it went down, Chief."

That teen. The liar and sneak.

The girl no one believed.

The chief frowned, moving his gaze between the two of them. "It's not like you to be sloppy, Miranda."

"No, it's not. Which is probably why I didn't recall it right away."

"What did you touch?"

"I don't remember. There was a lot going on. I—"

"You better damn well remember, because you're going to have to account for it."

"Yes, sir."

"Write it up, both of you. I want it in both your reports." He slid a folder across the desk. "Take it. It's everything we've got so far."

She did and they started for the door. Buddy stopped her. "Miranda, a moment alone."

She turned to face him, heart thundering in her head like a war drum. She schooled her features. "Yes, Chief?"

"That's the way it all went down, right?"

"Yeah, that's right." *God help her.*

"I expect better from you. That was sloppy police work."

"Yes, sir. It won't happen again."

"Make sure of it. And Miranda?"

She looked over her shoulder at him.

"I'm trusting you. You wouldn't lie to me, right?"

That girl. Untrustworthy. A liar.

She didn't blink, though she felt like she was dying inside. "You know me, Buddy. Do you think I'd lie to you?"

"No, I don't."

He'd hesitated, just a fraction of a second. That moment spoke volumes. "I'll keep you posted, Chief," she said, and exited the office.

CHAPTER ELEVEN

9:05 A.M.

Miranda left Buddy's office and went straight to her desk. Wordlessly, she handed the envelope to Jake.

He looked at it, then back up at her. "Are you okay?"

She grabbed her jacket, holstered her phone. "Why wouldn't I be?"

"That grilling in there."

"Whatever."

"Not whatever." He lowered his voice. "That was messed up."

"Tell me about it."

She started for the main entrance, aware of him directly behind her. She needed some time and space to think through what just happened. She couldn't do it with Jake attached to her hip.

"Mason," she said to the desk sergeant, "we're out. Following up on a lead in the Stark homicide."

She didn't wait for him to acknowledge her and pushed through the double glass doors and stepped outside into the overcast day. She was halfway to her car before Jake caught up with her.

"Is that it, Miranda?"

She met his eyes, angry. "What? You want me to thank you for backing me up? Thank you."

"I'm not the enemy." He grabbed her arm. "In there, that . . . interrogation. That was messed up. We need to talk about it."

"Not here," she said, jaw hurting from clenching it. "In the car."

They climbed in, buckled up, and Miranda backed out of the space.

"Where are we going?"

"Away from here."

They didn't speak again until she turned into University Place, a neighborhood located within walking distance of the ULH campus. She parked in the shade of a big, old oak tree but didn't cut the engine.

"I meant it. Thanks for backing me up."

"That's what partners do."

"Well, you shouldn't have." She glanced at him, then back at the street. "A lie's always the wrong choice."

"I know you, Miranda. It was the right choice. The only one."

She couldn't look at him. He'd see the regret in her eyes. The guilt. He'd know he'd just backed the losing horse.

The first drops of rain splattered on the windshield.

"We've got to talk about this," he said. "What's going on here?"

She nodded, preparing to tell him the truth about those prints, share that she thought somebody might be setting her up for Stark. How did she explain something in a way that made sense—when it didn't even make sense to her?

"The Chief," Jake said. "Something's not right with him."

She looked at him then, surprised.

"That, what just happened, it didn't make sense. You've never given him a reason to doubt you."

Not in fourteen years, anyway.

Until today.

Jake stared out the windshield, eyebrows pulled together in thought. "You're a decorated officer, Miranda. A ten-year veteran of the force."

"Apparently that doesn't mean much."

The bitterness she heard in her own voice could have curdled cream. She wished she could take it back but knew she couldn't.

He didn't seem to notice. "That's what I'm talking about. Hear me out before chiming in, okay?"

She nodded and he went on. "After the responding officer, Cadwell was the first to the scene. He went himself, in the middle of the night. Odd behavior number one."

She started to comment, but he held up a hand to hold her off. "So he goes to the scene, then calls you. Only you. Oddity number two."

She nodded—she'd thought the same thing that night.

"And here's number three. Cadwell tells you you're in charge of the case, has you contact me and the Sheriff's Department, then leaves the scene to notify the victim's next of kin—alone. You should have been there. Or at the very least, another officer."

He was right. Someone else to assess and record the next of kin's first reactions. That was a one-time deal.

"Odd, all of them, I agree. But I also understand where Buddy was coming from. Stark's an important figure in the community, and Buddy knew how fast the story could blow up. He went to the scene first to assess the situation, and to Stark and his wife out of respect."

"I get all that," Jake continued, "but he shared details of the crime scene? And of our potential suspect?

By the way, in my book that's oddity number four. All of it's a major breach of protocol."

He had her there, Miranda admitted. She'd thought the same about each, had even been shocked at the chief's lapse of judgment.

Still she balked. "I get it all, Jake. Yes, all of it is very unlike Buddy. But look at this case. That crime. Do you really think his parents could be involved? It's obvious they weren't."

"Nothing's ever obvious—until it is. Especially in a crime as violent and personal in nature as this one."

Jake angled in his seat to face her. "Ready for the big number five?" He didn't wait for her to agree. "That interrogation back there. Stark accuses you of impropriety and Cadwell takes his side? Pretty much one hundred percent? After ten years working with you on the force, he acts like you'd do that, no question about it?"

The clouds opened up and the sprinkle became a downpour. The rain thundered against the car roof and she raised her voice to be heard over the din. "Thanks for reminding me."

"It was screwed up, big time. Why would he take Stark's side over yours?"

"I don't know." It was true, she didn't. She searched aloud for an answer. "They've known each other for years. I suppose he respects him and wants to protect him . . . and by association, the university. Stark wields a lot of power in this town."

"Exactly. Cadwell knew it was Stark's kid who'd gotten whacked. He wanted to be first to the scene, so he could protect him if necessary."

Miranda gripped the steering wheel. Buddy Cadwell had taken her under his wing. He'd modeled the kind of cop she should be. There was right and wrong, no shades of gray in between. He'd taught her there was no place in police work for personal agendas.

"He wouldn't have tampered with evidence," she said. "Not Buddy, no way."

"You heard President Stark. We can't let these details out, he said. It would reflect badly on him and the university."

The rain eased, then let up, stopping almost as quickly as it had begun. The clouds parted, the sun peeked out. She looked at Jake. "All this, is it why you lied for me back there?"

"I backed you up, Miranda, because whatever team Cadwell's playing on right now, it's not yours or, for that matter, mine either. And as far as I'm concerned, your word stands. Period."

A lump settled in her chest. She had to tell him the truth, she realized, convinced by his absolute trust in her word. She'd opened her mouth to do just that when her cell went off.

"Detective Rader," she answered.

"Detective, this is Jessie Lund's neighbor, Max. You were by here last night looking for her."

"Yes, Max. How can I help you?"

"You asked me to let you know if she showed up. And she did."

"She's there now?"

"Yeah. But I don't think for long. I saw her putting stuff in her car. Like she's moving."

"Thanks, Max." She cranked the engine. "We're on our way."

CHAPTER TWELVE

Jessie Lund lived in one half of a small duplex on the west side of town. Most of the properties in this area were rentals, and university students occupied many of them. And it looked it: bikes chained to porch rails, trash cans sitting at curbs, overrun garden beds, and cars parked on lawns.

Miranda drove up to see Lund stuffing a cardboard box into the backseat of her small SUV. The head of a teddy bear poked out the top of the box; he seemed to be staring at her. Miranda parked directly behind Lund's vehicle to prevent her from fleeing.

Miranda and Jake climbed out of the car, slamming their doors in unison. The girl looked up and her eyes went as wide and vacant as the stuffed bear's.

"Jessie Lund?" Miranda said, holding up her shield. "Harmony PD. We need to ask you a few questions."

"I didn't do anything."

"We're not saying you did. We have a few questions, that's all. How about we go inside?"

She silently agreed and started up the walk, tripping on the first porch step.

Jake caught her arm, steadying her. "You okay?"

She nodded and led them the rest of the way inside without incident.

The front door dumped them directly into the living room. Miranda moved her gaze over the space. Typical college, garage-sale decor—basic, mismatched, and well-worn. It was also in a state of chaos: half-filled boxes, stacks of books and various other items, a trash bag filled with what looked like clothes.

Miranda crossed to the bag and peered inside, then looked up. "You moving, Jessie?"

The girl sat hard. As if her legs refused to hold her a moment more. "Yes."

"Where to?"

"Back home. To my mom's house."

"Why's that?" Jake asked.

"I'm not in school anymore and I'm unemployed. I can't afford my rent."

"Makes sense," he said, tone easy.

From the corner of her eye Miranda saw Jake take a note, and she stepped back in. "You were a grad student at ULH, is that correct?"

"Yes."

"And a graduate assistant to Professor Richard Stark?" Lund nodded and looked down at her clenched hands. "Jessie, you are aware of what happened the night before last? That Professor Stark was murdered?"

"Yes," she whispered.

"You don't find all this—" she motioned the boxes, "—a bit of a coincidence? Coming just after Professor Stark's murder?"

Her chin trembled. "Why would I?"

"Because it is. You were his graduate assistant for a year and a half. A month ago you quit school—and your job. Now he's dead and you're running away."

"I'm not running away! I told you, I can't pay my rent."

"You were almost done with your master's, am I right?" Lund agreed with her again. "So, why'd you drop out? A couple months, that's all you had left."

"A family emergency."

"What kind?"

"It's personal."

"It must have been a big emergency, really serious, to make you drop out of a degree program when the finish line was so close."

Her chin trembled. "It was."

"Can I share something with you?" Miranda leaned forward, the way a girlfriend with a secret would. She lowered her voice. "I probably shouldn't tell you this, but . . . a woman killed Professor Stark."

Lund swallowed so hard Miranda heard it. "Are you sure?"

"Oh, yeah, and we think we know why. Because she was in love with him and he wasn't in love with her."

With a strangled cry, she brought hand to her mouth, jumped to her feet, and ran to the bathroom.

Miranda followed, waiting outside the door. She heard the girl retch, and several moments later the flush of the toilet followed by running water.

Miranda tapped on the door. "Are you okay, Jessie?"

"Leave me alone."

"I'm sorry, Jessie," she said gently, "but I can't do that. Either you come out or I come in."

Silence followed and Miranda glanced at Jake. "Check the fridge. See if there's a soda or something for her. If not, get an ice water."

Miranda turned back to the door. "Detective Billings is getting you something cold to drink. Come on out.

We only want to talk. I'm on your side, Jessie. We both are."

The lock turned over and Jessie emerged, pale and shaking. Miranda took her arm. "Come sit down. It's going to be okay."

She led the young woman back to the lumpy couch and Jake handed her a drink. "Sprite," he said.

"Thanks." She took it and sipped. After a few moments some color returned to her cheeks.

"Feel well enough to talk some more?" Miranda asked.

"I guess."

"Good." She kept her tone low and soothing. "You remember what we were discussing before you got sick?"

The young woman's lips trembled; she pressed them together and nodded.

"You were in love with Richard Stark, weren't you?"

"Why do you think that?"

"We were told by several other students."

Her eyes filled with tears and she looked down at her lap.

Miranda worked to keep her voice low and soothing. "That's why you dropped out, isn't it? You told him and he rejected you."

"I was an idiot, the worst cliché. The plain Jane egghead in love with the handsome professor."

"You were angry. And hurt. I get it." Miranda smiled, encouraging. "So you made a plan. To make him pay for not loving you back."

"What?" She shook her head. "I quit, dropped out. He wasn't interested. When I saw the pity in his eyes, I fell apart. I couldn't be around him anymore. It was—" her voice broke, "—torture."

Tears rolled down her cheeks. Jake handed her a box of tissues.

"When was the last time you saw him?"

"The week before I dropped out."

"Where were you the night before last?"

She looked confused. "Where was I—"

"The night Richard Stark was killed?"

"At my mom's. I've been there the whole week."

"Funny, I was there yesterday. She told me she didn't know where you were."

"I asked her not to tell."

"You're saying she lied?" The young woman nodded. "And if I call her, right now, she'll back that up?"

"Yes!" She looked at Jake, then back at Miranda. "But you don't have to call. She's on her way over. To help me pack."

CHAPTER THIRTEEN

10:05 P.M.

Miranda stood on her small back deck, looking out at the soupy night. Her cabin backed up to wooded wetlands, alive with all manner of buzzing, chirping, and humming.

Familiar, she thought. All of it. The magnolia tree she'd planted just after she bought this place, the row of azalea bushes that lined the deck, the cypress trees where the wetlands began, their knobby knees poking up from the ground.

And the smell. She breathed deeply. Earthy and fecund.

So why did it all feel so strange tonight? So foreign? As if she had been transported to a new world that was the same—but different.

Miranda turned away from the night and went back inside. The day had been long and tumultuous. From Buddy's fingerprint bombshell and the way he had looked at her, to the lie slipping past her lips with ease, to Jake's confidence in her and Jessie Lund's mother's confirmation of her daughter's version of events.

Otherwise, Lund's mother had been tight-lipped and obviously angry. But why? And even more, why had that anger seemed to be directed at Miranda?

Miranda massaged her right temple and the headache that throbbed there. And why would Buddy take Ian Stark's side against her? Jake was right. Ten years of dedicated service and an impeccable record, and he looked at her that way? Like she was untrustworthy?

And then she had been, proving him right.

"I took off my gloves to call Jake. The touch screen doesn't work with them on."

Suddenly chilled, Miranda rubbed her arms. She glanced up. The ceiling fan, directly overhead. Spinning . . .'round and 'round . . .

The way the ceiling fan had that night, forcing the cooled air from the Harmony PD's derelict AC window unit down on her head. Officer Clint Wheeler, squinting at her, seeming oblivious to her discomfort, even as she shuddered and hugged herself.

"Where'd you get the weed, Randi? And you'd better tell me the truth."

She had told the truth, but he didn't believe her.

Of course he didn't.

Because Randi Rader had proved herself a liar so many times before.

No, Miranda thought. She wasn't going there, not tonight. She marched to the wall switch and turned off the fan. Someone was setting her up. It was the only explanation for her fingerprints being at the scene.

She'd wrestled with the idea all day. Told herself she was crazy. That the notion was too outlandish to be true. Set up as a killer? Why? What had she done? And why Stark? She didn't even know him.

Unless she did.

That was the answer, the reason, she kept circling back to. The same one that explained Richard Stark having that news clipping tucked into his desk drawer.

Richard Stark was her tormentor from that summer

night fourteen years ago. The beautiful monster in the Alabama ball cap. It was the only explanation that made sense.

Her knees went weak.

Sense, Miranda? Really?

She brought the heels of her hands to her eyes. How could she not have recognized him, even in death? He'd populated her every nightmare all these years. He was the creature under the bed, the thing lurking in the dark, the owner of the soft footfalls behind her.

He was the reason she'd become a cop.

What to do? Miranda struggled to find her breath, clear her head. Who could she tell?

No one. Not even Jake. That would play right into the hands of whoever was setting her up. The pieces of the investigation would fit nicely into place and she would be found guilty. Hell, from the way Buddy had looked at her, folks were just waiting to find her guilty. To slip up and be that girl again.

After all, a leopard can't change its spots.

No one would believe her now. Just as no one had believed her then.

Tears stung her eyes and she blinked furiously against them. Angry tears, she assured herself. Not ones of hurt or vulnerability. Not evidence of weakness.

The other girl would believe her. She had been real—despite the fact that nothing ever appeared in the local media, not news of a missing girl, not a reported rape or homicide. No Jane Doe.

What ever happened to her? Miranda had wondered that hundreds of times over the years. Had agonized over the question—did she escape? If so, why say nothing? And if not, why no missing-person report?

She curved her hands into fists. She wasn't a liar; she wasn't that girl. Today was an aberration; she'd needed to protect herself from whoever was setting her up. She didn't have a choice.

Let it go, she told herself. Pretend today didn't happen. Get back on track by finding Stark's killer. Which would lead to who was setting her up—and why.

She was a good cop. She could do this.

The room seemed to close in on her, her thoughts to choke the breath out of her. Too much alone. Too many questions with no answers.

Too much . . . Randi Rader.

Miranda snatched up her car keys from the kitchen counter and her purse from the back of the kitchen chair. She knew just where to go.

CHAPTER FOURTEEN

11:00 P.M.

The Toasted Cat was a hole-in-the-wall joint that'd been around since the sixties. The vibe was low key and old school; it catered to a working-class crowd as far removed from the frenetic clubs the kids favored as it was from the pretentiously cool places the intellectuals frequented. It was mostly a drinking spot, but had a limited menu of a few sandwiches and a soup or chili, depending on the weather.

As she stepped into the bar, the bartender, Summer Knight—who also happened to be the joint's owner—looked her way and smiled. "Hey, girl, what're you doing out tonight? The chief give you time off for being awesome?"

Miranda laughed and shook her head. "Like that would ever happen." She slid onto a barstool. "Knew I couldn't sleep, figured a drink might help."

"You got it. The usual?"

She shook her head. "A shot of tequila and a beer."

"That's hardcore for a school night."

"If you haven't noticed, I'm not in school anymore."

Summer set the shot and draft in front of her. Miranda sucked on the wedge of lime, then tossed back the tequila.

Summer watched her, eyebrow cocked in question. "Feel better?"

"Actually, I do." The numbing effect of the tequila was almost instantaneous and she motioned for a second, then took a long swallow of the beer.

Summer poured herself a splash of red wine. "Ready to talk?"

"About what?"

"You tell me."

Miranda glanced around. Other than a few other patrons—a couple cuddling in a corner booth, another couple at the opposite end of the bar from her, silent, staring at the cocktails in front of them—the place was empty.

"Quiet tonight," she said.

The eyebrow went up again. Summer folded her arms across her chest. "Okay, I'll play. Fair crowd earlier. Not too bad for a weeknight. Your turn."

Summer never missed a thing. And she never let those things pass. She had the kind of dry humor that encouraged confidence. A sort of cool familiarity with slightly sharp edges. Never mean, just . . . really direct.

They'd become fast friends.

So Miranda gave in. "It was a big day. I knew I wouldn't be able to sleep, so I came here."

"You couldn't crawl into a bottle at home?"

She bit down on the second wedge of lime, then shot the tequila. This one burned going down. "You're a pain in the ass, you know that?"

Summer smiled. "Absolutely."

"Okay, it wasn't just a full day, it was totally screwed up, too. Home alone wasn't an option."

"You needed your best friend the bartender. Aww, that's so sweet. I'm touched, I really am."

Exactly right, as usual. But the blow was softened

by her sarcasm. Miranda grinned. "The way you read people, you should be the cop."

Summer laughed. "Me with a gun? Not my style at all. Excuse me, I'll be right back."

Summer went to the other end of the bar to check on the couple there, cleared their tab, then returned.

"You heard about the murder?" Miranda asked.

"This is the kind of place where folks come to talk. That's pretty much all I heard about today. You working the case?"

"I am. What was everybody saying?"

"It seemed like a lot of speculation. Let's see . . . one version had it that he was shot during a robbery. Another that he killed himself and y'all are trying to cover it up."

"A cover-up of a suicide?"

"President Stark's orders. So his kid doesn't look bad."

Miranda shook her head. "That's nuts."

"I didn't say it made sense."

"What else?" She took another swallow of the beer.

"Here's another good one: The professor was juggling one too many ladies and one of them had enough and whacked him."

"Yeah? Who said that?"

"A group of ladies."

Made sense. "You have names?"

"A couple of 'em paid with a credit card. I could look it up."

"I'd appreciate that." Miranda finished the beer but refused a refill. "Stark, he ever come in here?"

"A few times, yeah."

"What did you think of him?"

"Besides that he was ridiculously good looking?" She rested on her elbows on the bar. "He was always with a group, sat at a table so we never really interacted. But I seem to recall he tipped well."

"The groups he came in with. Students? Other faculty?"

"Young people, a couple times, maybe. Mixed-looking groups."

"Never the same?" She shook her head. "How about one-on-ones? Maybe him and a woman?"

Summer took a sip of her wine. "Not that I recall."

"You observe him when he was here?"

"Depends on how busy I was. You know me, I observe everybody."

Miranda nodded. "So, what did you observe?"

She paused, lips pursed in thought. "Seemed liked. By other guys, but especially by the ladies. Hard not to be, with that face."

She indicated her glass. "Another shot?"

"God, no. I can't feel my toes as it is. I better settle up, get out of here."

Summer waved her off. "It's on the house."

Miranda moved to go, then stopped. "Do you ever feel like you're on this journey and you know who you are and where you're going? And then, out of nowhere, it seems like . . . you don't?"

Summer shrugged. "I suppose everybody feels that way sometimes."

"Do they? I don't. Didn't," she corrected. "Until today. It's like this fork in the road comes along and—"

"You have a choice. This path or the other?"

"Yeah." Miranda looked down at the bar, at the wet ring left by her glass. "How do you decide? One way's safe, because it's familiar and you're sure of the results. The other is the antithesis of comfortable or safe."

Summer leaned toward her, eyes sparkling. "Is this about a guy?"

"Sorry."

"Okay, I say take the fork." She smiled, expression rueful. "That's what I did and look at me, thirty years old and tending bar."

"You own the place."

"Technically, I'm only part owner. Bank owns the rest." Summer drained the splash of wine. "Look, four years ago I had a good job in liquor sales, and I was engaged to pretty great guy. I knew exactly where my life was going."

"You were engaged? You never told me that before."

"I'm not proud of the way it turned out. Point is, I was comfortable. Sure of myself and my future. House in the burbs. Kids. Marriage to a good guy."

"So, what happened?"

"The wreck."

Summer had told her about the car accident that had nearly taken her life. Hydroplaning on the interstate, crashing down an embankment into a tree.

"I woke up in the hospital three days later and knew."

"Knew what?"

"I couldn't do it. Marry the guy, do the sales, have the kids."

A single tear rolled down her cheek. A lump formed in Miranda's throat. Summer was the least likely person to cry that she knew.

"I almost died, Miranda. I was saved. I don't know why. But I knew that the path I was on . . . wasn't me."

Another tear escaped and she wiped it away. "I can't believe I'm telling you all this."

"What was his name?" Miranda asked softly.

"Scott. I hurt him. I didn't mean to or want to . . . and he didn't understand that it wasn't him, it was me. I had unfinished business. And I couldn't do that to him . . .

or any kids we might have. And I couldn't do it to me either."

Miranda reached across the bar and squeezed Summer's hand. "That took guts."

"Yeah, it did. It would have been so easy to just . . . let him love me." Her voice turned raspy and she cleared her throat. "At first he insisted I was just 'confused' because of the accident. Then, as the weeks passed, he accused me of being afraid. Of running away."

"He didn't get it," Miranda murmured. "That's what you were doing before."

"Yes." Her eyes filled and she looked away. When she turned back, she had her emotions in check. "So, I started looking around for something to do, saw this business up for sale, and here I am."

"I'm glad," Miranda said. "Or else I wouldn't know you."

"Oh, no, you don't." Summer said, freeing her hand. "Sobfest is officially over and it's time for you to go home."

CHAPTER FIFTEEN

1:20 A.M.

Jake was waiting for her when she got home. He sat on her front porch, his strong profile illuminated by the light filtering through the front window.

Handsome, she thought, stepping out of her car. She'd thought it before, but tonight he seemed particularly so. Not in the bulging, macho way of some men, but long and lean with a warm, brown gaze that never wavered.

Miranda started toward him. "Hey, partner. What're you doing here?"

"I needed to talk to you about something."

Unlike her dad or brothers, Jake was a stand-up guy. Real and in the moment. Quietly there. It made him a good cop. And a good partner.

And sometimes, when he looked at her, she thought he saw her more clearly than she saw herself. Times like tonight.

Uncomfortable, she broke the connection and glanced at her watch. "It couldn't wait? It must be really important."

"It is." He shoved his hands into his pockets. "You're out late."

"Visiting the Toasted Cat."

"Getting toasted?"

She was, she realized. Slightly crispy anyway. "That wasn't the reason, but it seems to be the result." She climbed the porch steps and crossed to the door. "C'mon in."

She unlocked the door and dropped her keys and bag on the front table. "Beer? Coffee?"

"Beer." He trailed her into the kitchen. "Big day today, huh?"

"You could say that." She looked over her shoulder at him. "I couldn't sleep."

"Me either."

"Sit." She waved in the direction of the counter stools, then reached in the fridge for the brew. She popped the cap and handed it to him, then went back and retrieved a bottle of water for herself.

Miranda leaned against the counter. "What did you want to talk about?"

"Today. What happened in Cadwell's office."

"Which part?"

"The part where I backed you up."

She waited. As the seconds ticked past, something about the energy between them changed. She didn't know why, but suddenly it was prickly, somehow electric.

"I told you I backed you up because I believe in you."

"Yup." She brought the bottle toward her lips. "No longer true?"

"Only partially true."

Miranda suddenly knew what was coming next. The swallow of water caught in her throat. She forced it down.

"The whole truth is because—"

"No, don't—"

"I love you, Miranda. I'm in love with you."

His words knocked the wind out of her. This was not a young man, saying whatever necessary to get into a woman's pants, not shallow, in love with himself and the effect of his words, not greedy or selfish.

This was Jake. Partner. Friend. Totally present Jake.

"You don't have to say anything. Because of today . . . I had to tell you. I couldn't keep it to myself anymore."

In love with her? How, she wondered. Why? The questions came out sideways. "Are you sure?"

He half-laughed. "Miranda, of course I'm sure."

She pressed her lips together a moment. "But you don't really know—"

"You? Yes, I do." He stood and crossed to stand directly in front of her. "I know you, Miranda."

That direct, steady gaze. Deep and warm brown. The way those eyes crinkled at the corners when he smiled. She dropped her gaze to his mouth. The chiseled cut of his upper lip. The hint of a dimple at the corners.

She felt lightheaded in a way that had nothing to do with the booze.

He searched her gaze. "I know you've never looked at me that way. But what do you think? Maybe you want to give it a try?"

Today . . . tonight, everything was different. Richard Stark was the beautiful monster from her nightmares. She knew it without proof. In her gut. That's why her fingerprints were at the scene. It's why the news clipping about her was in his desk drawer.

Stark saved it, all these years.

Everybody thought Richard Stark was a paragon. But she knew the truth. And so did someone else. The person who killed him, the one who planted her fingerprints at the scene.

Jake drew his eyebrows together. "Miranda, say

something. I'm hanging out here in the wind, feeling like a complete idiot."

Should she take a chance? Cross this line?

Everything was different tonight. She was different. *Take the fork in the road, Miranda. Do it.*

She cupped his face in her palms, stood on tiptoes, and kissed him. She felt his surprise, then his relief, as he drew her closer and deepened the kiss.

He tasted of the beer; smelled faintly of aftershave and the night. His body felt strong against hers and she let herself revel in that strength. She could be weak in this moment, she told herself. Just for now. With him she felt safe—something she hadn't allowed herself in a long time.

"The bedroom," she said against his mouth, the sound raspy with arousal.

"Where?"

"End of the hall." She tightened her grip on his shoulders. "Hurry."

Without breaking the kiss he lifted her. She wrapped her legs around his waist and arms around his neck. Within moments, the bed rose up to meet them. They tugged at one another's clothing, impatiently pushing garments aside, wriggling free of clinging fabric, greedy for what came next.

She wanted to feel him. His skin against hers, their joined heat. And she wanted him on top of her. Inside her.

She called his name and he understood. He rolled her onto her back, pinning her to the mattress. For a moment that seemed an eternity, he held her gaze. When it seemed she couldn't wait a moment longer, he entered her with a slow, deep thrust.

"I've got you, Miranda," he said against her ear. "I've got . . . *you.*"

CHAPTER SIXTEEN

5:05 A.M.

Miranda opened her eyes to see Jake, one leg in his pants, hopping to balance himself as he inserted the other leg.

She smiled sleepily. "Hey."

He fastened his pants and looked her way. "Hey. Sorry I woke you."

She yawned. "What time is it?"

"Five."

"Couldn't wait to get the hell out of here, huh?"

He laughed and crossed to the bed. He bent down and kissed her. "Obviously, my timing sucks."

"Your timing's great. No complaints here."

He knew she was referring to the night before and grinned. "Glad to be of service."

"Stud." She stretched and moaned, muscles heavy with sleep and sore in ways they hadn't been in a long time. "You don't have to go."

"Small town. Figured you'd prefer it if no one saw me leaving this morning."

Small town. Partners.

Major complications.

She sat up and pushed the hair out of her eyes. "Wait. We need to talk."

"Uh-oh, the 'talk' already."

He sat on the edge of the bed. She couldn't help but notice how beautifully molded his chest was. She recalled how those ripped muscles had felt against her palms and she averted her gaze.

"This probably wasn't such a good idea," she said.

He smiled. "I figured you were going to say that this morning."

"I'm that predictable?"

"I know you that well."

She arched an eyebrow. "Okay, so what was I going to say next?"

"That we're partners. We have to work together. This can't get in the way of that."

He was right, nearly word for word. "And I was going to be right about that."

"I know. This won't get in the way."

She smoothed the crumpled sheet, needing something to do with her hands. She didn't want to hurt him, but she had to be completely honest. "There's more. This wasn't fair to you . . . *I* wasn't fair to you."

"Because you're not in love with me?"

She met his eyes. "No, I'm not. I'm sorry."

"Yet." He leaned toward her, cupped her face in his palms. "You're not in love with me . . . yet."

She laughed and gave in, laying her hands on his chest, caressing. "Confidence. I like that, partner."

"An optimist," he teased, then grew serious. "I'm a patient man, Miranda. As long as it takes, no pressure."

A lump formed in her throat. Last night he'd said 'I love you' and she'd believed he thought he did. They were pretty words, but words—pretty or not—were cheap. Thrown easily about, no need to be backed up with action. Most often they weren't.

But he was backing his words up, offering to wait for her. To give her time and space. No one had ever done that for her before.

She kissed him. Tenderly. Deeply. Drawing him into her. Offering him something more precious than what she shared the night before.

They made love again, slowly this time. Taking time to linger on one sweet spot, then another. To taste. And savor.

His hands, then tongue, were magical instruments that made her body sing. She arched up against him with a cry of release as he entered her. The motion extended her pleasure, one spasm after another rocking her until he joined her. Finding her mouth, he captured their joint cries and rolled onto his back, bringing her with him.

Miranda rested her forehead against his shoulder, fighting to catch her breath. "Oh, my God," she said. "Mind. Blown."

He laughed softly and wrapped a strand of her hair around his finger. "You did seem to enjoy that."

His heart thundered against her breast, and Miranda smiled. "You, too."

"Oh yeah."

"Not sure what we could do for an encore."

"I'll think of something."

She smiled. "I bet you will."

Her cell went off and she groaned. "That's just rude."

He retrieved it from the nightstand and handed it to her. She looked at the number and frowned. A five-zero-four area code. New Orleans. The number seemed to pluck at her memory, but she didn't know from where.

"Not the chief," she said.

"Who?"

"Don't know. New Orleans number." She tossed the phone. "If it's important, they can leave a message."

"Did you happen to notice the time?"

She didn't want to let go of this moment, not yet. "Did you?"

"Unfortunately." He eased her off him. "I guess I blew my exit strategy."

"That's not the only thing you blew."

He made a sound that was a cross between a laugh and a snort. "I can't believe you said that. Maybe you are a bad girl after all."

A bad girl. Clint Wheeler's voice, from that night in June, sounded in her head. *"You're a bad girl, Randi Rader. And everyone 'round here knows it."*

"What did you say?"

His face fell. "I didn't mean anything by that. It was supposed to be funny."

What had she been thinking? Sleeping with her partner? Falling right back into the mold folks around here expected her to fill?

"You were right, you better go." She climbed out of bed and grabbed her panties and T-shirt and started for the bathroom. Stopping at the door, she looked back at him. "This is a small town, we're partners, and what we're doing is not okay. I'll see you at headquarters."

CHAPTER SEVENTEEN

*That night in June
2002*

Sobbing, Randi stumbled through the underbrush, branches and thorns tearing at her bare legs. She tripped on a root and went skidding forward, landing on her hands and knees. Pain shot up her arms, but she scrambled to her feet and started forward again, hoping and praying she was on her way to somewhere. A house or road. Someplace, anyplace, that had a phone or a driver willing to take her to the police.

Her prayers were answered—the forest thinned, then opened up to a road. Two lane, deserted. No lights, no buildings. Like a sadistic trick one of her brothers would play on her. She looked left, then right, no idea where she was or which way to go.

Something her mother used to say popped into her head: *"Stay on the right path, Randi. It's hard for women out there, you'll see."*

A hysterical sound passed her lips. Why hadn't she listened? Now it was too late . . .

Randi started to run, the slap of her sandals on the pavement morphing, becoming the other girl's screams. How could she still hear them? What was he doing to her?

What if he killed her?

No, please God . . . not that. It's not too late.

She pushed harder. Her chest burned; she was light-headed, her legs trembling, feet in agony. She couldn't go much farther, she thought, hysteria rising up in her. But she couldn't stop. She couldn't.

And then, a miracle. Headlights, cutting across the curve in the road ahead. She tripped, righted herself, and darted forward, waving her arms wildly.

Cherry lights; the short scream of a siren.

A police cruiser. Her legs nearly buckled in relief and she stumbled toward it.

A cop emerged, gun drawn. "Stop where you are! Hands above your head!"

She reacted automatically, hands shooting into the air. And then she saw who it was and her heart sank to her toes. Wheeler. Why'd it have to be Wheeler?

"Well, if it isn't Randi Rader, out past curfew on a Friday night."

"I need help. This guy . . . he picked me up and—"

"Slow down, Missy. What're you up to?"

"Back there," she said, turning and pointing, "there's another girl. This guy, he tied her up and—"

"The guy's name?"

"Steve. He said his name was Steve."

"Last name?"

"I didn't ask. I—" She saw by his expression that he didn't buy it so she made a name up. "Smith."

"Steve Smith?"

"Yes, Billy-Bo kicked me out of his—"

He holstered his gun. "Billy Boman?"

Why wouldn't he let her finish a sentence? She wanted to scream in frustration. "Yes! Just listen to me!"

The moment the words left her mouth, she knew it was the wrong thing to say.

She was right. "You've got that backwards, Missy. You listen to me. Have you been drinking?"

The lie slipped automatically past her lips. "No."

"See that center line? I want you to walk it."

Her legs shook so badly she could hardly stand, let alone walk a straight line.

"I can't."

"Finally, something true from that lying mouth of yours." He shined the light directly into her eyes. "Empty your pockets."

"We're wasting time! The other girl . . . Cathy . . . she's in trouble. He tied her up . . . he raped her. . . . I got away and—" Her voice broke. "I promised I'd get help!"

"Cathy who?"

She grabbed the first name that popped into her head. "Smith."

"Steve Smith and Cathy Smith? You sayin' he raped his sister?"

"I meant Stevens! Cathy Stevens. That's why I got confused."

"I've got another theory on that. You want to know what it is? Weed makes you stupid. Empty your pockets, one at a time."

She emptied the first, revealing a piece of Trident gum and two quarters. She stuck her hand in the second and froze, stomach dropping to her toes. The bag of weed she'd lifted from Billy-Bo.

"Empty it," he said.

She pulled her hand out, held it open. "Nothing in that one."

Her voice sounded high and tinny to her own ears—like she was scared to death.

She was.

"Empty your damn pocket. Inside out, now."

She pulled out the bag of weed. "It isn't mine."

"Of course it isn't." He took it from her. "That's why it was in your pocket."

He motioned to the cruiser. "We're taking a little ride."

"Please, just go look. We're right here. If you do, I'll come quietly—"

"You'll come quietly because I said you will. Hands behind your back."

"What? Why?"

He snapped a cuff on one wrist, then the other. "In the cruiser."

"Cathy needs our help! Right back there." Randi started to cry. "Why won't you listen to me?"

He didn't respond, just shoved her into the backseat and slammed the door. She looked over her shoulder at the spot where she'd stumbled out of the woods, trying to memorize it as it disappeared from sight, red lights twirling crazily, the effect like a funhouse on crack. She felt sick to her stomach and turned quickly away, praying she didn't puke.

"Back there, you asked me why I wouldn't listen to you." Wheeler met her eyes in the rearview mirror. "It's because you're a liar, Randi Rader. You've proved that a hundred times over. And leopards don't change their spots."

She wanted to deny it, but those hundreds of times flew to her mind. A bitter taste rose in her throat.

"I'm on to what you're up to, Missy. That whole story back there was a diversion. You were going to lead me on a wild goose chase and when I wasn't looking, you were going to toss the pot. Sorry to spoil your plan."

Randi pressed her lips together and looked away. She caught a sign: BELLHAVEN PLANTATION AND NATURE PRESERVE, 2 MILES AHEAD.

The Preserve. That's where they'd been, she realized. In the sixth grade she'd taken a field trip there. She recalled being wide-eyed at the size of the house and the forlorn beauty of the overrun gardens and grounds.

"I feel so bad for your poor mama," Wheeler was saying. "She and I went to school together, did you know that?" He didn't seem to notice her silence and went on. "She was a pretty girl. Not all beaten down like now. A real shame."

He fell silent a moment, then went on. "Your mama, she wasn't from the best family, but how many of us from around here are, right? But what she saw in your daddy . . . I'll never understand."

He snorted. "And now look, all three of her kids headed for the same place. Your brothers both have one foot in a jail cell already and after tonight you're not looking much better off."

He clucked his tongue. "Lord almighty, you'd think one of you would want to do better than your—" He stopped a moment before adding, "—daddy."

He'd been about to say "no-good daddy," Randi knew, but had held back. He needn't have, she thought, she knew it was true and so did everybody else around these parts.

"So how about it, Randi?" He met her gaze in the rearview once more. "You gonna end up like your mama? Or worse?"

Worse, Randi thought, stomach heaving. Turning her head, she puked on the seat beside her. Much worse.

CHAPTER EIGHTEEN

8:10 A.M.

When Miranda emerged from the bathroom, Jake was gone and her cell phone was ringing. She snatched it up off the bed, glanced at the display, and answered. "Hey, Summer."

"Morning, princess. Headache, I presume?"

"You presume wrong. Clear as a bell."

"Interesting. You're not as out of practice as I thought."

Miranda pictured the night before, her and Jake tangled together, and her mouth went dry. Summer was referring to her tequila consumption, but wouldn't she enjoy knowing how close to home her words were?

"Underestimating me as usual. What's up?"

"I've got those names for you. The group of ladies who were talking about Richard Stark."

"You're amazing. Thank you."

She laughed. "There's more. After I closed up, I went over to Metro, talked with a friend over there. Name's Skye. She said Stark used to come in there a lot, hit on some of the cocktail waitresses, a couple of the bartenders. You might want to look her up."

Summer rattled off the names, promised to keep

Miranda posted if she heard anything else, then hung up. As Miranda went to set down the phone, she remembered the earlier call that she'd ignored. They'd left a message and she accessed her voice mail.

"Hi, little sis, this is—"

Her brother. Robby. Miranda dropped the phone like a hot rock. Her hands shook. Her heart formed a knot in her throat. Why today? She hadn't heard from Robby—or any other member of her family—in over two years. The silence had been a blessing.

She breathed deeply, in through her nose and out her mouth, working to center herself. The last family member she'd talked to was her mother, calling for help. Wes had been arrested again. Drug charges, again. Miranda was a cop, couldn't she do something?

As politely as possible, Miranda had explained that her job was upholding the law, not making life easier for criminals. She'd urged her mother to contact an attorney, then ended the call.

Remembering her mother's emotional plea made her angry. Where was that mom when Miranda needed help? Fifteen, that's how old she'd been. The same woman, now desperate to help her precious son the drug dealer, had washed her hands of Miranda.

"Six months in juvie will do you good, girl. Maybe it'll open your eyes and straighten you up."

Boy, had it opened her eyes. Enough to know she didn't want anything to do with her mother, father, or the rest of her no-good family ever again. She decided that when she was old enough to escape them, she was out of there.

Miranda bent, snatched up the phone, and deleted her brother's message. Hopefully it would be another two years until she heard from any of them.

She strapped on her shoulder holster, then slipped on her jacket. She grabbed an apple and protein bar and hit the road.

She dialed Jake from the car. "Hey," she said when he answered. "You at HQ yet?"

"On my way now. What's up?"

"Got a lead from Summer. A group of women in the Cat yesterday, talking about Stark. Said something to the effect he was probably killed by one of the many women he was juggling. Thought I'd track them down this morning, see if they can point me toward anyone in particular."

"Sounds like a plan. I'll bring Buddy up to speed and catch up with you."

"Perfect—"

"Miranda?"

Something in his voice suddenly sounded different. Personal. *Complications, they were starting already.* "Yeah?"

"Nothing. It's cool. Talk to you later."

Naomi, Caroline, and Emma. All three attractive and married, all three with money and too much time on their hands. They were more than happy to talk to her.

Miranda met them at their tennis club. She couldn't help admiring their tennis gear and knock-it-out-of-the-park bling. Naomi, she quickly noted, was the pack leader.

"The man was an absolute dog," Naomi said. "Always sniffing around."

Emma squealed and jumped in. "Didn't matter if the woman was young or old—"

"Married or single—"

"He was interested."

"So, he hit on all of you?"

"Of course," Naomi said. "And more than once."

"Did any of you bite?"

"Absolutely not," Naomi answered for them all. "We take our marriage vows seriously."

Miranda noticed that Caroline seemed the least animated of the group. She looked directly at her. "What about you? You ever take the bait?"

"No." She shook her head and said it again, more firmly, "No."

Miranda wasn't convinced and made a note to catch up with the woman later, without her buddies riding shotgun.

"Do you have any idea who might have wanted him dead?"

"Honey," Naomi drawled, "have you even been listening? Half the female population of Harmony, that's all."

"I need names."

"Names?" she repeated, looking shocked.

"As much as I enjoy a girl-time gabfest, I'm looking for a killer. Someone hurt enough, angry enough, or just so damn jealous they wanted Richard Stark dead."

That shut all three of them down, even Naomi. They only had suspicions, they said. They'd heard rumors and, of course, seen the handsome professor in operation. But specific names? They had to do some thinking about that.

Miranda left the three and called Jake from the car. "Yo," she said. "Where're you at?"

"Leaving HQ. I've got Jones with me."

Another member of the investigative team. "Jones? What's up?"

He didn't answer that question, instead asking another of his own. "Did you get anything?"

He sounded off. "Pretty much a bust. Basically more of what we already knew. Stark was a player and the three ladies liked to talk. That's about it."

"Buddy wants me and Jones to question Jessie Lund's mother again, this time without her daughter present."

She frowned. "Without me?"

"Uh-huh. Got Stark's cell records in. Guess whose number was on them?"

"Lund's?"

"Yup. Calls in and out."

"I'll follow up a few leads here, run down some of the other phone numbers. Keep me posted."

"You too."

"And Jake? Tell Jones good luck filling my shoes."

"Will do."

Miranda hung up. She didn't know what Buddy was up to, sending Jones in her place, but she sure as hell wasn't about to let it fly.

CHAPTER NINETEEN

8:40 A.M.

Miranda found Buddy in his office. He was leaning back in his chair, boots propped on his desk, reading the newspaper.

She tapped on the door. "Chief, you have a moment?"

He waved her in. "Does it look like I have a moment?" Grinning, he set aside the paper and brought his feet to the floor with a thud. "Just catching up on what's happening in New Orleans and Baton Rouge. We are blessed to live in Harmony, that I know for sure."

She closed the door behind her, took one of the chairs in front of his desk, and looked him in the eyes. "You sent Jones with Jake this morning. Why?"

"You were otherwise occupied. I thought Jones was a good call."

"Am I lead on this case?"

"Yes, of course."

"Are you sure? No second thoughts? Because now's the time to share them."

He frowned. "You're my most seasoned detective; this is a big case. No second thoughts, Miranda."

"Then Jones should have been my call. Not yours."

He narrowed his eyes. "In case you've forgotten,

Detective Rader, every call is my call." He tapped his chest. "See that sign on the door? It reads Chief Cadwell."

"With all due respect, Chief, I should have been alerted to phone records having been acquired. As lead I should be aware of every piece of evidence as it comes in. At the very least, you should have consulted with me. What's going on with you?"

Red crept into his cheeks. "That's quite enough, Detective."

"I've worked under your command for ten years. I've worked hard to become a good cop. The kind of cop you are, Chief. You've been a mentor and a friend, a good one at that."

He shifted slightly in his seat. "I appreciate that, Miranda."

"In those ten years, have I ever let you down?"

"You have not."

"Have I ever given you reason to doubt my integrity?"

"Of course not."

She unclipped her shield and laid it on the desk. "You want my badge? Here it is."

"Hell no, I don't want your badge." He pushed it back towards her. "What's this about, Miranda?"

"The gloves," she answered. "President Stark's complaint about me. After ten years, you doubt me. After a decade working together, you believe I'd behave in an inappropriate manner with a witness. Flat out, I don't get it."

"It was a major slipup, Miranda. Your fingerprints at a murder scene? How could I not take that seriously?" He leaned forward. "Coupled then with a complaint from a witness that you were acting like you had an ax to grind with the victim? What should have I done? You tell me."

"Given me the benefit of the doubt. Maybe questioned why President Stark would say such a thing about a trusted member of your team."

Buddy let out a long breath. "Ian Stark's a powerful man in this community."

"So his word means more than mine?"

"Let me finish. He can make life . . . difficult. For me. And for you."

"So I should bow down to him? What are you afraid of, Buddy?"

He went from flushed to furious. "That is enough. You have no clue the pressure on a man in my position. What it's like to have everyone depending on you, expecting you to have all the answers. The responsibility of it can . . . consume you. It cost me my marriage and my family, you know that."

"I do know that," she shot back. "I was there to help you pick up the pieces. Remember?"

He didn't reply and she stood, laid her palms on his desk and leaned forward, gaze fixed on his. "You say you don't want my badge? Then let me do my damn job."

He gazed at her for a long moment, an expression in his eyes she hadn't seen since the morning he shared that his wife had left, taking the kids with her. Was it lost? she wondered. Or trapped?

He broke the contact, looked away a moment, then back at her. "Agreed, Miranda. Just—" He paused a moment before continuing. "For the love of God, try not to step on Stark's toes."

Miranda nodded and started toward the door. When she reached it she stopped, looked back. Stark was pulling Buddy's strings, that much she was certain of. But why was Buddy letting him do it?

"Stark's phone records," she said. "Where are they?"

"There's a copy in your inbox."

She held his gaze a moment, then nodded again. "I'll be in touch."

As promised, the list was waiting for her: Numbers in and out and separately, recent text messages.

She downloaded the record of all Starks calls from seven days prior to his murder, then sent the document to the printer. Her desk phone rang as she stood to retrieve it.

"Detective Rader."

"Miranda? It's your old schoolmate, Paula. You gave me your card the other night at the vigil."

Miranda kept her surprise from her voice. "Hey, Paula. What can I do for you today?"

"I wondered if . . . maybe we could get together for coffee? Catch up?"

The two of them, catch up? They had nothing to catch up on—other than reminiscing over how different they were from each other in high school and how neither would have been caught dead hanging out together. If that was the real reason she was calling, which Miranda doubted. Her old classmate had something else she wanted to talk about and her gut was telling her it had to do with Richard Stark.

"That's really nice, Paula, but I'm buried in this investigation right now. Maybe another time?"

A moment of pregnant silence followed. Miranda waited, mentally crossing her fingers.

"Actually, I thought we could talk about that as well. For old times' sake."

Bingo. "I'd like that. I know a quiet place we can meet. Coffee's not great, but no one will bother us there. Ever heard of the Toasted Cat?"

CHAPTER TWENTY

10:00 A.M.

When Miranda arrived at the Toasted Cat, Paula was already there, standing beside her car. She looked anxious. "This is a bar, Miranda."

"Exactly. You're not going to run into anyone you know here this time of day."

Paula indicated the CLOSED sign in the window. "We're not going to run into anyone, because it's not open for another thirty minutes."

"I know the owner," Miranda said, starting for the door. "She's here and knows we're coming."

Miranda texted her friend that they had arrived. A moment later, Summer opened the door. She didn't look well and Miranda made a mental note to check on her when she and Paula finished.

Miranda introduced the two women. "Summer's a good friend and owner of this magnificent establishment."

Summer laughed and held out a hand. "I don't know about magnificent, but I'm glad to have you here. The daytime bartender will be arriving soon, but other than her, you'll have the place to yourselves for a while." She indicated the bar. "Brewed a fresh pot. Cream, sugar, and cups are all there. I'll be in my office."

They both thanked her and fixed themselves a cup of coffee. Miranda gestured toward the back of the bar. "How about the booth in the far corner?"

Paula nodded and followed her to the booth. They sat. Paula had called the meeting so Miranda waited for her to initiate.

After several moments of awkward silence, she did. "How's your family?"

"The same as they were back then."

"Oh. Sorry."

Miranda's lips twitched. "Not your fault. How's your family?"

"They're good. Mom and Dad moved to Atlanta to be close to my sister and her kids."

"Nice."

"You're not married?"

"Nope, never even close. How about you?"

"Me either."

Miranda looked down at her cup, then back up at the other woman. "I may be wrong, but I don't think you called me to chitchat about our families or our matrimonial states?"

"No." Paula let out a long, soft breath. "I wanted to talk to you about . . . Richard."

Excited, Miranda leaned slightly forward. "You knew him better than you first said, didn't you?"

She caught her bottom lip between her teeth and shook her head. "Not really, but I've . . . heard things about him."

"What kind of things?"

"That he—" She stopped. "This was a mistake. I shouldn't have called you. It's all just . . . gossip. And there's nothing you can do with hearsay—"

Miranda reached across the table and caught her hand. It was balled into a tight fist. "Not everyone's an eyewitness. We depend on hearsay and personal opinions. They provide trails for us to follow."

The bartender—a young woman named Tara—arrived, but didn't even glance their way. Her presence seemed to increase Paula's anxiety.

Miranda squeezed her hand, hoping to reassure her. "You called me for a reason, Paula. Talk to me. Tell me what you've heard."

She swallowed, glanced toward the bartender, then back at Miranda. "I could be fired."

"For talking to me? That would actually be against the law."

"They'd find something . . . some reason."

"They?"

"Stark. His cronies. You know how the system works."

"What system?"

"Every system where there are people at the top and people at the bottom who depend on them for their livelihood. It's the human sickness. One of them, anyway."

"You, the preppy cheerleader, a cynic now?"

"Not a cynic, a realist. And you, of all people should be one too."

"And why me?"

"You know." She leaned closer. "That's been your whole life."

The words took her breath. The cold, hard truth of them. It had been the story of her life. And as much as she had tried to escape, it still was.

"Tell me about Richard Stark. Tell me what you heard."

Paula hesitated a moment, then began, voice just above a whisper. "He wasn't a nice guy. That was an act."

"Then what was he, Paula?"

"A . . . predator. He took advantage of stupid women. Women—girls—who fell for his charm. His position and pretty face. Women who trusted him because of all that."

Miranda noted Paula's hands, clasped so tightly her knuckles were white; she noted the look of trauma in her eyes. Maybe her old classmate had intimate knowledge of Richard Stark's true character. "And what did he do to those trusting women?"

She shook her head. "I have to go."

Miranda reached across the table and caught her hand once more. "He raped them, didn't he?" Paula didn't respond and Miranda went on. "How'd he do it? Did he drug them?"

She tugged her hand free. "I just wanted you to know, that's what I've heard."

"From who? Students? Other faculty? Help me, Paula. Give me names."

"I can't do that." She stood. "I've got to go."

"Wait." Miranda followed her up. "Was it you, Paula? Did he rape you?"

She paled. "Thanks for the coffee, Randi. I'm really glad you're doing so well and I . . ." She took a step toward the door, then stopped. "I know you were telling the truth back then."

Miranda opened her mouth to speak, her throat so tight she didn't know if she could. "How," she managed to ask, the word coming out a croak.

"I didn't back then. But now . . . I wanted you to know that. And I wanted to tell you . . . I'm sorry."

Miranda blinked against the tears that stung her eyes. "For what?"

"For being such a jerk back then. And for not believing you."

"Paula, wait . . . you've got to tell me. Were you raped? Did Stark rape you?"

She shook her head ever so slightly, but Miranda couldn't tell whether she was saying she hadn't been or she just couldn't talk about it.

"Thanks for doing this, Paula." She paused. "All of it."

"I didn't do . . . anything. And, Randi? We didn't talk. Promise me, okay?"

Miranda did promise and walked Paula to her vehicle. "You've got my number. Call me. Anytime."

Paula nodded, climbed into her sedan, and drove away. Miranda watched her go, wondering what she would have done if Paula had said yes, Stark had raped her. Brought her in for questioning? Grilled her? Made her recount every moment of the "alleged" rape and her whereabouts the night of the murder? Wasn't that standard operating procedure?

What did she do now? Miranda wondered, tipping her face to the cloud-studded sky. What was usually so clear to her, was now anything but.

Her hands were shaking and she stuck them into her pockets, turning to head back into the bar and say goodbye to Summer.

As the door shut behind her, the bartender came running out of the back, expression panicked.

"Miranda, come quick! Something's happened to Summer!"

CHAPTER TWENTY-ONE

Summer lay sprawled on the floor, halfway between her desk and the door, her body twitching uncontrollably. Miranda knew exactly what was happening and rushed to help her.

"She's having a seizure," Miranda said to the bartender. "We need to roll her onto her side."

Tara joined her and they carefully eased her onto her side. Miranda checked her airway, saw it was clear, and let out a relieved breath.

"Is Summer an epileptic?" she asked the bartender.

The younger woman looked completely freaked out. "I don't know. I don't even really know what that is."

"This will pass in a minute; she'll probably be thirsty. You get a glass of water. I've got her."

Tara nodded and ran to retrieve the drink. By the time she returned with it, the seizure had passed and Miranda was helping Summer into a sitting position.

"Is she okay?"

"I'm right here and can speak for myself," Summer said. "I'm fine."

"I brought you some water."

"I see that." She held out her hand for it.

Miranda saw that Tara's hand was shaking as she gave it to her.

"You going to be okay, boss?"

"I said, I'm fine. But I'd be better if you stopped making a fuss over me and went and worked the bar. Anyone could wander in and rob us blind."

Miranda smiled Tara. "Yup, I think she's good."

"Grumpy." Tara wagged a finger at Summer. "You really scared me! Don't do that again."

"Wish I could make that promise," Summer muttered and waved her toward the door. "Now . . . go."

"How do you really feel?" Miranda asked when she and Summer were alone.

"Ridiculous. Help me up."

Miranda squatted beside her. "Hold on, let's make sure you didn't bump your head and give yourself a concussion."

"Another happy thought."

"How's your head?"

"Hurts."

"Let me check."

Summer pushed her hand away. "I'll check my own head, thank you."

Miranda watched as she gingerly explored her scalp. "Got a little bump. Not too bad."

"May I?" Miranda asked.

Summer agreed, albeit grudgingly. Miranda felt the lump and nodded. "We should probably go to the emergency room just in case."

"That's not happening. Now, will you please help me up?"

Miranda bit back a smile and held out a hand. "I see you're one of those kind of patients."

Summer scowled and clasped Miranda's hand. A

moment later she was on her feet. She stood a moment as if making sure she was steady, then crossed to the desk and sat.

"So, what's the deal?" Miranda asked. "You're an epileptic?"

"Yeah." Summer took a swallow of the water. "The frequency of my seizures has increased since the car accident. Lucky me."

"I'm surprised you never told me."

"Should I have?" Summer retrieved a vial of pills from her desk drawer, then looked up apologetically. "Sorry to snap at you like that. I hate feeling so helpless."

"I get it, believe me," Miranda said as her friend opened the vial. "What's that?"

"Anti-seizure medication." She popped a capsule into her mouth and washed it down with the water. "How did the meeting with your old friend go?"

"You know we weren't friends."

She arched an eyebrow. Miranda was glad to see the color had come back into her cheeks. "Do I?"

"Yeah, old friends don't need to meet somewhere no one will see them."

She smiled ruefully. "True." She dropped the vial back into the drawer. "It was about the case, wasn't it? Stark's murder?"

"I can't comment on that."

"Right." She jerked her head toward the door. "So maybe you should get out of here and get back to work?"

"Not until I know you're fine."

"You're worse than my mother. I'm fine. Now get the hell out of here and go solve a murder."

CHAPTER TWENTY-TWO

12:10 P.M.

Miranda sat in her car, engine running, working to slow her thoughts. Struggling to push aside the image of Summer sprawled on the floor, body uncontrollably convulsing.

She took a deep, calming breath. Summer was fine; she was under a doctor's care and there was nothing Miranda could do for her right now.

She had a job to do.

Focus, Miranda. What next?

Paula's words popped into her head. *"He was not a nice guy. He only acted like one."*

So how could she prove it? She frowned. Nobody wanted to talk, so she needed to find the proof someplace else. Where?

Stark's house. The first time through she had been looking for evidence that would lead to the arrest of Stark's killer. Now, she needed to search with another mindset, one set on proving that Richard Stark was not the paragon this community made him out to be. He was a sexual predator, one who had hurt an untold number of women and gotten away with his crimes for a long time.

Her cell went off. Jake, she saw. "Hey," she answered. "Where are you?"

"We're on our way back, about ten minutes out. Lund's mother didn't budge, insisted her daughter spent the night of Stark's murder in her childhood bedroom. Refused to say any more."

"I can't say I'm surprised. She seem as angry as yesterday?"

"Oh, yeah, big time."

"There's something she wants to say but is holding back," Miranda said. "And she's not happy about it."

"Agreed. Chief wants us to bring Lund in, question her at the station. See if we can rattle something loose."

Miranda wanted to rattle something loose, too, but she figured it'd be something way different than what the chief was looking for. "You picking her up?"

"Sent a patrol unit."

Miranda checked the time. "I'll meet you there."

Huddled in the interview-room chair, Lund looked younger than her twenty-three years. Miranda wasn't sure if tears had scrubbed every trace of cosmetics from her face or if she had been dragged straight out of bed. Her brown hair fell across her face as she gazed down at her clasped hands, concealing her expression.

Miranda didn't need to see her face to know what she was feeling. Fear. And confusion.

She understood because she had been in this same place before—afraid, uncertain, and surrounded by people who didn't believe her.

Miranda closed the interview room door behind her and Jake. "Hey, Jessie," she said softly. "How are you today?"

"Not good," she whispered.

"Can I get you something? Water? A soft drink?"

She shook her head but didn't look up, and Miranda took the seat across from her. "You know why we brought you here?"

"You need to ask me some questions. About Richard."

"Yes. And about the night he died."

"I don't know anything about that night."

Miranda sent Jake a warning look and he bit back whatever he'd been about to say.

"We know you lied to us, Jessie."

"I didn't."

"Sweetie, you called Richard Stark the night of his murder. In fact, you called him three times. We have his phone records."

She looked up then, pale as a ghost.

"We just want to know why you called him and what you talked about. That's all."

"I didn't kill him."

Miranda smiled reassuringly. "We didn't say you did."

"But that's what you think."

"I don't think that, Jessie. But I do believe there's something you're not telling us."

She paused to give her words a moment to sink in. And to offer Lund the time to respond.

When she didn't, she went on. "Jessie? Look at me."

She did, eyes wide and watery. The expression in them vulnerable.

"You were in love with Richard. Isn't that right? In love with the man you thought he was?"

"Yes," she whispered.

"When did you realize he wasn't that man?"

"I don't know what you mean."

"Yes, you do," she coaxed. "He wasn't a nice person, was he? That's what you found out."

"Detective," Jake broke in, "could I have a word with you out in the hall?"

"Not now, Detective Billings." She turned back to Lund. "When did you realize you'd been wrong about him?"

She hugged herself. "I don't want to talk about it."

"I know it's difficult, but you can trust me."

Jake jumped in. "Why did you lie to us about having talked to Richard that night?"

"I was scared. I knew how it would look."

"Like you're guilty," he said. "Right?"

"Yes. I thought . . . I was afraid you wouldn't believe me."

"Why should we? You've done nothing but lie to us."

"That's not true! I swear it!"

"I believe you," Miranda said.

"You do?"

She looked so hopeful, Miranda's heart hurt. "I do. There was a time, a long time ago, that I was in a similar position. And no one believed me."

"What happened that nobody believed?"

"I was attacked." She saw Lund digesting the information, hope easing toward trust. "Were you attacked, Jessie? Is that what you're afraid no one will believe?"

Jake made a sound of surprise; Miranda half expected him to grab her arm and drag her into the hall. Truth was, she wouldn't blame him if he did. She was going way out on a limb with this.

"Richard," Lund began, voice quivering, "he . . . I think he—"

She bit the words back, shook her head and looked away.

"You can tell me," Miranda coaxed. "Did he rape you, Jessie?"

Jessie flinched; her gaze flew to Miranda's, wide and

terrified. She opened her mouth as if to respond, then shut it as the interview-room door burst open.

"Detective Rader," Buddy snapped, "I need you out here. Immediately."

Miranda stood, knowing she would not be returning. She held Lund's gaze. "Don't be afraid to tell the truth, Jessie. It's always the best path."

"Detective, now!"

She smiled reassuringly at the young woman. "It's going to be all right."

When the door clicked shut, the chief faced her, features tight with fury. "What the hell was that?"

"I was playing the good cop to Jake's bad cop. Earning her trust—"

"Bullshit. You were leading the witness. Putting ideas in her head and trying to put words in her mouth!"

"I was making progress."

"Progress in what? Your own agenda? Dragging Richard Stark through the mud? Stark's the victim here, Miranda. Not Lund."

"That's where you're wrong, Chief. She's a victim, too, I'm certain of it. And if you'll give me five more minutes with her, I know—"

"You're not to have any contact with her, do you understand?" His face turned an angry red. "Not one more minute, not one more word. And if I learn you've defied my order, I'm taking your badge."

"But Chief—"

He held up a hand. "You're done for the day. I hate having to do this but you've left me no choice. Go home and get your priorities straight. Your job is to find a killer, not to vilify the victim. If you can't do that, you don't have any business on this case."

CHAPTER TWENTY-THREE

8:20 P.M.

The knock on Miranda's door didn't surprise her. Nor did seeing that it was Jake standing on the other side of it. She hadn't contacted him after Buddy relieved her of duty for the day, and he hadn't called her.

But even so, she'd known he would come.

"Hey," she said, opening the door and stepping aside so he could enter.

"Hey," he said back. "You okay?"

"As well as can be expected. Want a beer?"

"Sure."

She motioned toward the couch as she passed it on her way to the kitchen. She got them each a bottle of Abita Amber, popped the caps, and carried the bottles back to the living room.

She handed him his and he took a long swallow. He looked tired, she thought. And tense. The same as she must look. How different from the way they had been that morning, sleepy and satisfied, relaxed with each other.

And hopeful, she thought. For the day, the future. Maybe even a romantic relationship between them. Now, that seemed impossibly optimistic.

The memory was bittersweet, and Miranda forced it

aside and sat in the chair directly across from him. "What happened with Lund?"

"She clammed up after you left. Her mom showed up with a lawyer."

Miranda lifted the bottle in a mock toast. "Clammed up and lawyered up, no surprise there."

"Tracked down a local dominatrix. Calls herself a lifestyle mistress."

She nearly choked on her swallow of beer. "Lifestyle mistress, no kidding? And right here in little old Harmony, Louisiana."

"She said Stark contacted her six or so months ago about interviewing her for a book he was writing. They met several times."

"You ask whether he was into the real thing?"

One corner of his mouth lifted in a grimace. "He had no interest in the submissive role."

"But the dominant?"

"Asked if he could watch her and a client. Strictly for research."

"Right." She rolled her eyes. "And?"

"She had a client that was into it. So she made it happen."

"Name of the client?"

"She wouldn't say. Not sure it would help us anyway."

"What else did she say about him?"

"What do you mean?"

"She say he was a nice guy?"

"Actually, yeah, she did."

"Figures," she muttered, taking another swallow of the brew and making no attempt to mask her incredulity and disapproval.

He frowned, looking confused. "What gives, Miranda?"

The elephant in the room, she acknowledged. Sitting squarely between them.

"This is about what happened to you all those years ago, isn't it?"

She glanced away, then back at him. "Yes. But probably not in the way you think."

"What am I thinking?"

She lowered her gaze to her hands, clenched around the beer bottle. "Not this, I'm confident of that."

"Then tell me. Miranda—" He lowered his voice. "Look at me."

She did, and in his eyes she saw her future. It was a crazy, weird sensation, like a reel of a lifetime playing out in a glance.

She could trust him. He wasn't like anyone else.

She let out a pent-up breath. The release was almost painful, as if with it she was opening a part of herself that had been sealed shut for a very long time.

"Richard Stark—" She had to force the words out. Saying them aloud, sharing them with another, made them real. Once she did, she could never take them back. "It was him, Jake. He's the one."

"The one what?"

She didn't look away, didn't even blink. She lifted her chin as if in challenge. "He's the one who abducted me and the other girl. He's the one who tied us up, who raped her and meant to rape me."

For a long, silent moment he simply held her gaze. Then, finally, he asked, "Are you sure?"

"Yes."

"What's your proof?"

"I don't have any. Yet."

"That night . . . you recognized him? Why didn't you say something before now?"

"I didn't recognize him, not at first. I've come to re-alize who he was. I know I'm right about this, Jake."

"Oh man . . ." He dragged a hand through his hair, skeptical too mild a term to describe his expression. "How, Miranda? How do you know?"

"It's why he had the clipping," she went on. "And it's why he was killed."

"You think."

Too anxious to stay seated, she stood and began to pace.

"I got a call this morning. From a woman—"

"Who?"

"I promised her complete confidence. I can tell you she knew Stark from the university. She said he wasn't a nice guy. All that kindness and charm was just a front."

"Listen to yourself, Miranda. That's one woman's opinion. A woman who doesn't want to be identified, one whose motivation could be anything. Maybe he re-jected her?"

"That's what men always think, isn't it? That women accuse men of rape because they're jealous, or rejected, or just plain liars?"

"Wait, now we're talking about rape? This woman claimed that Stark raped her?"

"She stopped just short of it, yes. That he drugged her, then raped her."

He shook his head. "Do you really think this guy, this handsome, successful guy—the same one women were drooling over—you think he drugged women so he could have sex with them?"

"Not sex, Jake. Don't you get it? Sexual assault isn't about sex—it's about power, control, and punishment."

"Why hasn't anyone come forward?"

"It's obvious—just replay your last comments. Who would believe them?"

"So, what's your plan?"

"Lund's one of his victims, I'm certain of it. And so is the woman I talked to this morning."

"So that's where today came from?"

"Yes." She stopped, met his gaze. "Stark raped her. And Lund was ready to admit it when Buddy yanked me out of there."

"Big problem, Miranda. You put the thought in her head. And if she is guilty, you gave her a strong motive."

"She didn't kill him."

"Then who did? That's what we're supposed to find out." He paused a moment. "It's what we're paid to find out."

"We're paid to protect and serve. All citizens. All victims."

He dragged a hand through his hair again, leaving it standing on end. Oddly, she recalled the way his hair had felt when she ran her hands through it.

"What are you hoping to prove?" he asked. "What's your outcome?"

"Justice."

"For Stark?"

"No. For everyone he hurt."

"He's dead, Miranda. Someone violently took his life. It was a horrible, terrifying death. You don't think that was enough?"

"That was vengeance, Jake. This is for every woman he violated, every woman he took something from that wasn't his to take. When the truth comes out, they'll be heard. And they'll be believed."

He crossed to her, took the beer from her hands, and

drew her to her feet. He cupped her face in his palms. "I'm so sorry that happened to you back then."

"It's over."

"Is it?"

They both knew it wasn't. She'd been foolish enough to think she had moved on. Before Stark's murder. Before the news clipping found in his desk, before her fingerprints uncovered at the scene. Before Lund and Paula.

It seemed like a long time ago.

Miranda searched his gaze. "Are you going to stay?"

"Do you want me to?"

"Yes," she said, standing on tiptoes. "Stay."

And then she kissed him.

CHAPTER TWENTY-FOUR

6:00 A.M.

The next morning, Jake was gone when Miranda awakened. He left her a note of apology—he wanted to let her sleep, and considering the events of the day before, thought it better if he wasn't seen leaving her place in the morning.

Although Miranda agreed, she acknowledged a feeling of loss. She climbed out of bed, chastising herself for it. He was being smart. The way she prided herself on being.

So why this tug in the pit of her gut? What was wrong with her?

Miranda pulled on a pair of sweats, grabbed a T-shirt, then headed to the kitchen to start the coffee. There, as she watched the dark, fragrant brew drip into the pot, she realized there was nothing wrong with her. It was simply that everything around her was upside down and inside out.

Her cell went off and she darted to the bedroom, certain it would be Jake. Or headquarters. Who else called at six in the morning?

Her brother, Miranda saw when she snatched up the phone. Heart in her throat, she stared at the display, at the number shouting at her. Two calls in two days. It must be important.

To him. Not to her. She owed him nothing. He hadn't stood by her back then; none of them had.

Miranda tossed the phone onto the bed and headed back into the kitchen for coffee. It had finished brewing and she filled her ULH travel mug, added cream and sugar, and carried it with her to the bathroom.

She took a sip and the university's mascot, a hornet with a vicious-looking stinger, reflected back at her from the mirror.

"He wasn't a nice guy. He only acted like one."

Stark's house. Proof. That's where she had been headed before the Lund interview pulled her away. Why not do it now?

In fifteen minutes, Miranda was showered, dressed, and on the road. She forced herself to go the speed limit—the last thing she needed to do was call attention to herself. She reached Stark's neighborhood, then turned onto his street. It was the first time she'd been by since the night of the murder and as she got closer, she experienced the oddest tingle in her fingertips and toes. Like a heightened awareness of, or a connection, to the scene.

Miranda flexed her fingers in an attempt to shake off the sensation. Stark's house came into view; the crime-scene tape was gone and a silver Infiniti sedan sat the driveway.

She stopped at the mailbox and climbed out, scanning the area. Other than the car, the property seemed deserted. She approached the vehicle cautiously, peered inside, and confirmed it was empty.

Miranda turned her attention to the home's entry. Upon their exit of the scene the other night, the Sheriff's department had sealed the home's entrance. That seal was still intact. Once law enforcement determined they had gathered everything they needed from the scene, it would be cleared, the seal removed. That was Buddy's call to make.

She peeked through the front window. Again, nothing.

A neighbor could be using the driveway, she thought, although with the driveways on either side of this one empty, that was unlikely.

She went around to the back entrance. This door, however, stood slightly ajar, and she eased her weapon from her holster and made her way inside.

Ian and Catherine Stark. He rifling through drawers, she standing slightly behind, a framed photograph clutched in her hands. She saw Miranda and the photo slipped from her grip and hit the tile floor with a loud crack of the glass shattering.

At the commotion, Ian Stark swung around, whatever he'd been about to say dying on his lips.

Miranda lowered her weapon. "What are you doing in here?"

He glared at her. "I could ask you the same question."

"I was driving by, saw a vehicle, and came to investigate."

"Now that you know it's us, get out."

"I'm sorry, President Stark, but breaking the seal on that door was a crime."

"That's ridiculous. This was our son's home. It belongs to us now. We have every right to be here."

Miranda ignored him and looked at his wife. "I'm so sorry, Mrs. Stark, but you'll have to wait to collect any valuables until the home is cleared for entry."

"There are a few things . . . family things—" He

gaze dropped to the shattered photo. "I wanted to make certain they were . . . safe."

Her voice trailed off and Miranda felt bad for her. "Ma'am," she said softly, "I'm so sorry for your loss. But you don't want to be here, not yet."

"Don't tell my wife what she wants. You have no idea."

Miranda looked him straight in the eyes. "I think I do. This no place for your wife, your son's mother, to be. Not yet, anyway. Whatever your problem is with me, don't subject her to this."

Catherine Stark whimpered and plucked at his sleeve. "Let's go, Ian. Please."

"It's our property. You have no right to deny us access."

"Take it up with the Sheriff's Department or Chief Cadwell. I suspect you can get him to clear it, but until then, if you don't immediately vacate these premises, as a sworn officer of the Harmony Police Department I'll be forced escort you out, forcibly if necessary."

Catherine tugged at his arm. She looked a hair-breadth from completely falling apart. And suddenly so did he. It was as if all the bluster that had puffed him up evaporated, leaving him looking small and shrunken. She wouldn't have thought she could ever feel sorry for the man, but she did.

Miranda escorted them out, a hand on Catherine's elbow to help support her. She helped her into the ve-hicle and the woman's faded eyes held hers for a long moment. In them Miranda saw regret, so palpable a lump formed in her own throat.

"Be well, Mrs. Stark," she said softly, and slammed the door.

Miranda watched them drive off, then went to her car and retrieved a pair of gloves.

Stark was going to call Buddy as soon as possible; he may be on the phone with him already. She had missed something the first time through, because they hadn't been certain what they were looking for. She was now.

And she was on the clock.

She fitted on the gloves and headed back inside.

CHAPTER TWENTY-FIVE

Miranda shut the kitchen door behind her. Oddly, it seemed as if Ian and Catherine Stark's presence still hung in the room. Her gaze dropped to the broken picture frame and shattered glass. She bent and picked it up.

A young Catherine Stark with a handsome little boy. Miranda stared at the image, heart hurting as she thought of what the woman in the picture had already lost—and how much she would suffer if this search proved successful.

She slid the photo out from what was left of the frame and tucked it into her pocket.

The kitchen was as good a place to start as any. Obviously, Ian Stark had been looking for something here. But whatever it was, she didn't think he'd found it.

Miranda began her search to the right of the refrigerator and moved clockwise. Every drawer and cabinet. She moved as quickly as she could while still being thorough. Thumbing through paperwork, sifting through items in a catch-all drawer—bits of this and pieces of that. She shuffled through the pots and pans, peeked inside mixing bowls, and checked beneath every plate.

Nothing. Nothing yet, she told herself. She had a feeling of purpose. And urgency. It thrummed in her blood and spurred her on.

The pantry was nearly empty. That made things quicker but possibilities dimmer. She looked beneath each can, shook boxes, bags, and multipacks.

Still nothing.

The refrigerator was next. Again, very little on the shelves. Leftover pizza and Chinese. Catsup and mustard. Alcohol—champagne, beer, chardonnay, Irish cream liqueur—the guy obviously liked to drink more than eat.

Or he just entertained a lot.

Miranda checked the cheese and meat drawer—salami and several cheeses—then the fruit and veggie drawer, finding only strawberries and grapes, both well past their prime.

She took a deep breath and moved on to the freezer. More in here. Meat—steaks and chops and hamburger patties. A carton of ice cream—she checked it—no-frills vanilla. Several mystery meals in plasticware; she wondered if his mother had prepared those for him.

There, tucked in back was a lone box of frozen peas—with the exception of the mold growing on the cheese, the only green in the man's entire kitchen.

She knew even before she closed her hand around the box, before she saw it was already open, before she looked inside, that she had found what she was looking for.

Hands shaking, Miranda lifted the box's side flap and peered in. Tucked inside was a zip-style plastic bag. She eased it out. Not peas—small, round, white pills. A dozen of them.

Miranda knew exactly what they were. Rohypnol, commonly called roofies. The drug most often used in drug-facilitated sexual assault and no longer legally sold in the US.

Anger took her breath. That was how the bastard was doing it. He'd gotten a lot slicker in the last fourteen years. No more tape and rope—who needed that when he could render a woman unconscious and unable to resist with nothing more than a smile and a little white pill?

A metallic taste filled her mouth. Her anger became fury, mixed with hopelessness and pain, rising up in her until she feared it would spew from her with the force of a volcano erupting. She hugged herself and doubled over, fighting to hold back the howl of rage.

She couldn't. The sound ripped from her, bouncing off the walls and empty rooms, seeming to reverberate to her very soul. Goosebumps flew up her arms, over her belly and down her back. She gagged at the taste of bile in her throat.

Still hugging herself, she dropped to her knees. All the women he must have hurt over the years. Were she and the other girl his first? Or were there others before them?

A tear rolled down her cheek. She could have stopped him, protected all those women—if she had been a different girl. One who didn't lie. One who was cautious instead of reckless. The kind of person people believed.

Back then no one believed her.

Her fury eased, replaced by steely determination. They would now.

She slid the bag of pills back in the box, then tucked the box back into its spot at the back of the freezer.

If she collected the bag, it would be useless. Tainted beyond repair. She was here alone and without official authorization; it would be her word against *everyone's*.

She checked the time. Almost seven-thirty. Even as

she told herself she had enough and her best move was to come back with a team, something pressed her to search the rest of the house. Unlike the kitchen, she searched quickly, neither as methodically nor as stealthily as before. The clock, she knew, was ticking down to zero.

The garage was last. Her gaze landed on his car—a five-hundred-series BMW. His tastes hadn't changed, she thought bitterly, not in the cars he drove nor how he liked his women—immobilized and unwilling.

He'd left the sedan unlocked. Miranda thought she heard a car door slam out front, but continued her search anyway. She rummaged through, between the seats, under them, in the console.

A key. Small. Oddly shaped. Not to a door. A safe, she thought. Or lockbox.

"What the hell, Miranda?"

Jake. She curled her fingers around the key, slipped it into her back pocket, then emerged from the car.

He looked shocked. And disappointed. The last cut deepest.

He shook his head. "When the chief called, I was certain he was wrong. No way were you here—" he motioned around them, "—doing this. Not you, Miranda."

"I can explain."

"Don't bother. President Stark called Buddy. He sent me over. You're to cease and desist immediately."

"I saw a car in the drive. . . . The scene was still sealed, so I checked it out. It was Stark and his wife."

When he didn't comment, she rushed on. "He was looking for something . . . going through the kitchen drawers. He broke the seal, not me."

"So you kicked him out?"

"Yes."

"Why are you still here, Miranda?"

"Looking for what we missed."

"We didn't miss anything."

She pictured the key, the bag of roofies. "I think we might have. In fact—"

He held up a hand, stopping her. "Don't say another word. I don't want any part of whatever you think you're doing."

"The night of the murder, we were looking for something that would lead us to his killer. Turn that around—if he'd been a suspect, our search would have been different. Right? Different perspective, different—"

"Stop, Miranda. You're losing it. Richard Stark is the victim, not the perpetrator."

"He's both, Jake." Her voice shook and she fought to steady it. "I know it. Hear me, please."

"You've got to get your head on straight. If you don't—"

"I found something—"

"I don't want to—"

"In the kitchen, the freezer—"

"I can't know, Miranda! Don't you get it? Then we'll both be off the case."

She bit her words back. "You're right. I'm sorry. I shouldn't be here."

"No, you shouldn't. I'll escort you back to your vehicle and lock up."

She started for the door, then stopped. "Buddy's going to clear the scene, isn't he?"

"Yes."

"It's a mistake."

"No," he countered, "what you're doing is the mistake."

"Because I'll get yanked off the case? Or fired?"

"Yeah to both. And maybe worse."

Maybe worse, she thought. Like knowing the truth but nobody believing you. Like a scream echoing in your head and not ever knowing what happened next. Or living with the fact that it could have been you, and the help you promised never came.

The fight drained out of her and he walked with her to her car. She climbed in. "I'll see you back at head-quarters."

He nodded, slammed the car door, but didn't make a move toward his own vehicle.

Miranda cranked the engine and drove off. Before she turned at the end of the block, she glanced in the rearview mirror.

He still hadn't moved. As if he felt her glance, he lifted a hand in good-bye.

CHAPTER TWENTY-SIX

8:25 A.M.

In the ten short minutes it took Miranda to drive from Stark's home to headquarters, the certainty of what she needed to do took form: Tell Buddy about the roofies and convince him to put together a team to go in and retrieve them right way.

She was a good enough cop to know she'd screwed up and that Buddy was going to let her know it. But she was also good enough to know something could be salvaged from the discovery.

She took a deep breath and tapped on his partially open door. The chief waved her in, expression a thundercloud. "Shut the door, Miranda."

"Should we wait for Jake—"

"No. Take a seat." She did and he fixed his furious gaze on her. "What the hell were you thinking?"

"Hear me out, Chief. If you still want to come at me with both barrels, I'm right here and an easy target."

He nodded slightly, although his flush didn't reassure her this was going to end well. "Ian Stark and his wife were the ones who broke the law. I drove up, saw a car in the victim's drive, and went to investigate."

"Why were you in Stark's neighborhood in the first place?"

"To check on the scene. I had no idea the vehicle belonged to them."

He looked her straight in the eyes. "And until that moment, you had no previous plans to enter the home?" Her hesitation gave her away and he swore. "Dammit, Miranda! You know better than—"

Jake tapped on the door and poked his head in. "Chief, you want me to—"

The chief waved him in. While Jake got settled, Miranda took over. "I had this feeling we'd missed something." She rushed on before Buddy had a chance to respond. "I was right. I found something, Chief. It's pretty big."

She felt Jake's gaze; the chief stilled, suddenly alert and waiting. "Roofies," she said. "A bag of them. In the freezer, stuffed into a vegetable box. Green Giant sweet peas, to be exact."

Buddy looked at Jake. "Did you know?"

He shook his head. "No. I found Miranda in the garage, going through Stark's car."

He didn't mention her attempt to tell him, which was probably for the best.

"Where are they now?" Buddy asked.

"I put them back where I found them."

"And what, to your mind, does this have to do with this investigation?"

"As you very well know, Chief, roofies are used for one thing: drug-facilitated sexual assault."

"I repeat, what does that have to do with this investigation?"

"You've got to be joking."

"I'm dead serious." He folded his hands on the desk in front of him.

"Richard Stark was a bad guy. A really bad guy. And the bag of drugs proves it."

"That's not your job, Rader. Your job is to find Richard Stark's killer."

"There's only one thing those roofies—"

"Alleged roofies."

"—are used for. They prove Richard Stark was a sexual predator."

"Even if it's true—"

"It is."

"Even if it's true," he repeated, "we're not looking for a sexual predator. We're looking for a murderer."

Was he being deliberately obtuse? How could he not comprehend the ramifications of her discovery? She glanced at Jake, saw no help would be coming from that direction, and refocused on Buddy.

"It widens the field and gives us a motive. What we don't know is how big the victim pool might be. Five? Ten? Twenty-five?"

"For God's sake, Miranda! Victim pool? Get a grip!"

She went on as coolly as possible. "The killing, the brutality of it . . . his castration, for God's sake. . . . Come on, Chief, it supports this being a vengeance killing, one hundred percent."

Jake stepped in. "She has a point, Chief. Stark's death was a case of serious overkill."

Buddy stood, face red. "I will not let you drag a good man through the mud—"

"A good man?" she repeated, outraged, launching to her feet. "If I'm right, he was a sexual predator! Rohypnol, Chief! A dozen in the bag. A dozen!"

"What if you're wrong? Think about his family, the pain this would cause them. And the university, its reputation. Just the rumor could be devastating to enrollment. A popular professor a sexual predator? What parent's going to send their daughter to ULH?"

"You sure that's whose reputation you're worried about, Chief?"

He went dead still. "You're out of line, Detective."

She refused to look away or back down. "I'm not wrong about this."

"What do you propose?"

"We go back into Stark's house and retrieve the evidence."

"It's worthless now."

She looked at Jake. "When you showed up, did I have my gloves on?"

"You did."

Buddy dismissed the idea. "What difference does that make?"

"Somebody's prints will be on that box and the bag in it. I was wearing my gloves so they won't be mine."

"Stark's," Jake said, looking at the chief. "She's right—the man's dead so there's no way the evidence could have been planted."

"But it was tampered with. It won't hold up in a court of law."

"It doesn't have to. We're not trying to convict with this evidence. We're trying to support our line of questioning."

"And that's it? Because I won't tolerate any attempt to use this as an opportunity to blame the victim."

Jake stepped in. "That's it, Chief. I'll see to it."

For a long moment, Buddy was quiet; then he nodded in Jake's direction. "You bet your ass you will." He turned back to Miranda. "We do it together. I want the photographic documentation and someone from the Sheriff's Department along. They sealed the scene, so they should be there when we go back in."

"Thank you, Buddy," she said. "You won't regret it, I—"

He held up a hand, stopping her. "We do this, then you're off the case."

"What?" She shook her head. "No. That's not right, I'm the best person for—"

"No, you're not. Not anymore, Miranda. You've lost your objectivity." He turned to Jake. "You're lead, Jones assists. My decision's final."

CHAPTER TWENTY-SEVEN

9:50 A.M.

It took nearly an hour to assemble the team. The three vehicles pulled up to Stark's home, one with Miranda and Jake, another the chief, and the last the Sheriff's Department crime-scene van. The officers exited their vehicles in unison and started silently up the walk. Miranda fitted on gloves as she did so, willing her racing heart to slow, her turbulent thoughts with it.

She'd never been removed from a case before, never had to endure the heavy silence in the squad room as she passed or the way her colleagues averted their gaze. They were embarrassed for her.

But they didn't get it. The truth was on her side. Justice was on her side. All she had to do was stay calm. Once Buddy saw the box, the bag it contained, he'd come to his senses and put her back on the case, even if it was only as second in command.

The sheriff's man cut the seal; the team filed in, making their way to the kitchen. Miranda waited while the tech readied the video camera. When he signaled the go-ahead, she opened the freezer and reached inside, making certain the camera caught and recorded her every move.

And it did: Her disbelief and momentary confusion, then her stunned expression as the realization dawned.

The box, along with its damning evidence, was gone.

Miranda stood beside her car, mind reeling and hands shaking. The box had been there. She'd held it in her hands, counted the pills in the bag. A dozen. There'd been a dozen.

She wasn't delusional, although she had looked that way, rummaging wildly through the refrigerator, thinking maybe, in her excitement, she'd stuck the box there by mistake. Even though she knew she hadn't—she clearly remembered placing the box exactly where she'd found it.

She hadn't been able to look at anyone. Had been afraid to speak. What could she have said? Begged them to believe her? Stomped her foot or burst into tears, like an unhinged two-year-old?

So, she did something she never would have thought possible for her to do. Simply, without a word, she'd walked out.

And here she stood, waiting for the others. Feeling ridiculous and beaten. How long had it been since she'd felt this way, this soul-stealing combination?

The home's door opened; the team emerged. Jake and Buddy started toward her; the sheriff's techs headed straight for the van, neither glancing her way. No doubt they'd have a good laugh at her expense, a great story to share over beers later.

The breeze worked some hair free from the clip holding it back; Miranda tucked the strands behind her ear. Buddy and Jake stopped in front of her. She looked at Buddy. "I don't understand, Chief. It was there."

"Miranda—"

"It was. You have to believe me. Someone's a step ahead. They knew what I found—or what was there—and in the time between—"

He cut her off. "I don't know what's going on with you, Miranda. Maybe it's some sort of PTSD, but you haven't left me any choice."

She heard pity in his voice. Resignation. She suspected what was coming next and shook her head. "Don't do this, Chief. . . . Buddy, please—"

"Give me your badge, Detective Rader."

She felt the words like a blow and took an automatic step back. This couldn't be happening. She wasn't that person.

He held out his hand. "And your service weapon." He shifted his gaze slightly. "It's temporary, until we get a handle on what's going on with you."

"Nothing's going on with me. The box was there! Inside it was a zip bag with twelve round, white pills—"

She stopped and looked at Jake. He stood slightly behind Buddy, hands jammed into his pockets, eyes averted. No help, she thought. No champion or ally, just like fourteen years ago.

It hurt and she steeled herself against the emotion. She squared her shoulders and narrowed her eyes. "I'm fine," she said softly but with steel in her tone. "I didn't imagine any of this, and someday you'll admit it and regret doing this."

"Take some time off," he said. "I want you to make an appointment with the department shrink. We'll see how it goes."

She didn't respond and he went on. "I've cleared the scene. You set foot on this property again, and you're trespassing." He narrowed his gaze on her. "Do you understand?"

"Of course."

"Your badge," he said again.

She handed it over, then her holster and weapon. By some miracle her hands and gaze were steady. "Jake, I presume you'll catch a ride back with Chief Cadwell?"

He looked at her then, expression stricken. "I'll do that."

She nodded curtly, climbed into her car, and without a backward glance, drove off.

CHAPTER TWENTY-EIGHT

Noon

Miranda stepped from the bright light of midday into the perpetual evening of the Toasted Cat. Summer looked up from the newspaper she was reading, spread open on the bar in front of her.

"I heard," Summer said.

"Bad news travels fast."

"Jake called me. He figured you'd come here."

Miranda slid onto a barstool. "How much did he tell you?"

"Only that you'd been suspended." Summer set a glass of water in front of her. "Honestly, I thought it was a joke."

"I wish."

"That was a while ago. Where've you been?"

"Just driving."

"I'm sorry," she said. "This really blows."

Yes, it did. "How about a cup of coffee?"

"Just made a fresh pot."

She poured them each a cup and set out the carton of half-and-half and the sugar caddy. "What happened?"

"I followed a hunch."

"The Stark murder?"

"Uh huh." Miranda doctored her coffee, then took a

sip. "Took it upon myself to go back to the scene, conduct a search."

"And you found something incriminating?"

"Damn right I did."

Her eyebrows shot up. "And Cadwell wasn't dancing for joy?"

"He would have been," she said bitterly, "but it incriminated the wrong party."

Summer rested her chin on her fist. "Sweetie, that doesn't make a bit of sense. You know that, right?"

"Oh, it does. Unfortunately for me." She shook her head, knowing she'd already said too much but going on anyway. "So, I left said incriminating evidence where I found it and convinced Cadwell to assemble a team to go back and collect it."

"And?"

"When we got there, it was gone."

"Holy crap."

"That pretty much covers it. And not only am I unprofessional, I look like I've lost my mind as well."

Summer went for the coffee, refilled her own cup, and topped off Miranda's. "And Cadwell didn't believe you?"

"He suggested I might be suffering from PTSD. I have to see the department shrink before he'll even consider reinstating me."

"That's a crock of shit. You're the most stable person I know."

Miranda laughed, the sound choked. "Maybe I am suffering from PTSD. You know what happened to me when I was fifteen? This case has dredged it all up, and maybe I'm cracking."

Summer made a face. "You don't believe that. I know you don't."

"I don't know what to believe anymore."

"That's just—" Summer grimaced slightly and rubbed her temple. "Bullshit."

Miranda realized she'd seen Summer do that earlier, as well. "Are you okay?"

"Headache, that's all."

"From your expression just now, it looks like a doozy. Have you taken something for it?"

"I hoped the coffee would take care of it, but maybe I should." She rummaged in the drawer under the register and came up with a couple tablets.

She took them, then returned to their conversation. "First off, I believe you. I believe in you, Miranda. You didn't imagine any of this. You didn't make it up. So don't start the 'I don't know what to believe' crap. And second—" Summer leaned toward her. "What happened today, that evidence disappearing, you know what that means."

She did, and nodded, feeling as if she was coming back to life. "That between the time I left and came back with the team, someone took it."

"That's right. How long was that?"

"Two hours, tops." Miranda narrowed her eyes. "It had to be Ian Stark. He was there when I got there, in the kitchen, obviously searching for something."

"Who else could it be?"

"His wife, Catherine. She was with him, but . . . I don't see that."

"Anyone else know you found something?"

"The chief. But he never left HQ after I told him. And Jake. But he was—"

She bit back the words and Summer frowned. "What about Jake?"

"Nothing. He was with me, too. The whole time."

Except for the few minutes between when she left the

scene and he showed up at headquarters. She'd told him about the freezer, that she'd found something that supported her claim about Stark. He hadn't wanted to hear more, so she'd stopped.

How long was it between when she arrived back at HQ and Jake did? Ten minutes? Certainly enough time to go to Stark's freezer and see for himself. He was smart; he would have recognized the box as being out of place right away, just as she had.

Enough time to take the box.

No, not Jake. Why would he? To protect Stark? To further his career? Neither sounded like the Jake she knew.

"Miranda? What's wrong?"

She blinked, focusing on her friend's concerned expression. "Sorting it out, wondering who I can trust."

"Sounds to me like you can't trust anyone."

Maybe she couldn't. Maybe it was time to go. Pack up and move on, the way she'd always promised herself she would.

She told Summer that, and her friend frowned. "Where would you go?"

"Anywhere. Away from here."

Summer wiped a water ring from the bar. "I think they call that running away."

"Yeah, so what?" She drained her coffee. It had gone cold and grown bitter.

"You're not a quitter, Miranda."

"You so sure about that?"

"A quitter would have walked away from this place a long time ago. Just saying."

Dammit. Summer was right on both counts. "So, what do I do?"

"Do about what? Getting your job back?"

"Yeah, but not just my job. My reputation."

Summer nodded, her gaze shifting to the door and the boisterous group coming in. "You get them to believe you. Whatever it takes."

CHAPTER TWENTY-NINE

11:10 A.M.

For Miranda, the next twenty-four hours passed in a fog of pacing and moping, of channel-surfing and simply staring at the ceiling and wondering what the hell she was going to do with her time. She wrapped her days around her job. That's what she did. It was all she had.

Jake had called twice. Both times she'd let it go to voice mail. Both messages had said pretty much the same thing—he wondered how she was, he was worried, and he asked her to please give him a call.

She hadn't. She wasn't ready.

Summer's words kept coming back to her.

"Seems to me, you can't trust anyone."

Could she trust anyone? Jake had the opportunity to take the box and its evidence. She shook her head. No, she couldn't see it.

But what about Buddy? He hadn't left the department, so she knew beyond a shadow of a doubt he hadn't had the opportunity. But could he have called someone, asked them to do it.

Who? Someone under his command? And chance tarnishing his reputation? No way. So who else? Ian Stark?

She stood and began to pace. Stark had the most to

lose. His son's reputation and by association, his own as well. Perhaps worse, it'd be a blow to the university—a popular professor—and son of the university president—drugging and raping his students?

It didn't get much more damaging than that.

Ian Stark had known what his son was. She didn't have proof, but would stake her life on it. So had Catherine Stark. They were the most likely to have retrieved the damning evidence.

The key, Miranda remembered. She hadn't thought of it since Jake surprised her and she stuffed it into her pocket. She hurried to the bedroom and retrieved the pants she'd been wearing. The key fell out of the pocket, landing at her feet.

She picked it up, curling her fingers around it.

What did the key belong to? A lockbox of some sort, she thought. But there hadn't been one at Stark's house. Not in his faculty office at the university either. So where?

His parents.

She could imagine him asking his parents to keep it for him. Or him storing it in his childhood bedroom, tucking it there on the top shelf of his closet.

Make them believe you. Do whatever it takes.

Miranda straightened, crossed to her closet and the jacket she'd worn the previous day. There, in the inside pocket, the photo of the sweet little boy who would become a monster.

She gazed at young Richard Stark's cherubic face, an idea forming. With her first sense of purpose in twenty-four hours, she headed to the shower.

Miranda pulled up in front of Ian and Catherine Stark's home. Before coming here, she'd driven by the campus administration building. A silver Infiniti sedan had been parked in the spot marked RESERVED FOR PRESIDENT.

Perfect. With Ian Stark tied up at work, maybe she'd have a chance to connect with his wife.

Miranda took a deep, fortifying breath, collected the tissue-wrapped package from the passenger seat, and tucked it into her purse. She climbed out of her car and headed up the walk.

Catherine Stark herself answered the door. When she saw it was Miranda, she grew visibly upset. "I can't talk to you," she said, and began to close the door.

Miranda stopped her. "Wait, please. I have something for you." She handed over the package. "It's my fault it was broken."

The woman peeled away the tissue. When she saw what it was, tears welled in her eyes and rolled down her cheeks.

"I couldn't salvage the frame," Miranda said. "So I bought a new one."

She didn't look up, didn't acknowledge Miranda in any way. Just gazed at the photo of a smiling toddler and his adoring mother.

"He was a beautiful little boy," Miranda said softly.

"Yes," she whispered and looked up. "And very sweet." She lightly touched the glass. "He was my heart."

"I'm terribly sorry for your loss, Mrs. Stark." And she was. Not just for the physical loss of her only child, but for the loss of the sweet little boy she'd loved. That loss, Miranda knew, had come long before his murder. "I can only image how difficult this has been."

"We couldn't have more children," she said, almost to herself. "We tried. We . . . it was me. I couldn't carry another child."

A lump formed in Miranda's throat. She didn't respond because she wasn't sure she could.

"Maybe I loved him too much," she whispered, gaze returning to the photograph. "Maybe we both did."

"I don't think anyone can be loved too much." Catherine Stark didn't respond and Miranda went on. "I want you to know, I have nothing against you or your husband. I'm just trying to do my job."

The woman lifted her gaze. "Why did this have to happen? Why . . . him?"

Again, Miranda had the feeling she wasn't talking about the murder—or only the murder—but about the loss of the sweet boy her son had started out to be. "I don't know. I wish it hadn't happened to you."

"Thank you for . . . bringing this. It was very kind."

"If you need anything, don't hesitate to call me."

She nodded and started to close the door. Miranda stopped her. "Wait, Mrs. . . . . Catherine?"

"Yes?"

"We found a key at Richard's. It appears to go to a lockbox of some type. Do you know . . . did your son have one?"

Mrs. Stark seemed to freeze a moment, then shook her head, movement stiff. "How would that help you find his killer?"

Miranda lifted a shoulder. "We're not sure, but it raises questions. Perhaps the killer took the box?"

"Good-bye, Detective. I hope you find what you're looking for."

What, not who, Miranda thought as the door snapped shut. From the other side, she heard the click of the deadbolt falling into place.

Miranda hurried back to her car. The quicker she exited, the less likely she was to be seen here. If Buddy got wind she was pursuing the case on her own, she'd never get her badge back.

Miranda reached her car, climbed in, and started it up. She pulled away from the curb, letting out a breath she hadn't realized she'd been holding. She had planted the seed; she could only hope that something grew from it. If nothing did, she had no idea where she'd turn next.

CHAPTER THIRTY

Jake was waiting for Miranda when she got home. As she turned into her drive, he climbed out of his vehicle and started toward hers. She hadn't realized until that moment how angry she was at him. Or how hurt.

She exited her car, slamming the door behind her. "What are you doing here?"

"I need to talk to you."

She folded her arms across her chest. "You didn't stick up for me, Jake."

"How could I, Miranda? What could I have said?"

"That you believed in me. You could have told Buddy that if I said that box was there, it was. That's belief in someone, that's having their back."

"I'm in love with you, Miranda—"

"Funny way of showing it."

She ducked by him, heading to the front door. He caught her elbow, stopping her before she reached it. "If you'd just listen—"

She looked over her shoulder at him, spoiling for a fight. The anger, betrayal, and helplessness of the past few days boiling up in her. "Did you take it?"

"Take what?"

"The box, with the roofies. I told you I found

something, that it was in the freezer. You had the opportunity—"

"No. God, no. How can you even ask me that?"

"Because someone did."

"I believe you," he said.

She jerked her arm free. "Too late. You had your chance in front of Buddy. That's the moment that counted."

She unlocked her door and stepped inside. He stopped her from closing it in his face. "I believe you," he said again. "I saw it, Miranda. I saw the box."

"What did you . . . what do you mean, you saw it?"

"After you left Stark's, curiosity got the better of me. I decided to look in the freezer. I saw that lone box of vegetables."

Her heart beat heavily against the wall of her chest. "Did you look inside it?"

"No."

"Why not? You were that far. Why—"

"I got a grip on myself. I acknowledged that what I was doing was pretty stupid. Whatever you'd found had been compromised enough; my messing with it would only make it worse."

She digested that. "Why didn't you say something?"

"I couldn't. If I had, Buddy would've pulled me off the case, too. Then you would have had no one on the inside."

She arched an eyebrow. "Are you suggesting I should be grateful you didn't stand by me?"

"Of course not." He flashed her a smile. "But yeah, maybe."

She steeled herself against the smile. "How do I know I can trust you?"

"You should just know, Miranda."

Simple. Straightforward. And true.

Just like Jake.

For better or worse, she did trust him. "Come on in."

He stepped into the foyer, and closed the door behind him. "I can't stay too long. Buddy's been watching me like a hawk."

"Speaking of trust."

"Exactly." He turned back to her. "Buddy's protecting Stark's reputation. Both the Starks', I imagine."

"I can't believe he would do this," Miranda murmured. "I trusted him, looked up to him. To protect a serial predator by covering up evidence? A week ago I would have called the notion impossible."

"He might not have done it, Miranda."

"I gave him the benefit of the doubt before, when you pointed out his odd behavior concerning this case. Now it all makes sense. His going to the crime scene first, his going to Stark, taking his side against me. He was never impartial."

Jake crossed to her and caught her hands in his. "Were you? Impartial?"

A damning question. One they both knew the answer to.

"I couldn't be," she said softly, a catch in her voice. "Once I knew Stark was . . . the one."

She lowered her gaze to their joined hands, then returned it to his. "Buddy was right to take me off the investigation."

"Yes." Jake rested his forehead against hers. "But he did it for the wrong reasons."

She swallowed past the lump in her throat. "Thank you."

"I didn't do anything." He cupped her face in his palms. "Yet anyway."

He kissed her, deeply. Once, then again.

With a sound of regret, he ended the embrace. "I

need to go, but I've got news about the case. It's about Jessie Lund."

Miranda held her breath. Something in his tone warned she wouldn't be happy with what he was about to share.

"We've gotten ahold of her phone data and it's not good news for her. Records show she was not at her mother's the night of the murder. At least not the entire night."

"Dammit," Miranda muttered.

"More like damning," Jake said. "She called her mother just after one in the morning. The call lasted twenty-seven minutes."

Miranda's heart sank. Around Stark's estimated time of death. A hysterical girl calling her mother? Maybe.

Jake took several folded papers from his pocket and handed them to her. "A copy of Lund's phone log."

Miranda scanned them. Starting in mid-January, a steady stream of calls between Lund and Stark. The number grew, seeming to reach a crescendo, then stopped dead. Right around the time Lund quit school.

"Fifty calls," Jake said, as if reading along with her. "Then nothing, until a flurry of calls leading up to the night of the murder."

"The first of those," she noted, "was initiated by Stark."

He raised his eyebrows in question. "So?"

"He was reeling her back in."

"That's one interpretation. Here's another. Lund has a major crush on Stark; she thinks he reciprocates, but he rejects her. Playing devil's advocate here, he does it firmly, but as gently as he can."

"I think I'm gonna puke."

"You know that's what any prosecutor worth his salary's going to say."

"Fine," she said. "Let's hear the rest of the fairy tale."

"She gives up her assistantship and drops out of school. He feels bad. He didn't mean to hurt her, so he calls, to try to make it right. Because he's a good guy with a big heart."

"That's a pretty picture you're painting of Stark. Let's look at a different one. What if he knew she had a crush on him and he took advantage of her? Or maybe it's worse than that? Maybe he's a predator, he hunts for the weak and vulnerable, then incapacitates them and sexually assaults them?"

"You're counselor for the defense; prove it," Jake said. "Prove it and use it to lighten the sentence against Lund, because she's still guilty of murder."

"She didn't do it."

"She may have, Miranda."

"No way."

"Well, somebody did. And my bet is, if it wasn't Lund, it was somebody like her."

"I've got to talk to Lund."

"That's not going to happen. Besides, you heard the chief—you talk to her and he finds out you did, you lose your badge permanently. He might even charge you with interfering with an investigation."

"It might be worth the risk."

"Think that through carefully, Miranda. It could change your life forever."

This already has, she silently acknowledged. "Is she being charged?"

"They don't have enough, but they're holding her as long as they legally can."

She couldn't wait that long. "Her mother," Miranda said, meeting his eyes. "This is why she's been so angry. She knows what Stark did and she's furious because we're treating her daughter like she's the criminal."

"So, why's she keeping quiet?"

"My bet? At first her daughter made her promise not to say anything. And now she realizes, or their lawyer has advised, that the truth supplies the police with a strong motive."

"That's true, Miranda. You know that, right?"

"But when we expose the sheer number of women he's done this to, it dilutes that motivation and widens the field of suspects. Suddenly, Lund won't seem like such a slam dunk."

"You've got a steep hill to climb."

Miranda's mind was racing. If she couldn't get to Jessie Lund, she'd go for the next best. "I'm going to try to connect with Lund's mother. See if I can get her to talk."

"I didn't hear that." He moved toward the door. "And I certainly didn't mention that said mother has a room over at the Harmony B&B on Franklin."

CHAPTER THIRTY-ONE

5:05 P.M.

Located in the university area, the Harmony B&B was one of the few unique places to stay in town. Built in the eighteen-hundreds, the Victorian-style home had been purchased by a couple from New Orleans looking for a slower-paced lifestyle in the country.

Miranda knew the owners from responding to various calls over the years, and unless word had spread about her suspension—which she doubted—she wouldn't need to show her badge to get the information she wanted. And if the innkeeper had heard, Miranda figured she'd still get the information. Carolyn Ramsey liked to talk.

Miranda smiled and crossed the foyer to the front desk. "Evening, Carolyn. What's for dinner tonight? It smells amazing."

"Shrimp creole over rice, green beans almondine, and bread pudding with praline sauce."

Miranda's mouth began to water. "And those tiny cheese biscuits?"

"You know it." Carolyn smiled broadly. "I made extra, like I always do. How about I bag up a couple for you?"

"I can't believe I'm saying this, but not tonight. I'm here to talk to Susan Lund."

"Oh." Carolyn glanced toward the door, a frown creasing her brow. "She must have forgotten. You just missed her."

"She checked out?"

"No, went for a walk." Carolyn leaned forward. "What's going on with her daughter? When she checked in, she told me she was visiting her daughter. I assumed it had something to do with a university event, but our yardman said he saw her coming out of the police station the other day, and Betty from Coffee & More said—"

"Now, Carolyn," Miranda said lightly, cutting her off, "it doesn't matter how small this town is; you know I can't talk about that."

She looked so disappointed, Miranda figured the woman wouldn't be offering her biscuits again any time soon.

"Just tell me this—" Carolyn leaned forward and lowered her voice. "Does it have anything to do with that professor's murder?"

Keeping her features neutral, Miranda asked, "Why would you say that?"

"People are talking, that's all."

"I tell you what, Carolyn, you hear anything that sounds like more than gossip, give me a call." She slid her card across the counter. "Call my cell, not the department."

The woman looked thrilled. "You've got it, Miranda."

"Any idea where Mrs. Lund may have gone?"

"I suggested the trail around the duck pond. It's so pretty this time of day."

Susan Lund had taken the innkeeper's suggestion;
Miranda found her on a bench at the halfway point,
staring at the lake. As Miranda approached, her shoulders slumped and she dropped her head into her
hands.

"Mrs. Lund . . . Susan, I was hoping to have a minute
of your time."

She looked up, face blotchy from crying. "Leave me
alone. I don't want to talk to you."

"I understand," Miranda said softly, "more than you
know."

"My Jessie didn't do anything. She's the one who
was hurt! And now, you people—" She bit the last back
and stood. "Don't follow me."

"I know Jessie didn't do anything," Miranda called
after her. "Except fall for a bad guy."

She stopped and turned slowly back to Miranda.
"What did you say?"

"You heard me. I know your daughter did not kill
Richard Stark. And I know what he was."

Several different emotions sped across the other
woman's face: hope, suspicion, fear. "How?"

Miranda motioned to the bench. "Can we sit
down?"

Susan hesitated a moment, then nodded and returned
to the bench. Miranda sat beside her and together they
stared silently out at the water.

Several seconds ticked by. Then without looking at
her, Lund asked, "What did you mean when you said
you knew what Richard Stark was?"

"That's the thing, Susan. I need *you* to tell me. What
Richard Stark was and what he did to your daughter.

She twisted her fingers together. "I can't."

"I know what he did, but if I say it and ask you to
confirm, I'm leading you. I can't do that."

"She's my baby. She had her whole life ahead of her!"

"She still does. She's not going to jail for this. She didn't do it. Susan, look at me."

The woman did, the anguish in her eyes heartbreaking.

"I saw the crime scene, and I talked to your daughter. There's nothing about Jessie that speaks to that kind of rage. As I'm sure your lawyer told you, they don't have enough to charge her so they're going to have to let her go."

"I am not going to say anything that you'll use against her."

"Not me," Miranda said. "I'm not even working the case, not anymore."

"So why . . . why are you here?"

"Because Jess's not the only girl he . . . hurt." Miranda realized her hands were balled into tight fists and consciously relaxed them. "I'm not going to let him get away with it."

Lund's eyes brimmed with tears. They spilled over and rolled down her cheeks. "Why do you care? What is my Jessie to you?"

"Another innocent victim." Miranda paused, turned her own gaze to the lake and paddling ducks. "A long time ago, he did it to . . . someone very close to me."

Lund broke down then, sobbing into her hands. "I tried to get her to go to the police . . . but she said she didn't have proof . . . that no one would believe her. She just wanted it to go away. And now look!"

"I'm so very sorry," Miranda said, voice thick with emotion.

"I trusted the university. I trusted you, the police, to keep her safe! You let me down. You let her down, all of you! I'm so angry . . . what do I do with it?"

Miranda didn't know. How could she tell Lund what to do with her anger when she didn't know where to put her own?

So she simply sat and waited until the woman composed herself and stood. She looked down at Miranda. "What do you want from me?"

"Confirmation that I was right. And, I guess, for you to know I'm not the enemy."

She nodded and let out a tired-sounding breath. "I'd do anything to protect my daughter. Anything, detective."

Tears pricked the backs of Miranda's eyes. How must that feel, she wondered, to have a mother who would do anything for you? Who supported and loved you, no matter what?

"She's very lucky to have you for a mother, Susan. Some daughters never know that kind of love."

Miranda watched the woman walk away, acknowledging how emotionally spent she was. How tired.

She stood and headed back to her car. Once inside, she texted Jake:

Heading back home. Talked to mom. Have news.

CHAPTER THIRTY-TWO

8:45 P.M.

By eight that night, Miranda was crawling the walls. She had left Jake two more messages since that first one—and she still hadn't heard from him. She was torn between relief—his silence surely meant he was still leading the investigation—and frustration. She wanted news, and she wanted it now.

When her doorbell rang, she ran to answer it. Finally! She yanked the door open, but Jake's name died on her lips.

Not Jake. Her brother, Robby. She would have recognized him anywhere, even though he'd changed immensely in the ten years since she'd last seen him.

He was fully a man now; gone were the last visages of youth. He'd filled out—his shoulders, neck, and chest—his beard had filled in. She remembered his exasperation over the bare spots that had kept him from sporting the cool, scruffy look that had been popular at the time. His hair was still thick and dark, his hairline receding only slightly.

They had the same features, she realized. The same wide-spaced, hazel eyes. The same straight nose and stubborn chin. It hadn't been so obvious when they were kids, but now their blood connection was undeniable.

"Hello, Randi," he said.

"Robby. What are you doing here?"

"We haven't seen each other in years and—"

"Ten," she said, cutting him off. "To be exact."

"—and that's the first thing you want to say to me?"

"Yeah, it is." She folded her arms across her chest. "What are you doing here?"

"You'd know if you had called me back."

"But I didn't. That should have told you something."

"Did you even listen to my messages?" He saw by her expression she hadn't and shook his head. "What's happened to you, Randi?"

"Stop calling me that. That girl doesn't exist anymore. I have a new life now, an honorable one. And I built it without any help from anyone."

"You think you can run away from your past, is that it?"

"I didn't run away, I left it behind. That's not the same thing."

"But I'm still your brother, no matter how much you wish it wasn't true."

"I don't care enough to wish that."

"And mom's the only mother you've got, like it or not."

Her mother. Screeching at the JD officer from the doorway of the double-wide. *I can't do nothin' with her—she's as wild as a billy goat. . . . Maybe they'll teach her somethin' at that place.*

Miranda folded her arms across her chest. "What do you want, Robby?"

"Mom's sick. She had a heart attack, a big one complicated by her COPD and diabetes."

Her own heart seemed to skip a beat. "When?"

"Three days ago. It was touch and go at first, but she's going to make it."

"I'm glad for her and for you, but what does this have to do with me?"

"She wants to see you, that's all. You're her baby girl."

Her baby girl? She had never felt wanted that way. Not ever.

"What a joke. I'm wild and bad and she doesn't know what to do with me. Those are her words, Robby."

"Her dying wish is to make peace with her baby girl. *Those* are her words."

Miranda snorted. "I thought you said she was going to make it."

"It's what she asked before she was stabilized, and I promised her I would try."

"Well, you've done your duty now and proved yourself a good son. Gold star for you."

He cocked his head, studying her, a crease forming between his eyebrows. "You never used to be mean. Stubborn, headstrong, but not mean. When did that change?"

The words stung and she steeled herself against the feeling. "Mom washed her hands of me when I was fifteen. I'm sorry she's unwell, but there's nothing I can do for you."

"You say you've built an *honorable* life, so honor your mother. Do this for her."

"She didn't believe me, Robby. She didn't stand up for me. Do you have any idea how scared I was? I was fifteen. Fifteen! And completely alone."

"I was a kid, too, Randi."

"You were eighteen! You were my big brother!" She looked away, tears burning the backs of her eyes. She refused to allow them to fall.

When she met his eyes once more, hers were completely dry. "And you dare call *me* mean? '*I don't know what really happened to you tonight,'"* she mimicked him from all those years ago, *"'and it's not my problem. If you think I'm going to come cover for you and get my butt busted, you're crazier than I thought. You were stupid and got caught. Deal with it.'* And then you hung up on me."

"I'm sorry," he said, voice thick. "I regret a lot of things I've done in my life, but nothing more than that. I live with it every day, Randi, and every day it rips a little chunk out of me. That's the thing about regrets—they don't care what you've got going right in your life or the good you're trying to do; they hang around to remind you what a piece of crap you really are."

"Is that supposed to make me feel sorry for you?" Even as she asked, she acknowledged it did. She called herself a fool. "Well, it doesn't."

He held out a hand. She noticed it was callused from a lifetime of physical labor. She noticed, too, the dark circles under his bloodshot eyes. "You're not the only one who's twisted into knots by the past and our dysfunctional family-of-the-year."

"I'm not twisted up." She stuck her hands into the front pockets of her jeans. "I'm doing just fine, thank you."

He made a sound of disbelief and dropped his hand. "Right. That's why you won't go see mom. That's why you don't return calls to your brother."

She opened her mouth; he cut her off. "You may not have another chance. She could die and then it'll be too late to make your peace. You don't want that regret living inside of you."

He waited a moment as if to see some softening in her, then shook his head. "Good-bye, Miranda."

"Robby, wait!"

But the words sounded only in her head. Instead, she

watched silently as he climbed into an SUV and without a look back, drove off. When his taillights disappeared from view, she stepped back into her house, shutting and locking the door behind her. As she did, the air-conditioning kicked on and goose bumps raced up her arms.

She curved her arms around her middle and sank to the floor.

CHAPTER THIRTY-THREE

That night in June
2002

Randi huddled in the plastic chair, so cold her teeth chattered. Directly above her, the air-conditioning vent pumped out icy air, most of which was aimed at her. On the wall across from her, a clock ticked out the minutes with agonizing repetition.

Officer Wheeler had dumped her here and warned her not to move. She hugged herself and stared at the clock. How long had it been since Wheeler picked her up? How long since she'd freed herself and raced into the woods?

How long since the other girl screamed?

The sound of it tore through her head again, and Randi flinched in response. She had to help her . . . she'd promised! Someone had to believe her before it was too late.

Unless it was too late already.

The clock clicked over another minute. The woman at the front desk was talking to the one of the cops. She had teased-up hair and cat glasses, and sounded real country.

"Can you believe it's still ninety degrees outside?" she drawled. "For heaven's sake, what's goin' on with this dad-gum weather?"

"Rader!"

Wheeler. She twisted to look at him, standing in a doorway on the opposite side of the room. "C'mon, phone's free."

She jumped up and followed him into the hallway. He pointed to the wall phone. "There you go."

"Do I have to call my mom?"

"Well, last I heard your daddy was locked up, so yeah, I think you do."

"How about one of my brothers? Robby's eighteen."

With a sly smile, Wheeler agreed. "Then he can confirm parts of your story. I like that, two birds, one stone."

Miranda wasn't certain what he meant by that, but was relieved it was okay. She dialed her brother's cell number, praying he'd answer.

He did and the words spilled out of her. "Robby, it's me. I need your help."

"Randi? What the hell? Nice move pissing off Billy-Bo! Geez-us, girl, you stole his pot!"

"You gotta listen, Robby . . . I'm at the Harmony PD. You have to come get me."

"Hell, no, I'm not coming to get you. What'd you do this time?"

"Something bad's happened. They don't believe me. You've got to tell 'em!"

"Tell them what?" He sounded annoyed. "What don't they believe?'

"About you and Wes having Billy pick me up, and how he kicked me out of his truck and how I stole his pot—"

"They found the pot?"

"It was in my pocket and—I need you to tell them what happened."

"You're out of your damn mind, girl, I'm not telling them that. You're just crazy."

"You don't understand—"

"'Course I do. You're trying to throw me, Wes, and Billy under the bus because you were stupid and got caught."

"No . . . no . . . after he kicked me out, I hitched a ride with a guy and this other girl. We were partying and—" Her voice rose. "I passed out. When I came to, I was tied up. . . . That guy . . . he raped the other girl and he was gonna rape me, but I got away!"

For a long moment he was silent. When he finally spoke, his voice was low. "What kind of bullshit story are you telling them?"

"It's not bullshit. I promised her I'd get her help but nobody believes me!"

"Add me to that list."

"You're my brother. You've got to believe me. I'm not making this up. Please," she begged, voice cracking. "You're eighteen, they'll believe you."

"Yeah, and send me to jail. Call mom."

"The guy raped her! He was gonna rape me but I got loose and—"

"Bullshit."

"You're my brother," she said again, feeling as if her heart had just been ripped from her chest. He didn't believe her. Her mother wouldn't either. Her other brother? She wouldn't waste her breath. Bitter tears stung her eyes. Maybe her no-good daddy up at Angola could lend a hand.

"Look, Randi, I don't know what really happened to you tonight, and it's not my problem. But if you think I'm going to come cover for you and get my ass busted, you're crazier than I thought. Deal with it and call mom."

He hung up. The click resounded in her head and she

glanced over her shoulder at Wheeler. He smirked at her. "Having a problem?"

She had nobody, she realized. Same as always.

She jerked her chin up and glared at the man. "You could say that. My brother's an asshole. What's your excuse?"

CHAPTER THIRTY-FOUR

9:20 P.M.

The shriek of her phone startled Miranda from the past to the present. She wiped the tears from her cheeks, stood, and hurried to her phone. "This is Rader," she answered.

"Miranda?" A woman. Her voice high-pitched and hysterical.

"Yes. Who is this?"

"It's Tara. From the bar."

The image of Summer grimacing and rubbing her temple filled her head. "What's wrong?"

"It's Summer. She collapsed again. I couldn't get her to wake up—"

"Call 911."

"I did. They're here now, loading her into the ambulance. I can't leave the bar. . . . We're busy and—"

Miranda grabbed her purse and started for the front door. "I'm on my way. I'll keep you posted."

Eight minutes later, Miranda wheeled into the emergency room drive, stopping behind an ambulance. An EMT was slamming the vehicle's rear doors.

She hopped out. "You just drop off Summer Knight?"

"We did. They're admitting her now."

She thanked them and rushed inside—and saw that

the hospital staff was trying to admit her. Summer was alert and mighty pissed off.

"Ms. Knight," the nurse said sharply, "we're just trying to help you."

"Then get me off this damn thing!"

Miranda hurried over. "Summer, what's all the fuss about?"

Summer looked relieved to see her. "I don't have a clue. I wake up in an ambulance, for God's sake, and nobody will tell me anything!" She glared at the nurse.

Miranda stepped in. "Tara called me. She said you passed out at the bar and she couldn't rouse you."

Summer scowled. "That girl's overexcitable."

"She did the right thing. It's you who's acting like a horse's behind." Miranda looked at the nurse. "She had a seizure a couple days ago as well. I was there when it happened."

"I have epilepsy," Summer muttered. "This happens."

The paramedic returned with his paperwork. He looked tired. When he spoke, he sounded tired, too. "And as I told you ma'am, what I observed was not consistent with an epileptic seizure."

Miranda frowned, then looked at Summer. "I don't like the sound of that. You're here. Just stay and let them run a few tests. You might have hit your head—"

"Which is why we're going to take you down to get a CT scan. If everything looks all right, you're out of here."

"Nope. I'm out of here now." She sat up and swung her legs off the side of the gurney.

She seemed to wobble and Miranda darted forward to steady her. "Summer, please be reasonable—"

She jerked her arm free. "You're either my friend and you help me out of here or you're not and I call an Uber and do this alone. Either way, I'm leaving."

Both the ER nurse and paramedic looked flummoxed. "Ma'am, I strongly suggest you stay. One CT scan, that's all."

"No." She stood, confronting Miranda. "Well?"

Miranda glanced apologetically at the nurse, then nodded. "I'll take you home."

All Summer's bluster seemed to evaporate. "Thank you."

The nurse shrugged. "We can't make you stay. But we have some forms you'll need to sign before you leave. They state that it was your choice to leave the hospital and you won't hold us responsible should anything happen to you as a result."

Ten minutes later Miranda had Summer settled into her front passenger seat. She turned to Summer before she pulled away from the curb. "You're sure about this?"

"Yeah, I'm sure. Just take me back to the bar."

Miranda made a choked sound of disbelief. "That's so not happening, girlfriend."

Summer leaned her head back and closed her eyes. "Figured you'd say that."

Summer lived in a quirky condo on the far edge of the university area. Miranda parked and ran around to help her; Summer waved her off.

"C'mon in, we'll talk."

Summer unlocked the door and stepped inside, flipping on the light. Miranda followed her in, then stopped in surprise. The place was a mess, unread mail and newspapers stacked about, shoes that had obviously been kicked off and left, empty soda cans, a couple beer bottles. It wasn't exactly awful—no dirty dishes or food sitting out—but it didn't hold up to her friend's usual standards.

"You have been feeling bad."

Summer ignored that. "Something to drink?"

"How about a beer? I'm not working tomorrow."

"It's a pretty night. Let's sit on the patio."

Miranda wandered out; a moment later, Summer returned with two bottles of Blue Moon. They sat at the small table and Miranda eyed the beer. "You sure that's a good idea?"

"What I have, a little alcohol isn't going to hurt."

"Yeah?" Miranda brought the bottle to her lips. "And what's that?"

Again, Summer ignored her and redirected. "I know I seemed kind of like a jerk back there—"

"Kind of like?"

"My kind of friend, honest to a fault." Summer lifted her bottle in a mock toast, then took a swallow before continuing. "The deal is, I already know what's wrong with me and they weren't going to be able to make it better."

"Hardheadedness? A screw loose? Or maybe, wound too tight?"

"Funny—" She brought the bottle to her lips once more. "Considering."

Miranda frowned. "Considering what? You're sort of scaring me now."

"I have cancer."

Miranda felt like a two-hundred-pound, drug-fueled perp had just punched her in the gut. "You didn't just say—"

"Yeah, I did."

"What kind?" Miranda managed, voice thick.

"The worst kind."

"I don't know what that means."

"Brain."

Miranda sucked in a sharp breath. "Okay . . . so what's your plan?"

"Live out the rest of my life here, not in a hospital."

"What about your treatment plan? Is it underway?"

"It is," she said. "Because I'm not doing treatment."

"Wait . . . what?"

"You heard me." Summer looked her in the eyes. "The tumor's inoperable. The drugs will make me sick as hell, and I'm not interested living my last months that way."

Months, not years. Miranda swallowed past the lump in her throat. "But won't treatment extend your life?"

"Define life." She leaned forward. "This is a fast-growing, high-grade tumor. I have drugs to help with symptoms, but I choose not to seek treatment. It's terminal, Miranda. I've dealt with that fact, and I've made my decision about how I want to live out the rest of my life. I hope you can support me in this."

What could she say? It was Summer's life, her body, and her decision what to do with it. With every fiber of her own being she wanted to scream, *"Fight!"* and *"Miracles happen!"*

But that was her reaction, not Summer's. And how could she judge? Until faced with the same prognosis, she couldn't. Nobody could.

So she nodded, went around the table, and hugged her friend.

Holding on to each other, they cried until they laughed.

CHAPTER THIRTY-FIVE

11:45 P.M.

Miranda left because Summer asked her to. It felt one hundred percent wrong leaving her friend alone, but Summer insisted that's what she wanted.

Miranda started her car but just sat, staring at the dark road ahead of her. Summer had made up her mind how her story would end. Miranda respected that, but it wasn't the way she wanted her own story to go. Alone, fighting her battles without an ally. No one by her side to share the victories or the defeats. The joy or, like now, the despair.

She despaired, not just for her friend, but for herself as well. Summer was dying. It hurt.

She didn't want to be alone.

Jake. She wanted to be with Jake.

Miranda plucked her phone from the console and punched in his number.

"Miranda?" he answered, sounding groggy.

She didn't know why the sound of his voice made her start to cry, but it did. "Hey," she managed.

"What's wrong?" The change in his voice was immediate; she heard the rustle of bedclothes.

"Summer's sick. Real sick. I just found out and—" Her nose was dripping and she fumbled for a tissue with her free hand. "I'm so . . . can you come over? I need you, Jake."

"I'm on my way."

They arrived at her place simultaneously and without speaking, went inside. There, in the dark foyer, he folded her into his arms and held her.

"I'm sorry," he murmured.

She didn't reply, simply buried her face into the curve of his neck and shoulder. He smelled real, she thought, letting his scent fill her head. Like a man should—honest like the outdoors, and strong—like spice and sweat.

She slid her hands from his chest around to his back. The muscled ridge of his lats, the solid breadth of his shoulders.

The kind of shoulders a woman could lean on. A strong back to help carry a heavy load.

Had she ever leaned on anyone?

Not like this.

"Brain cancer," she said against his shoulder. He didn't respond and she went on. "She's . . . refusing treatment. It's terminal and—" She tipped her face up to his. "I feel like my heart's breaking."

"I'm here," he said. "Hold on to me."

He was, she realized. In a way no one had ever been there for her. Moral and loyal to his core, Jake didn't manipulate or cheat, didn't put himself or his own needs first. He stood up for what was right—and those he loved.

And he loved her.

She caught his hand, laced their fingers, and led him to her bedroom. There, they made love. Real love, she realized. Different from sex, this was something she hadn't experienced before. Beautiful and reverent, they melted into one another, becoming one. Not to give or receive pleasure, though they did—but to share the essence of themselves.

It was wondrous, surreal and . . . reverent. That word again. Not physical—not about reaching completion, some momentary feel-good climax, but a spiritual connection.

In this moment, twined with Jake, they were one person. For the first time in her life, she wasn't alone.

Miranda awakened with a start. Jake lay beside her, arm flung possessively across her back. She listened. His deep, rhythmic breathing, the gentle whir of the ceiling fan. A motor running, she realized. Out front.

Careful not to wake him, she slid out from under his arm and off the bed. He groaned slightly, then rolled over.

She grabbed his T-shirt and slipped it over her head, collected her personal weapon from the bedside drawer, and tiptoed into the hall. The sounds of steps on her porch, then the slam of a car door.

Miranda ran to the door, yanked it open, and darted across the porch in time to see a car round the corner, little more than red taillights on the dark road.

She turned to head back inside and stopped. Whoever had just sped off had left her something in a black plastic garbage bag. Heart thundering, she crossed to it. She nudged it with her toe. Whatever was inside was rigid and heavy—certainly nothing that was going to jump out and bite her.

Still moving cautiously, she opened the bag. A box, she saw. About the size of a shoebox, gray in color with a handle on top.

And then she knew what it was. A lockbox.

The lockbox, she knew. Stark's.

Miranda lifted it out and a folded piece of paper fluttered to the ground. She bent to retrieve it. Two words were written on the paper in a scrolling, feminine style.

I'm Sorry

Catherine Stark. It had to be. Miranda released a small, relieved breath, one she hadn't realized she'd been holding. The other day, she'd read Catherine Stark's feelings correctly.

Her gambit had worked.

She started to shake. In a moment, she would know. The contents of this box could break the case wide open or leave her as frustrated as before. This could be something big or just something more.

Miranda carried the box into her living room. She set it on the coffee table and went for the key, which she'd tucked into the change compartment of her wallet. From there she went to the coat closet to grab a pair of scene gloves from her jacket.

She slipped them on and knelt on the floor in front of the coffee table. Her fingers trembled as she fit the key into the lock. It could be nothing, she reminded herself. A disappointment.

"No," she whispered because somehow, deep in the pit of her gut, she knew that the contents of this box were going to change everything.

She turned the key; lifted the lid. A collection of things. Documents. A passport, a driver's license, a diploma. An envelope containing cash. She quickly counted—ten thousand dollars.

She picked up the passport, flipped it open. Richard Stark's face stared back at her. She shifted her gaze to the identifying information. Michael Weisman from Gainesville, Florida.

She moved on to the drivers' license and diploma and found the same thing: Richard Stark's photo, another man's name.

Every form of identifying information a person needed to travel, get a job, get married even. And cash. A lot of it.

This was Stark's get-out-of-jail-free box. His escape plan should he ever be found out. Bastard had gotten away with his crimes for at least fifteen years; he'd decided he would get away with them forever, even if it meant becoming another person and leaving the country.

Guess you didn't expect one of your victims to fight back. Sorry, dude, plan spoiled.

Miranda moved aside the diploma. Car keys and what looked like a padlock key. A contract with a self-storage facility—Grant's, near the I-12 east exit. As she picked it up, something shiny caught her eye, peeking out from under an envelope.

A button, she saw. Shaped like a flower, the petals made up of pink rhinestones, the center a faux pearl.

The breath hissed past her lips. Not any button. The one from the blouse she'd worn that night fourteen years ago.

CHAPTER THIRTY-SIX

That night in June
2002

The woman at the Harmony Police Department information desk pinned her with a bespectacled gaze. "Who do you have here, Clint baby?"

"One Randi Rader, welfare mama in training."

"You stop that, Clint Wheeler." She looked back at Randi. "How old are you, sweetheart?"

Randi's teeth chattered. "Fif-t-teen, ma'am."

"Don't let the big eyes and 'ma'am' fool you," Wheeler said. "She's practically a hardened criminal already."

"What's she here for?"

"Numerous reasons, but a pocketful of pot's the biggest."

The woman frowned and wagged a finger at her. "Sweetheart, that's not gonna get you anywhere in life. You listen to Miss Roxy, I won't steer you wrong."

Wheeler rolled his eyes. "Keep an eye on her, would ya? The first family member she tried wanted no part of her or her stories. She's thinking about who she wants to call next. When she's ready, let her use the phone."

"I can do that." She smiled at Randi. "Take a seat over there." She lowered her voice and leaned forward. "And, honey, you might want to button up."

Randi looked down at herself. Her shirt gaped open, revealing her cheap bra. Cheeks hot, she went to fasten it and discovered she'd lost a button. Her yellow blouse and its sparkly, rhinestone buttons—it was so pretty. Her favorite. Dirty and rumpled now, the prettiest part missing.

"I can't button it . . . the button, it's—" She started to cry. "I lost it."

"Don't cry, sweetheart," Ms. Roxy said, voice soothing. "I'll get you a safety pin. It's all gonna be okay."

No it wasn't, Randi thought, slumping in her chair, clutching her blouse to hold it together. Not for her and not for the other girl.

"Here you go, sweetie, this should do it."

Randi looked up, tears dripping off her chin. She took the pin. "Thank you."

"You go ahead and fasten that pretty blouse up. I'll stand here and make sure no one can see what you're doing."

"Got it," Randi said a moment later. "Thank you."

Ms. Roxy smiled reassuringly. "You're going to be okay, honey. Chief Cadwell's a good man. He'll make sure of it."

She turned to walk away and Randi stopped her. "Is he here?"

Ms. Roxy looked back. "Chief Cadwell?"

Randi nodded. "I really need to talk to him."

"He won't be back 'til morning, but I'm sure he'll—"

"No!" Randi shook her head. "I need to talk to him right away! Something bad's happening to this other girl but no one believes me!" Her chin began to wobble. "I promised her I'd get help."

Roxy's brow knitted. She sat down next to Randi. "What do you mean, something bad's happening to another girl?"

The story spilled out, along with more tears, the words tumbling one over the other.

When she finished, the woman looked distraught. "And you told Officer Wheeler this?"

"I did, but he said I was lying. But I'm not. I promise!"

"You don't worry another minute, sweet thing. I'm taking care of this right now."

CHAPTER THIRTY-SEVEN

2:30 A.M.

"Miranda? What's going on?"

She looked over her shoulder at Jake, standing in the doorway to the living room. Her expression must have said it all because his changed from sleepy to alert.

"What's wrong?"

She held out the button, perched on her gloved palm like an offering. "It was mine."

"I don't understand."

"It's from the blouse I was wearing fourteen years ago, when Stark abducted me."

"How did you . . . are you sure?"

Her eyes filled with tears and her hand began to shake. She curled her fingers around the button. "Yes."

He crossed the room and knelt down beside her. "I'm sorry."

"I'm not," she said, tone fierce. "Now I know for sure."

He shifted his gaze, seeing the lockbox for the first time. "What is that?"

"It was Stark's. Look."

She opened the passport, then the diploma. "His get-out-of-jail-free cards."

"Holy shit." He stood. "I've got gloves in my console,

I'll be right back." He returned with the gloves and after putting them on, studied each item from the box.

When he'd finished, he looked at her. "Where'd this come from, Miranda?"

"Someone left it on my porch tonight. I think it was Catherine Stark."

Jake's brow creased. "Why would she do that?"

Miranda explained about finding the key, then bringing Catherine Stark the reframed photo and asking her about a lockbox. "I could see it, in her eyes, that she felt bad about her son. That she knew about him, what he did to women. She knew about me."

"She said that?"

"No. But she brought me the box because she felt guilty and wanted to help. Look." She slid over the folded paper, with its two-word apology.

"Miranda, you lifted that key from a crime scene."

"I know, but I didn't mean—" She bit off what she was about to say. She'd stuck the key in her pocket. How could she say she didn't mean to? "I didn't plan on doing it," she said instead. "It just . . . happened."

He removed his gloves and dragged a hand through his already-rumpled hair. "This is really messed up, Miranda."

It was. And so was what she was about to ask him. "Don't tell anyone about this, Jake. Not yet."

"Too late. I already called Cadwell."

She couldn't believe what he was saying. "When?"

"When I went out for the gloves. This is big; he needs to know. You would have done the same thing."

She would have, what seemed like a lifetime ago. Everything was different now. She was different.

She couldn't look at him, not yet, she felt so betrayed. "Did you tell him everything?"

"What I knew so far."

"You told him about the button?"

"No, I didn't get that specific. I told him about the box, the general contents."

"This wasn't yours to share." She fisted her fingers. "Especially the button."

"Babe, you're talking crazy. We're in the middle of an investigation—"

"No. You're in the middle of an investigation. I've been sidelined."

"And I wonder why?"

Her cheeks heated. "Whose side are you on?"

"The side of what's lawful."

"Don't talk to me about the law! This is more important—it's about the truth. People need to know. The women he hurt need them to know."

"Including you."

"Yes, dammit! What's wrong with that?"

He reached for her; she jerked away. "Don't."

He looked hurt. "Miranda, what you're imagining isn't going to happen. Richard Stark being labeled a sexual predator? Women coming forward in droves? Why haven't they already? I'm sorry, it's just not."

"Yes, it will. I'm going to take this to the Sheriff's Department—"

"Babe, listen to me—"

"No." She shook her head. "You don't get it because it didn't happen to you!"

The words landed between them like a sharp slap. His expression softened. "You're right, it didn't. But if you do this they're going to drag you through the mud. Call you a liar. Crazy. Sick or jealous or bitter . . . whatever. You'll lose your job, your reputation, and your place in this community."

"I've got the box. I've got proof."

"Proof they'll say you manufactured. They'll claim

this was a setup, that you slept with me so I would be here when the box was 'left' on your porch. They'll argue you were manipulating me, so I would back you up, vouch for everything you said."

She wanted to deny he was right, fling the words back at him, but she couldn't. He was right. And it hurt. "What about the button? I have it. Surely someone will remember me losing it."

"You really think someone will recall you lost a button that night, fourteen years ago?"

"Ms. Roxy," she said, hearing the note of desperation in her voice. "She noticed it. She brought me a safety pin . . ."

But she'd died two years ago. Miranda remembered the funeral; the woman had been beloved and nearly the entire town attended the service.

Jake remembered, too; she saw it in his eyes. "Let's look at it this way," he said. "You believe the button's a trophy, correct?" When she nodded, he went on. "Think it through, Miranda. Why's your button the only trophy in the box?"

She stared at him, nonplussed. Her reaction to the button had been so visceral, she hadn't paused to ask that question herself—or truthfully, any other.

"I don't know," she said. "I lost the button and he—"

"Found it and kept it all these years?"

Jake was right. Her button was the only object like it in the box. Why? It didn't make sense.

And it didn't make this—tonight, her having the box, any of it—look good.

"Maybe I was the only one who got away?"

"Is that why he had that news clipping about you? The only news clipping we found in his desk?"

"I don't know, Jake. It doesn't make sense, but there's a reason. I know I'm right about it, all of it."

"When I called Cadwell, I told him somebody left the box on your porch, you opened it, saw what was inside, and contacted me and that I was on my way here to check it out. Here's what I propose: I collect the box, the note, and the bag and take them in as evidence."

She shook her head, although she knew she had no other choice. But she wasn't going to be anyone's victim, never again. "Cadwell's going to bury this."

"I won't let him."

"You can't stop him. And no way am I going to allow this to become his word against mine. Because I'll lose."

"What're you going to do?"

"Document everything here. At least I'll have photos to back up my claims."

"You'll have me, too, Miranda."

She hoped so but realized she couldn't be certain of that. Not anymore, not after his call to Buddy.

She didn't respond, and instead stood up and went for her phone.

Jake watched as she photographed all the items, as she'd originally found them and individually as well. Then she reloaded the box with everything but the button and relocked it.

"You're keeping your button?"

"I am." She looked at him in challenge. "Stark stole it from me and now I have it back. You have a problem with that?"

He did, she saw it in his eyes. But he didn't argue, just shook his head.

"It's all yours," she said, tone defiant.

"Buddy's going to want to talk to you."

She nodded, already thinking ahead to that meeting. "Tell him to call me. I'll be waiting."

CHAPTER THIRTY-EIGHT

9:00 A.M.

Miranda sat across the scarred wooden table from Buddy, the lockbox in the middle between them. Jake stood near the door, leaning nonchalantly against the frame, gazing with pretended disinterest out the door's small window, the way she had seen him do hundreds of times before. Only this time was different. She was on the other side now—of the table and the law.

Buddy had wanted her to come in and officially give her version of how she had come into possession of the box.

"Something woke me up," Miranda said. "I realized it was a car's engine, coming from out front. So, I went to investigate."

She paused a moment, then went on. "I heard someone on my front porch, but by the time I got there, they'd driven off. When I turned to go back in, I saw the garbage bag. I approached cautiously, only opening the bag when I was certain it was safe to do so. The lockbox was inside. When I picked it up, the note fell out."

"And what did it say?"

"I'm sorry."

Buddy's gaze never left hers. "Then you called Jake."

"No, I opened the box first. When I saw its contents I involved Jake."

"Why?"

"Why wait?" she asked. "Or why involve Jake?"

"Both."

"At first I had no idea what was in the box, so why would I involve him? Once I did know the box's contents, the why's obvious, I think. He's in charge of the Stark investigation. And I trust him."

Until that moment, Buddy hadn't blinked, but he did then. His words to her that summer night fourteen years ago popped into her head.

"You can trust me, Randi. I promise you that."

She couldn't anymore, she realized. And she didn't. Problem was, the sentiment seemed to be mutual.

"Do you have any idea who could have left the box on your porch?"

"It's my belief that Catherine Stark left it."

His eyebrows shot up. "That's some wild theory."

Her palms began to sweat. Here was where her story became damning. "Not so wild. The day I caught the two of them at their son's, I startled her and she dropped the framed photo she was holding. The glass shattered. I felt responsible, so I replaced the glass and brought it to her."

"You mean, you manipulated the situation to create a reason to approach her—after I specifically told you not to."

They both knew her action had been motivated far more by investigative ingenuity than kindness. If she'd done it in her official capacity, as a sworn officer working under his direction, Cadwell would have given her a high five and an "attagirl."

But not now. No, indeed. He was pissed.

"Of course not." She met his gaze evenly. "She's

obviously in a lot of pain. I was being a decent human being. While I was there," she continued, "I mentioned that we'd found a lockbox key at her son's, but no box, and asked if she was aware her son had one."

He frowned slightly and glanced toward Jake, as if in question, but Jake didn't seem to notice and continued to stare out the door.

The chief returned his attention to her. "And she said what?"

"Nothing. Just wished me luck." She waited a heartbeat before continuing. "Which brings us to tonight. The box turns up on my porch with a note that says, 'I'm sorry.' Coincidence? I think not."

"In my book, that's a stretch."

"Who else would have access to the box and those documents?"

"The killer."

"Maybe. But then why the note of apology?"

"Exactly—what does Catherine Stark have to be sorry for?"

"She knows what her son was."

Buddy shifted in his seat. "And what is that?"

"A sexual predator. The contents of the box prove it."

"It proves nothing."

His response wasn't unexpected but it still made her blood pressure rise. She flattened her hands on the table. "Unbelievable, Buddy. It's so obvious. Why else would he have this stuff?"

"It's only obvious to you, Miranda."

"C'mon, Buddy! A driver's license and passport in another name? Ten thousand dollars cash? He had all this in case he needed to disappear and start a new life."

"Why would he want to do that?"

"I already told you, but if you insist on playing this game—Richard Stark was a sexual predator. He knew it was only a matter of time before a victim stepped forward. He was ready for that day. A new identity and ten K to start his new life. I shouldn't have to explain this to you, Buddy. You're a better cop than that."

Face turning crimson, he pushed away from his desk and stood, glaring down at her. "Don't you lecture me. You're a better cop than this, Miranda. The roofies that didn't exist—"

"They did. Someone took them."

"Well, they don't now. Not to me, not to Jake or Jones, nor any cop worth their salt. And as for this—" He swept his hand in the direction of the box. "We have no way of knowing for certain why he did this."

"I know why he did it. And you do, too."

He flinched slightly. "The man's dead, Miranda. How're you going to prove this theory?"

She stared him down. "Maybe I take the box and everything in it to the Sheriff's Department? See what they think about it? And last I checked, falsifying government documents was a crime."

"The man's dead! You're obsessed with this case. It's like you're on some sort of vendetta. Don't you see? It's ruining you, Miranda."

"You're not going to do anything with this, are you?"

"I didn't say that, Miranda."

"You didn't have to. It's the same thing you've been doing all along, isn't it? Protecting Stark? Or is it his father you're protecting?"

Jake sucked in a sharp breath; Buddy turned an angry shade of red. "Watch yourself, Detective Rader."

"You watch yourself." She stood and started for the door. "I'm out."

"We're not done here!"

She glanced over her shoulder at him. "Oh, yes we are. We're way past done. Y'all have a good day."

Damning silence followed her from the chief's office through the squad room. On her way out of the building, she bought a Coke from the vending machine.

Miranda stepped onto the sidewalk. The sunlight stung and she jammed on her sunglasses. She crossed the street to her car, climbed in, and dropped her can of soda into the console drink holder. Only then did she realize how badly her hands were shaking. She gripped the steering wheel tightly.

"It's like you're on some sort of vendetta. Don't you see? It's ruining you, Miranda."

Was it? Ruining her?

A desperate-sounding laugh slipped past her lips. Her life was in shambles. Had she really just told her superior officer to watch himself? Had she really accused him of burying evidence to protect Ian Stark?

She was done at the Harmony PD. No way Buddy could reinstate her after that.

Where would she go? What would she do? She'd wanted to be a cop forever. A strangled sound caught in her throat. She certainly couldn't expect a glowing recommendation from him.

She'd come unglued over a case. Gone off on her own private vendetta, ignoring chain of command and investigative good practices and disrespected her superior officer.

Her cell phone went off; she answered and without thinking said, "This is Detective Rader."

"Miranda? It's Summer."

Her thoughts shifted immediately, filling with her friend's plight. "How are you this morning?"

"Alive," Summer answered. "That's a good thing. Heading into work."

"The bar? Are you sure you should?"

"It beats the hell out of lying down and dying."

"Not funny."

"I wasn't trying to be." She paused a beat. "I'm really sorry."

"For what?"

"Adding my problems to your plate."

A lump formed in Miranda's throat. Her problems were nonexistent compared to Summer's; the last thing she should be doing was whining about her life. "I'm glad you told me, and honored you trusted me with this." When Summer didn't respond, Miranda went on. "Are you sure I can't talk you into giving treatment a try? I promise to be with you every step of the way."

"Every step of the way," Summer repeated. "We both know that's not possible."

It was Summer's body under attack, not hers. Summer's life at stake, not hers.

"By your side then," Miranda corrected. "Holding you up."

"You're already doing that." Summer's voice was thick and she cleared her throat. "I've got to go."

"Wait! I'll stop by the bar."

"No, don't. Today's delivery day and it's going to be tough. I'll call you later."

She hung up before Miranda had a chance to respond—let alone argue—and Miranda admitted, as hard as it was, she had to give her friend space and privacy.

So, what the hell she was going to do for the rest of the day—let alone the rest of her life?

Disgusted with herself, Miranda cranked the engine and snatched up the Coke. She tapped the top with her index finger, then popped the top. The hiss of carbonated gas escaping and the puff of cool against her fingers was as familiar as summertime in the south. She brought the drink to her lips and took a long swallow, the addictively sweet taste filling her mouth.

Over the years, how many commercials had played on that sensory familiarity—the snap and hiss, the cold, sweet taste filling the mouth and the bubbly sensation as the beverage slid down the throat?

Over the years . . .

How many years?

Fourteen.

"You can trust me, Randi. I promise you that."

Miranda stared at the bright red can, the memory from earlier again unfurling her head.

CHAPTER THIRTY-NINE

That night in June
2002

Ms. Roxy, with the teased hair and kind eyes, handed her a Coke. The can was cold and wet, and although chilled to the bone, Randi clutched it with both hands.

"Don't you worry, sugar, the chief will be here any moment."

In the last twenty minutes, Ms. Roxy had said the same thing three times. But in a way, Miranda was glad he was taking so long. She was scared of what he would say, scared he would call her a liar and throw her in jail.

And Ms. Roxy was being real sweet to her. Staying right by her side except when she had to answer the phone or help one of the deputies, and then she would pat Randi's hand and promise she'd "be right back."

Randi marveled at her kindness and wondered if being nice was part of her job. She'd never met anybody this nice before, that was for sure.

Chief Cadwell finally arrived. Randi knew who he was—his face had been plastered all over Harmony during the recent election. At the time she'd thought he was kind of handsome for an old guy—especially compared to her daddy—but now, not so much. He was red in the face and rumpled looking, with bags under his eyes and deep groves around his mouth.

"Give me two minutes, Roxy," he said, not looking at Randi. "Then bring Miss Rader in."

He stepped into his office, closing the door behind him. Roxy glanced at Randi and winked. "Let's give him five instead."

Exactly five minutes later, the woman escorted her in. Chief Cadwell looked at her then, leveling her with his serious gaze. "Hello, Randi," he said. "Have a seat."

She nodded, a lump in her throat. When she was seated, he looked back at Roxy. "Roxy, could you bring me a cup of coffee? I'm beat. And grab a blanket from the first-aid closet. Randi here doesn't need to be shivering like that."

"You got it, Chief," she said, sending him an approving nod. "Be right back."

When the door clicked shut behind her, he turned his attention back to Randi. "That was quite a story you told to Roxy."

Randi swallowed hard. "Yes, sir."

"Abduction and rape. That's serious, serious business. You understand that, don't you?" She nodded and he went on. "And you still stand by it?"

She tightened her fingers on the can of soda. "Yes, sir."

"All right then, I need you to tell me the story. Starting at the beginning."

She hesitated, wondering how to weave the story so he would believe her but she wouldn't get anyone else in trouble.

As if he read her mind, he leaned slightly forward. "Be smart, Randi. You're in big trouble. Tell me everything and tell me the truth, the entire truth. Holding back to protect someone else will only make your situation worse. And frankly, I don't see anyone rushing in to try to save your butt."

And no one would, she thought. She was alone.

But not as alone as the other girl.

"You can trust me, Randi," he said quietly. "I promise you that."

She could, she thought, relief bringing tears to her eyes. They welled and spilled over just as Ms. Roxy re-entered the room.

"Your coffee, Chief," she said, setting a cup emblazoned with BEST DAD AWARD on the desk in front of him. "And a blanket for you." She opened it and laid it gently over Randi's shoulders, then gave them a re-assuring squeeze. "Anything else, boss?"

He said there wasn't and she left the room, leaving the door open a crack.

"You can trust me," he said again. "C'mon, Randi, tell me what happened tonight."

So she did, the story pouring out of her—all of it, every detail. She began with her brothers sending Billy Boman to pick her up, about the beers, the kissing, and his kicking her out of the truck when she wouldn't go all the way with him.

"He had a bag of pot in the console and I took it."

He made a note. "So, you're saying the weed was his?"

There would be hell to pay with her brothers, but she didn't see either of them hurrying down here to help her. She nodded. "Yes, sir. He made me really mad, so I took it."

"Did the two of you smoke weed together?"

"No." When the chief looked doubtful, she vehemently shook her head. "We drank his Dixies, that's all."

"What then?"

"I started to walk."

"No cell phone?"

This time it was she who looked disbelieving. "Not until I can pay for one."

"Okay. Go on."

"A guy pulled up—"

"Did you know him?"

"Nope, never even saw him before."

"What kind of car?"

She thought a moment. "Nice. Expensive looking. Black . . . maybe a BMW?"

"Maybe?"

"It was dark, and I was so glad he came along. . . . But it had a tan leather interior. I remember thinking how pretty it was."

Cadwell noted that, then returned his gaze to hers. "What did he look like?"

"He was good looking . . . but I didn't, you know, want to stare or anything."

"You were playing it cool?"

"Yeah. Oh, and he was wearing a ball cap."

"Anything on it?"

She shifted nervously, thinking of the other girl and aware of more time passing. "Maybe we should just go out there now? It's been so long . . . I promised—"

"We do this first, Randi. Keep on task and we'll be out of here in no time. Anything on the ball cap?"

"University of Alabama. I noticed it 'cause my brothers hate 'Bama so much."

"Anything else you recall about his face?"

Randi looked down at her hands, feeling stupid. "Like I said, it was dark and I was drunk and pissed off."

"And playing it cool?" She nodded. "So, he offered you a ride?"

"Yeah."

"And you took it?" Reprisal in his tone. An almost paternal disappointment.

She thought of her cockiness, climbing in the car, acting all tough and street smart. What a joke.

She lowered her eyes and forced "Yes" past the lump in her throat. "He said his name was Steve. He seemed real nice and . . . there was another girl with him and it didn't seem like there was—"

She bit back the words but they landed with a thud between them.

Anything to be afraid of.

Stupid, Randi. Stupid, stupid, stupid.

"The other girl have a name?"

"Cathy. She was older, seemed nice."

"Older?"

"Like in college or something."

He made a note on the pad in front of him. She realized he'd been doing that the whole time.

"Steve or Cathy have last names?"

"I didn't ask. . . . I see now how dumb that was."

He didn't comment or lecture but he didn't have to. They both knew she had learned a lesson she'd never forget.

"What happened next, Randi?"

"We drove around and partied."

"Partied. What does that mean?"

She averted her eyes. "We smoked weed."

"You got high?"

She nodded. "And I guess . . . I passed out."

"You guess?"

"'Cause I woke up . . . outside somewhere." Starting to shiver again, she pulled the blanket tighter. She had to force the words past her chattering teeth. "I couldn't hardly move and I didn't know why."

"And why couldn't you move?"

She still couldn't look at him. It was easier to get the words past her lips without seeing his fatherly disapproval. She was afraid she'd completely fall apart if she did. "I was tied up. With tape. The wide, clear kind."

"Packing tape."

"Yeah, I guess." Randi swallowed hard, her saliva bitter. "The other girl, Cathy, was crying."

"Where was she?"

"A few feet away. She said he . . . said he raped her. And that I was next."

"And where was he?" he asked, voice turning gruff.

"She said he went for food. Taco Bell." She sneaked a peek at him. He had an expression on his face, like he'd eaten something sour.

"And you believed her?"

"It was true. She was tied up, too. But with rope."

"Rope?" he repeated, eyebrows lifting. "You with tape, she with rope?"

"Uh-huh. Why . . . don't you believe me?"

"It's just odd, Randi. Very unusual for a perpetrator to use different materials, especially at the same scene."

"But it's true. Maybe . . . maybe, he didn't have enough rope for both of us?"

"But he had a roll of packing tape handy?" He shook his head slightly. "I'm going to be honest with you, Randi, your story's starting to fall apart."

"It's true!" She bunched her hands into fists. "I promise!"

"And you're not making this up to try to deflect our attention from the fact that you had an ounce of pot in your pocket? Maybe you're trying to make yourself look like a victim instead?"

"No!"

He jotted several notes, then looked back up at her. "What happened next?"

"I was hysterical, trying to get my hands free—"

"And how did you?"

"I chewed through the tape." She made a face at the memory. "It took a long time and tasted real nasty. But I got my hands free, then my feet, and went to help Cathy." Her voice rose. "That's when he came back. I saw the headlights . . . then heard the car door—"

Randi recalled every moment, from her wildly beating heart to the terror that had threatened to overwhelm her.

"He was humming . . . getting closer . . . I had to run! Don't you see? I promised I'd bring help . . . I promised her!"

He stood. "You think you can find where this Steve held you?"

She said she could, then burst into tears.

CHAPTER FORTY

Miranda decided on a brutal workout, then an equally brutal run. Tracks and treadmills couldn't compare to a good, old-fashioned country road, so she drove outside the city limits and parked in the lot of the closed-for-the-season Christmas tree farm.

She'd run this five-mile circuit before, knew each curve and turn, where to watch for traffic and where there was none. Her feet pounded the dirt shoulder in time with her heart, and her breath surged forcefully in and out of her lungs. She might not be able to move tomorrow, but for now the exertion and endorphins were doing their jobs, forcing both her past and the present to the back of her mind.

Up ahead, she saw the sign announcing Bayou Spring Trailer Park. Every rural, southern town had at least one trailer park. Some were shiny and manicured, but most were slightly seedy with more than a whiff of despair about them.

The way this one did. And the way the one where she'd grown up had. Miranda slowed at the entrance, glanced in. Clothes on a line, a couple young kids sitting in a homemade sandbox, two women in folding lawn chairs watching them.

She'd been called out to Bayou Spring a handful of times. Nothing she lost sleep over; most of the disturbances stemmed from one dumbass getting tanked up and pulling a knife on another dumbass. The rest were domestic disturbances or drug related.

Neither of the women looked her way and she ran on, rounding the curve in the road, her gaze landing on the rusted mailbox ahead. Her gait faltered. And some country folks got themselves a double-wide, planted it on a patch of ground, and let the world grow up around them.

The way Clint Wheeler had.

She stopped at the once-shiny mailbox, C. WHEELER hand-painted in bold black on its side.

Her legs just seemed to lock up. Wheeler had retired from the force a year before she'd joined it; when was the last time she'd seen him? She thought back. If she remembered correctly, it was a couple years ago. He'd won a tarpon rodeo, had the poor creature stuffed and mounted and brought it into the HPD to show it off.

"You're a liar, girl. Always was, always will be."

She stared at the crudely painted letters, the euphoria of the run evaporating and her breath turning hard and agitated. And as she stared at those letters a thought popped into her head, rooting and taking hold.

Confront him with the truth. Confront him with the pain he caused, tell him she knew who her attacker was. Perhaps he already knew.

Show him the button.

Miranda brought her hand to the hidden pocket in her jogging pants.

Car key.

ID.

Rhinestone button.

She'd tucked it in at the last moment, like some twisted good-luck charm.

Or maybe because the idea to confront former Officer Clint Wheeler had been taking root all along.

What did she have to lose? He might order her off his property, even threaten to shoot her if she didn't go, but she would have her say. He needed to understand what he'd done.

Even as she told herself to turn back, she started toward the trailer.

His gravel drive was overrun with weeds. Her steps made a crunching noise and the gravel occasionally shifted beneath her sneakered feet.

The strangest sensation came over her. As if déjà vu had just met destiny and she felt at once empowered adult and vulnerable teen. She narrowed her eyes in determination. No. She wasn't at his—or anyone else's—mercy, not anymore.

He'd built a small front porch onto the double-wide, big enough for a single folding lawn chair and a sawed-off pine log, turned on end to serve as a table. On it sat an overflowing ashtray. The smell of stale butts stung her nose and Miranda recalled the way he'd reeked of cigarettes. How the smell in the closed-up cruiser had made her gag.

And she remembered the way he had leered at her. The way it had made her feel—at once cold with fear and hot with shame.

Wheeler had the screen door open, presumably to let the spring air circulate through the trailer. Miranda climbed the two steps and crossed to the screen door, working to get ahold of her emotions. Fact was, she was mad and itching for a fight. A fight she'd been waiting fourteen years to have.

She glanced down. Sitting by the front door was a

New Orleans Saints garden gnome. And just like that, Miranda had herself completely in control. She would determine how this encounter went. It was her show and she would control it.

She was nobody's victim, not anymore.

She rapped on the door frame. "Officer Wheeler," she called, "it's Detective Miranda Rader." When he didn't reply, she tried again. "It's Detective Rader. I need a word with you."

She peered through the screen. From what she could see, the trailer was empty. She nudged the door handle and it lowered; with her toe she pushed the door open.

Odd, she thought. For a man like Wheeler to leave his door unlocked. Maybe he wasn't the tough old son-of-a-bitch she remembered. She considered going inside, then thought better of it and turned to go.

As she did she heard music playing, coming from somewhere behind the trailer. She exited the porch and went around back. The music, she realized, was coming from deeper on the property. She headed that way, using a well-worn path. A bayou ran through this area, the one the trailer park up the road was named after.

She thought of that stuffed fish and followed the trail toward the bayou. As she did, the music got louder. A country song about the joys of living in the Deep South.

Then she saw him. Sitting in a lawn chair on the edge of the bayou, fishing pole in hand, small cooler at his side. It was a little early for beer, but hey, Wheeler was retired.

"Officer Wheeler," she called. "I wonder if I could have a moment of your time?"

He didn't respond and she called again as she got closer. Her steps slowed as she saw he wasn't holding the fishing pole, that it was propped up by the folding chair, one that looked exactly like the one on the porch;

that the cooler at his feet was open but not one of the six pack of Dixie long necks had been opened; and that an inordinate number of flies buzzed around him.

And mostly, because of the blood. It stained the back of his white T-shirt, turning it an angry red.

The old bastard wasn't hard of hearing, at least not anymore. He was dead.

She walked around the chair to check his pulse, then stopped cold. A piece of packing tape was plastered across his mouth, a word scrawled in damning black across the tape.

LIAR

Miranda's hands started to shake, her mind to race. He'd called her the liar. So, was it a message to her? No, that couldn't be—how would the killer have anticipated her finding the body? She—or he—could have if they didn't know she'd been suspended.

Either way, the duct tape was definitely a message. To anyone who found him, then to everyone in Harmony via the press.

He was the liar, not her.

Miranda unclipped her phone and dialed Jake. As it rang, she considered hanging up and walking away. Let someone else find him, she thought. Let them call it in.

This wasn't going to look good for her.

Even as her brain registered the command to walk away, she pictured the two women at the trailer park, watching their children play; she recalled the cars that had passed her during her run, the cyclist whizzing past in his bright-colored Spandex.

Someone would remember seeing her, place her at the scene. And that would look even worse for her.

"Miranda?"

She realized Jake had answered. "Yeah, it's me."

"Are you okay?"

"I'm fine. I'm out here at Clint Wheeler's place—"

"Clint Wheeler's? What the hell—"

"He's dead. Somebody shot him."

She heard his sharply drawn breath, then nothing but a long, damning silence.

Finally, he spoke. "I'm on my way. Stay put. Don't touch anything."

CHAPTER FORTY-ONE

2:00 P.M.

Jake made it to the scene first. Miranda met him and together they walked toward to the rear of Wheeler's property and Wheeler himself, being circled by flies.

They stopped and Jake surveyed the body, then returned to her side. "Well, shit," he said.

She looked at Jake. "I'm not sorry he's dead."

He met her eyes, squinting against the light. "Don't say that again, Miranda. It's not smart."

"It's true, though." She glanced back at Wheeler. "Waiting for you to get here . . . I remembered what he said to me that night, how he treated me." Anger rose up in her, coloring her tone. "I was just a kid. And I was terrified."

"Don't say anything else, Miranda. Not to me. I don't want to know."

She blinked, realizing what he meant. "Do you think I'm confessing? I didn't kill him, Jake."

He looked toward the drive, then back at her. "Jones should be here any minute. Before he gets here, I have to ask you a question. That day the chief told you your prints were found at the scene and I backed you up, were you telling the truth? Did you take off your gloves to make a call?" At her silence he swore. "I lied for you."

"I didn't ask you to, and I didn't want it."

"You don't get it. I jumped to your defense because I believed you. I never questioned your version of events. It didn't even cross my mind to doubt you."

His words stung. She lifted her chin. "I didn't kill Stark. And I didn't kill Wheeler."

"How do I know that's the truth?"

There was nothing else he could have said that would have hurt her more. "I'm not going to dignify that with a response."

She turned to head back toward the house; he caught her arm, stopping her. "Is that what's been going on, Miranda?"

"What are you talking about?"

"You and me, the sex. Am I your ace in the hole?"

"Stop it." She tugged her arm free; he caught it again.

"Was I part of your plan? Just in case something went wrong, you'd have an advocate on the inside? One with a very personal reason to champion you?"

"Go to hell."

"Just tell me it isn't true, Miranda. Just look me in the eyes and tell me."

Jones arrived. They heard the crunch of tires on the gravel drive, the slam of a car door. Miranda looked Jake in the eyes. "I shouldn't have to."

Miranda stood to the side, watching Jake and Jones work. She couldn't hear what they were saying, but she didn't need to. She'd participated in the same back-and-forth discussion, making those same notations, many times before.

Jake squatting beside the body, pointing and mo-
tioning. *Trajectory of the bullet downward. The
shooter appeared to have been standing behind the
seated victim. Theory supported by blood spatter at
the victim's feet.*

Jones nodding, examining the victim's hands, his position in the chair. *No sign of a struggle. Victim either
didn't hear the shooter arrive or had already greeted
them.*

Both studying the taped mouth. The word written on
it. *Pre- or post-mortem? Post, obviously.*

*What of the word? A clue to motivation? Or a mes-
sage for someone? The police maybe? Or someone
else?*

Jake standing. Moving his gaze over the landscape.
Slowly. Taking it in, making his calculations. Best way
in and out: the road. The bayou sliced through the property, cutting it off. On one side the trailer park, on the
other side another residence. Perp would have wanted
to get in and out quickly.

If they tried to pin this on her, she'd have that going
for her, she thought. No car, no means of a clean get-
away. What would they surmise she'd done with the
gun?

The bayou. Yes, of course. Kill Wheeler, dispose of
the gun, call it in.

At the sound of car doors slamming, she turned. The
crime-scene van, Buddy, two more cruisers.

The team made their way over. Buddy went directly
to confer with Jake and survey the scene close up.

Then he made his way to her. He stopped beside her,
but didn't glance her way. After a moment of silence,
he spoke, tone low. "What are you doing, Miranda?"

Not how, but what. "Standing here watching something I should be a part of."

"Aren't you already? A part of it?"

She looked at him but he kept his gaze focused on Wheeler and the activity surrounding him. "If you have something to say to me, Buddy, spit it out."

"You know how this looks."

"I found Wheeler. I didn't kill him."

"Especially on the heels of Stark. And our last conversation."

He'd accused her of being on a twisted trip down memory lane. A psychological one, she'd thought. If she was reading him accurately, he was taking that a step farther.

"You can't truly think I killed Wheeler?"

He looked at her then, gaze steely. "I'm going to need to formally question you."

Miranda knew what that meant. Questioned at HQ. Being observed, videotaped. The entire department knowing what was going down.

"Fine," she said. "What time?"

"I'll have Taggert take you in." He motioned the young patrolman over. "I'll be there when I've finished here."

CHAPTER FORTY-TWO

6:20 P.M.

Buddy finally arrived. He carried a manila folder and a steaming cup of coffee. She could smell it and her mouth watered. "Sorry to keep you waiting so long, Miranda."

Classic bullshit. "Two hours, Buddy? Seriously?"

"It's been a busy day." He crossed to the table, dropped the folder on it. "Can we get you something?"

A lawyer, Miranda thought, but held back. She wanted to get a sense of where this would go first. "Guess that depends on how long I'm going to be here."

"That depends on you, Miranda."

More bullshit. "A bottle of water would be nice, something from vending."

He set his coffee on the table, stepped out into the hall, then returned a couple minutes later with the water and a Snickers bar. He stopped at the video camera and flipped it on.

"This is official," she said as he took a seat across from her.

"It's not playtime. One of ours is dead."

"How could I forget? I was the one who found him and called it in."

He took a sip of the coffee. "Why don't we get started."

"No Jake?"

"Not this time."

What did it mean? She sifted through the options, uncomfortable with them all. Jake knew more than she was willing to share with Cadwell . . . yet. But would Jake feel the need to keep her secrets? After their last conversation, she thought not.

"For the record," he began, "why were you out at Clint Wheeler's place today?"

"As I told Jake—Detective Billings—I was running. I came to his mailbox and stopped to say hello."

"Stop and visit, just like that? I didn't know you two were close."

"We weren't. But we were colleagues, former colleagues that is. I heard music coming from around back, so I followed it. You know what happened next."

"For the record, please."

"I found Clint Wheeler dead."

"You and Officer Wheeler had some history together, did you not?"

"You know we did."

"Yes or no."

"Yes."

"What was the nature of that relationship, apart from being HPD colleagues?"

If he thought he was going to make her squirm, he was mistaken. "When I was fifteen Officer Wheeler busted me for possession of marijuana. It's all a matter of public record."

"But there's more to the story, isn't there?"

She narrowed her eyes slightly. "Also a matter of public record."

He shifted on the wooden chair. "You spent six

months in juvie, all because of Officer Wheeler. Isn't that right?"

"No," she countered. "I spent six months in juvenile detention because of choices I made. Bad ones."

"Would it be fair to say you hated Clint Wheeler?"

"I did, a long time ago." She settled her gaze on his. "I grew up and left all that childishness behind."

He changed tack. "Tell me about the crime scene."

"You were there."

"From your eyes, Detective Rader. You're one of my best investigators. What would your report say?"

Miranda clicked through the facts. "Man, shot from behind, bullet's trajectory downward, suggesting perpetrator was standing behind the victim. Wound and blood spatter support that assessment. No sign of a struggle by Wheeler, which suggests he either knew the perpetrator and thought he had nothing to fear, or the perp somehow sneaked up without being heard. An improbable option, even with the radio."

She went on, falling into the rhythm, using the opportunity to go over the facts herself. "Cooler was open and full. Dixie long necks. The beer was warm."

"Excuse me?"

"It was warm, I checked. That means the cooler was open for a while before I arrived. A pretty fall day, they would have held their temperature longer."

Buddy made a note and she moved on. "The most interesting, and unusual, aspect of the scene was the tape on Wheeler's mouth. And the word written on it."

"Liar."

"Yes. Obviously a message, but what and to whom are the questions."

"What's your theory, Detective Rader? Why label Clint Wheeler a liar?"

Because he was, jumped to her tongue. She said

instead, "I don't have one. What's yours? You're chief of the Harmony PD."

"You know how this works. I ask the questions and you answer. Real easy."

Miranda folded her hands on the table in front of her. "Like I said, it seems like the perp was sending a message, maybe about Wheeler himself, maybe police in general. Are we done here?"

"Hardly." He shifted in his seat. "How'd the killer get in and out?"

"Only the killer knows that for certain, Buddy. But it seems to me the only reasonable option was by car."

"But you got to Wheeler's on foot."

"So? I didn't kill Clint Wheeler. C'mon, Buddy, you're fishing here. You have nothing worth a damn, and frankly, you're wasting both of our time."

"Let's talk about Richard Stark."

"Stark?" she repeated, surprised.

"Yes." He rocked back in his chair. "You have a theory about his murder."

"You know I do."

"Could you share it, for the sake of the video?"

Miranda understood what he was doing and it rankled. And she knew she should probably refuse and lawyer up. But it really pissed her off.

She looked directly at the camera. "I believe Richard Stark was a sexual predator and was killed by someone he abused."

She felt a rush of satisfaction at Buddy's surprise. He hadn't expected her to make that statement, and now that she had, it was part of the official record.

Take that, asshole.

"Were you that person?"

Now it was she who was taken aback. "What?"

"Did you kill Richard Stark?"

"No! Absolutely not. I didn't even know who Richard Stark was before I arrived that night."

"Your prints were found at the scene."

"I explained that."

"So you did."

The mildness of his tone slid along her nerve endings like an alarm. "Jake backed me up."

"He did." He paused. "At the time."

She told herself to play it cool, even as a sick feeling rolled over her. That Buddy knew everything. That Jake had come clean about the gloves, the key, and the button.

She cocked her head. "He doesn't anymore? I find that very . . . odd."

"Why's that? Because you two are in a relationship?"

For a split second, she couldn't breathe. The moment passed. "No. Because Jake wouldn't lie."

"But he is loyal, isn't he? And very . . . trusting."

"What are you trying to say?"

"Why do you think Stark had that news clipping about you in his drawer?"

"I told you before, I don't know."

"But you have a theory?"

"Yeah, some weird coincidence."

"Why'd you lie to me, Miranda?"

It felt as if her heart plummeted to her stomach. She didn't even blink. "Excuse me?"

"Why'd you lie to me?"

"When was that, Buddy?"

"This morning."

"You're mistaken."

He settled his gaze on hers. Several seconds passed before he spoke. "Where'd you get the key, Miranda?"

She played dumb. "What key?"

"To the lockbox." When she didn't respond, he went

on. "This morning, you said the key had been taken in as evidence from the Stark scene."

"I don't recall that."

He went on as if she hadn't spoken. "There are a couple problems with that. One, you must have had the key on you because you opened the box at your home, in the middle of the night. Just to be certain, I checked with the desk sergeant—you weren't in last night. And while I was at it, I reviewed the evidence log from the Stark scene. There was no key collected that night. Where'd you get the key, Miranda?"

She'd known it was a strong possibility Buddy would question that part of her account, but she'd taken the chance anyway. Now it looked like it might be her undoing.

"I'm not going to say another word until I have a lawyer."

"Of course." He stood but didn't move away from the table. "It's me, Buddy, you're talking to. I was there that night, all those years ago."

That night in June 2002. The night everything seemed to point to.

"You told Wheeler a story. One he didn't believe." He flipped open the folder on the table. Spun it around to face her.

A police report, she saw. She didn't have to read it to know exactly what it said.

"He didn't believe you, did he? It says right in the report." He tapped the page. "In fact, he called you a liar."

Miranda folded her arms across her chest, maintaining her silence.

"Before I came in here today, I reviewed this, Wheeler's report. I noticed something I'd forgotten. Something about the story you told him."

She cocked an eyebrow, playing it cool even as her mind raced. Where was he going with all this? And what else did he have?

"You said the person who bound you that night, bound you with packing tape. Isn't that right?"

She didn't respond and he went on. "Don't you find it odd—an uncomfortable coincidence—that the man who called you a liar was shot in the back, then branded a liar? Using the exact material you claimed to have been restrained with that night?"

He paused, waiting. When she didn't comment, he added, "And let's not forget, you just happened to be out running and 'found' the body?" He made quotation marks with his fingers.

"I asked for a lawyer. And I'm not saying another thing until I have one."

"If that's how you want to play this, fine. But you know what? I think we're done here for now."

He stood and crossed to the video camera and turned it off, then collected the folder from the table. He used the moment to bend down close to her ear.

"I feel real bad about what happened to you back then," he said, voice low. "But I've got a job to do. I hope you understand that . . . Randi."

He straightened and motioned to the door. "Thanks for your time. I'll be in touch."

CHAPTER FORTY-THREE

8:00 P.M.

Miranda walked out of the HPD a free woman. For now, she thought. Buddy wasn't done with her yet, of that she had no doubt. She nodded a casual greeting to a couple officers on their way in, the picture of ease. Like she didn't have a care in the world.

Inside, she was falling apart. She wanted to shout in anger, bang her fists in frustration, rail at the injustice of it. She settled for the vehicular equivalent—she tore out of the parking lot, tires squealing as she turned onto Railroad Avenue.

A moment later, acknowledging that drawing more attention to herself right now was not a good idea, she eased her foot off the gas.

Not knowing what else to do or where to go, she simply drove. She briefly considered going to Summer, but the last thing her friend needed right now was someone crying on her shoulder.

Head west, she thought. Jump onto I-10 and don't stop until you reach the Pacific Ocean.

She used to promise herself she'd do that. Escape to California and never come back. Escape her family, and every memory of this godforsaken place. Start over, new and shiny bright.

Instead, she never left Jasper, not really. Even tonight it drew her back. She rolled onto Main Street, acknowledging how small and broken down it was. Once upon a time, it had been the center of her universe.

Maybe it still was.

A lump in her throat, she eased through town, past the elementary and middle schools she'd attended, then the high school. She stopped in front of the latter, a hulking brick building where her memories turned darker. A teen spiraling out of control, hanging onto angry rebellion as one did a life vest—that anger, that rebellion had given her a place to belong, friends, and an identity.

The life vest had proved to be an anchor. After she returned from juvie, being a rebel wasn't so cool anymore. Besides, her former friends—like everyone else—wanted nothing to do with her. She was damaged goods; the girl who'd done time. The liar who would say or do anything to save her own butt.

She hadn't belonged anywhere.

She still didn't.

Miranda turned away from the thought and the school and headed back the way she'd come, pulling into the Sonic Drive-In she and her friends used to hang at and where she'd been a carhop for a week before being fired for mouthing off to her manager.

For old times' sake, she ordered onion rings and a Blue Raspberry Slush. The rings were greasier than she remembered, and the Slush sweeter, but she finished them anyway.

Miranda tipped the carhop big because she knew just how god-awful the job could be, and exited the drive-in. As if on autopilot, she headed toward home. Not her cozy cottage in Harmony, but to the trailer park where she'd grown up.

She stopped short, the quick jerk of the safety belt

knocking the wind out of her. Or was it surprise that took her breath?

The trailer park was gone. Replaced by a community of small, neat garden homes.

When had it happened? She should have known this. Homes didn't spring up overnight—how long since she'd driven by? It couldn't have been that . . .

She never drove by, she realized. Not here.

But still, why hadn't anyone told her?

Who would that have been, Miranda? You left everyone from those days behind. Even your family.

She pulled away from the development's entrance, spitting up gravel as she did. Just like back then, wanting nothing more than to leave this place—and all its memories—far behind.

But where could she go from here?

The place she had refused to confront for fourteen years, not since the night in June when she stood shaking beside the Harmony chief of police, her tenuously constructed world splintering into razor sharp, bloodied fragments.

Just like it was now.

Miranda found the spot—how could she not have? It was burned into her memory. The two trees. The picnic table. The trash barrel next to where Stark—he had a name now—parked the car.

The same spot she parked hers tonight. Miranda climbed out, moved her gaze over the area. In fourteen years, it seemed not to have changed. Impossible. Everything in nature changed. Things grew and blossomed, they withered and died.

But this place appeared to be frozen in time.

Or was it her mind playing tricks on her?

With leaden legs, propelled by sheer force of will, she started for the trees.

Her tree.

And the other girl's.

"Are you certain this is the place?" Chief Cadwell asked, voice heavy with doubt.

"Yes!" she cried. *"It was here!"* She turned to him, pleading. *"You have to believe me!"*

But he didn't. Why should he have? There proved nothing but her word to back her up—not even a shiny scrap of tape. To his credit he searched with her—he with a flashlight, she on her hands and knees.

Finally, in tears, she gave up.

"He must have taken her somewhere," she said, wiping her nose with the back of her hand. *"He cleaned the area up and—"*

"It's time to go, Randi."

"But what about the other girl? She—"

"I'm sorry. There's nothing here."

He looked at her strangely. Not with contempt, the way Wheeler had. With pity, she realized. He didn't believe her, but he felt sorry for her.

Same as he said to her today.

"I feel real bad about what happened back then, Randi. But I've got a job to do. And I'm going to do it."

Nothing had changed. Not in fourteen years.

With a strangled cry, Miranda sank to her knees. She'd left everyone from those days behind—everyone except that girl she had been. All these years, carrying her around like an invisible anchor.

The girl she had been.

And the one she still was.

She brought her hands to her mouth to hold back a sob. She'd promised herself she would never be that girl again. But the truth was, she'd never stopped.

Fourteen lost years. How did that happen? She swiped the tears from her cheeks. How had she gotten here? Back to where it all began?

Her brother's accusation popped into her head. *"Sounds like running away to me, Randi."*

He was right. Running away didn't equal change—it was cowardice.

Is that what she was? A coward?

Miranda dropped her hands and, curling them into fists, pounded the ground. She howled in rage and frustration; she wept at the futility of it. She'd spent her entire adult life trying to prove she wasn't a liar, giving up her family, the dreams she'd had. Pushing them all aside, intent on becoming the person in the position of authority, the one others trusted and turned to for support. Intent on proving she was worthy.

And here she was, right back where she started.

She sobbed until she was spent, with neither the tears nor energy to continue.

Let it go, Miranda. Let the past go.

She couldn't. She'd tried. All these years, but here she was. How did she leave the past behind when it was all around her? When it constituted the very fabric of her being?

Let. It. Go.

The fight drained out of her and she stilled, listening to her own heartbeat, breathing hard. In and out. The seconds ran together, becoming minutes. Her breath slowed to a deep, rhythmic pace, her tears dried, and the knot in her chest unfurled.

She was almost thirty years old . . . for God's sake, wasn't it time to move on?

Not run away. That's what she had been doing. Robby was right about that. The time had come to put it all to rest and find peace. With the past and all the people who populated it—including her family. The ones who had hurt her most.

Anger stirred in the pit of her gut, the cut of betrayal. The bitterness that came with both. The taste of it filled her senses, nearly choking her. Why should she make peace with them? They abandoned her. When she needed them they had been nowhere to be found.

Let. It. Go.

And suddenly, she understood. The truth rolled over her in a wave. The change she needed, the peace she longed for, didn't have a damn thing to do with anyone else's actions or attitudes. Healing change could only come from inside her, from deep down in her marrow.

The time had come to truly move on with her life.

And she knew just where she had to start. Miranda stood and brushed dirt and debris from her pants. Her hands hurt; she noticed she'd cut her right pinky. She must look a fright. The way she'd looked that night in June, sitting across the desk from Buddy.

Miranda made her way to her car. There, she stopped and took one long, last glance back, then climbed in and fired up the engine. She dug her phone out of her purse, noting that she'd missed two calls and voice mails from Jake. She ignored them, accessed her call log, and scrolled through. She found the number she was looking for.

Without giving herself a chance to change her mind, she tapped it. A moment later her brother, Robby, answered, sounding exhausted.

"It's Miranda," she said.

"Miranda?" he repeated in question, obviously surprised to be hearing from her. "What are you—are you all right?"

She almost laughed. Not at the question, but at the answer that sprang to her tongue despite the heap of trouble she was in. "Yeah," she said, "never better. Just . . . what hospital did you say Mom was in?"

CHAPTER FORTY-FOUR

11:10 P.M.

Robby told Miranda that their mother was at East Jefferson General Hospital. He hadn't said much else, but then she didn't give him the opportunity to. She hadn't wanted questions, congratulations, or even an "It's about time" from him. She was acting on emotion and gut instinct and the fact was, she still might back out.

It took all her strength of will to climb out of the car and walk into the hospital. The next test was stepping into the elevator and pressing the button for the third floor. And now, as the elevator lurched to a stop, exiting on her mother's floor.

Dead ahead stood the nurses' station; one of the nurses looked up at her. Miranda forced a smile and headed her way. "Good evening," she said. "I'm looking for Sally Rader."

"It's past visiting hours," the nurse replied. "Only family—"

"I'm her daughter."

The nurse's expression changed. "You're the police officer."

Miranda stiffened slightly. "I am."

"She was hoping you'd come visit. She's so proud of you."

Her mother? Proud of her? Since when?

Miranda cleared her throat. "I know it's late. . . . I don't intend to wake her. I just wanted to—"

What? Why was she *really* here?

"To sit with her awhile," the nurse finished for her. "That's perfectly fine. She's in room three-oh-eight." She indicated the hall to her right. "The chair reclines. Your brother's usually here, so there's already an extra pillow and blanket."

Miranda thanked her and started for her mother's room, aware of the nurse's gaze on her back. One step at a time, she told herself, praying she didn't take one look at her mother and run the other way.

Miranda stopped outside the partially open door. Her heart beat like a tribal drum in her chest. Fight or flight. Ridiculous, she told herself. She'd taken down perps twice her size and broken up fights between testosterone-fueled frat boys, and she was terrified of facing a sick, old woman in a hospital bed?

Not any woman.

The one who had broken her heart.

With a deep, steadying breath, Miranda slipped inside, her gaze automatically going to the bed. Her mother slept. She looked frail and . . . elderly. Way older than her fifty-some years.

Miranda moved closer, taking in her pallor and sunken cheeks, the gray in her hair. How long since they had been face to face? Six years? Eight?

As if she sensed Miranda's presence, her mother's eyes opened and settled on her.

"Mom," she said softly. "It's me. Miranda."

Her mother blinked, gaze going from unfocused to clear. "Randi? Is that really you?"

Her voice was small and crackly. Miranda's eyes burned. "It is, Mama. It's me."

Her mother tipped her hand over, and Miranda clasped it lightly. The skin felt thin and papery; the fingers almost skeletal. A tear slipped down Miranda's cheek. "I'm sorry," she said. "I should have been here before now."

"No." She rocked her head from side to side. "I'm sorry . . ."

Her voice trailed off and her grip went limp. For one heart-stopping moment, Miranda thought she'd slipped away. Then she saw the gentle rise and fall of her chest.

It went like that all night, her mother drifting in and out of sleep. Awakening, calling for Miranda, then drifting off again. The nurses came in and out, checking her mother's vitals, sending sympathetic glances Miranda's way.

Miranda drifted, too. Moments of sleep that ranged from deep and dreamless to ones of battling monsters.

When she awakened fully, sun cascaded through the window, and the hall outside the room bustled with activity.

"I was afraid I dreamed you."

Miranda turned her head. Her mother. Propped up in bed, watching her.

"I'm not surprised. It was so late when I got here." She found her ponytail holder, pulled her hair back, and crossed to the bed. "How do you feel this morning?"

"Better than I have in a long time."

"That's good." She curved her hand around her mother's. "Can I get you some juice or something?"

"I just want to look at you."

A knot of tears formed in Miranda's throat. "I'm not going anywhere, Mom."

"I'm glad." Her lips curved into small, shy smile. "You're so pretty."

Miranda squeezed her hand. "I thought you had a heart attack, not lost your mind."

Instead of smiling back, her eyes filled with tears. "I'm sorry, baby. For everything."

"Mom, you don't have to—"

"I think I . . . yes, I do. I made so many mistakes." She looked away, then back. "So many."

"Me, too," Miranda whispered. "It's in the past now."

"No." The pillow made a rustling noise as her mother shook her head. "It's not. But I want it to be."

"I do, too, Mom."

She went on as if Miranda hadn't spoken. "I was so afraid for you." She paused, as if to catch her breath. "I didn't want you to—"

"Don't, Mom. Save your energy, it's—"

"—end up like me."

"Don't say that."

Her watery blue eyes suddenly seemed focused not on Miranda, but something far away.

"Married to someone like . . . your daddy. He was sick in the head, Randi. Real bad."

"You could have left him, Mom. Why didn't you?"

"Where would I have gone? Three babies to take care of . . . no skills, no money . . ." She drew in a shuddering breath. "I couldn't leave the three of you, but how would I have cared for you and your brothers? I didn't even have a car."

She'd been trapped, Miranda realized. And felt powerless. How many women over the ages had felt the same way?

"I was so afraid for you. Your brothers, too, but not in the same way. I knew because they were boys, they'd have opportunities you wouldn't."

Miranda recalled what her mother said all those

years ago, about life being tougher for women. That was the only world her mother had ever known.

She'd never thought of her mother's situation quite that way. Had never thought of her as being a victim, too. She'd been too busy being angry and feeling sorry for herself.

It broke her heart.

"I let them take you away because I thought it was the only way. Maybe your only chance to . . . escape the life I had."

She went silent a moment, a tear rolling down her cheek. "I believed you, Randi."

Miranda caught her breath. "Wait—what did you say?"

"I knew you were telling the truth, about that boy and what happened."

Miranda struggled to get ahold of her emotions, her racing thoughts. "I don't understand, Mama. You believed me? Why didn't you say so? Why didn't you stick up for me?"

"What could I have done? Nothing. My opinion would have meant nothing."

Miranda opened her mouth to tell her it would have meant everything to her, that knowing somebody cared enough to fight for her would have meant everything.

Then her mother went on. "I needed you to get away from Jasper before you were ruined like me. So I lost you."

She started to cry and something deep inside Miranda broke free, all the things she'd imagined saying to her mother falling away with it—accusations about not being loved or protected. About a mother who didn't stand up for her child.

Now she saw that in her own way her mother had tried to protect her. And that she had been loved.

"You were right, Mama," she said, voice thick with tears. "I was heading down a really bad path. Juvie was the best thing that ever happened to me, because it changed me. I realized I didn't want to be that person I was becoming."

It wasn't the whole truth, but it was all the truth her mother needed to know.

"You were right," she said again, leaning closer, smoothing away her mother's tears. "I was wrong to be mad at you all this time. And I'm sorry, so very sorry, that I'm only realizing that now."

They were both crying when Robby walked in. He stopped in the doorway, looking confused. "What's wrong?"

"Nothing," Miranda said, smiling through her tears. "Mom and I were just catching up."

He frowned slightly, like that didn't make any sense at all to him. But instead of saying so, he crossed to the bed. "Morning, Mom. How're you feeling today?"

"Randi came," she said.

He chuckled. "I see that."

The aide arrived with a breakfast tray. Robby used the opportunity to motion Miranda out to the hall.

"I didn't expect to see you this morning," he said softly.

"I spent the night."

He seemed to digest that and nodded. "Thanks for coming. It means a lot to her."

"It meant a lot to me to see her." She paused. "Thanks for . . . letting me know. And for all you've done for her."

He seemed taken aback and cleared his throat. "Yeah, well, she's my mother. What was I gonna do?"

Honorable, she thought. Her brother had grown into an honorable and good man. Suddenly, absurdly, she felt like crying again.

She glanced away, cleared her throat. "What's her prognosis?"

"She needs to start taking care of herself. Eat right. Exercise. Take the medicine they prescribed. Apparently, high cholesterol and high blood pressure run in her family."

"They do?" she asked, surprised. "I didn't know that."

"Me, either. I just learned her mother died in her fifties from a heart attack. Did you know?"

She shook her head. "But she's going to be okay?"

"If she follows doctor's orders." He paused a moment before going on. "So, what now?"

"What do you mean?"

"You gone again?" he asked, not quite meeting her eyes. "Or are you going to come around sometimes?"

"Is it okay if I come around?"

This time it was he who looked overcome with emotion, he who glanced quickly away. "Yeah," he said. "That'd be good."

CHAPTER FORTY-FIVE

9:15 A.M.

"Since Mom's napping," Miranda said a short time later, standing and hooking her purse strap over her shoulder, "I'm going to grab a coffee and something to eat. You want anything?"

Robby looked up from his phone and nodded. "Coffee. As big as they've got."

"Done. Be right back."

She slipped out of the room and into the hall. As she cleared the room, her cell vibrated in her pocket. Jake, she saw. The last thing she wanted to do was talk to him, but she answered anyway.

"Hey, Jake."

"Hey. Are you okay?"

"Yeah."

"I'm glad to hear that." He paused a moment. "Miranda?"

"I'm here."

"I wanted . . . I needed to tell you I'm sorry."

"For what, Jake?"

He paused again, this time longer and more awkward than the first. The silence grew to deafening proportion. Still, she waited. He'd called her; she had nothing to say.

"I had to tell Buddy."

Her heart began to rap against the wall of her chest. She willed it to slow. "Tell him what?"

"That I lied about seeing you at the Stark scene with your gloves off."

Which explained one line of Buddy's interrogation and answered the question of whether Jake had come clean about that.

"I had to," he added, "considering the turn of events."

"I get it; you have a job to do."

Which didn't change the fact that it felt like a betrayal. Her chest tightened. And now, it was just her word about the prints. How much faith would Buddy put in that?

"Did he suspend you?" she asked.

"Not yet. But it's coming, I think."

"I'm sorry about that, Jake. I'd never want that to happen to you."

"You didn't ask me to back you up. That's on me."

"I'm still sorry."

"It's physical evidence tying you to the scene."

"I know. And there's nothing I can do about that. The fact is, I didn't kill Stark and I have no idea how my prints ended up at Stark's home. And like I told Buddy, I didn't even know who he was before that night."

"There's more." This time he didn't wait for a reply. "I told him about the button, and that I was there with you that night. That we're . . . in a relationship."

That hurt more than the other. Because it was personal. Because she'd asked him not to.

She felt exposed. Like that shivering fifteen-year-old, alone and exposed with no place to hide.

But she wasn't, she reminded herself. Not anymore.

At her silence, he went on. "He brought Catherine Stark in for questioning. About the box."

"And?" The word came out a croak.

"She said she didn't know what he was talking about."

"But I mentioned the key to her!" A couple passing in the hallway looked her way. She lowered her voice. "I asked her if she knew about a strongbox—"

"She acknowledged that, Miranda. But claimed she had no knowledge of the box and absolutely no part in it ending up on your porch."

"I don't believe her."

"I sat in on the interview. She was shocked by the suggestion, Miranda. Shocked."

"Then where did it come from?"

"You're going to need a lawyer. A good one."

"You can't be serious." But he was, she knew. "Is Buddy issuing a warrant?"

"Not yet."

"But you think he will?"

He hesitated. "Yeah, I do. Ian Stark's breathing pretty heavily down his neck."

"What, besides what we discussed, does Buddy have?"

"I don't know. And even if I did, I couldn't tell you. I'm sorry," he said again.

"It's crazy. He can't have anything because there's nothing to have."

"Stark says if Buddy doesn't do it, he's calling a press conference and going to the Sheriff's Department. I just wanted to give you a heads-up."

"I appreciate that."

"Miranda?"

"Yeah?"

"Where are you? I went by your place last night and waited."

"My mom's in the hospital. I'm here with her and my brother."

Although she'd never delved into the details of why with him, he knew she and her family were estranged.

Now, he seemed to digest the information. "Is she going to be okay?"

"It looks that way, yes."

"I'm glad."

"Yeah, me too." She pressed the phone closer to her ear. "Look, I've got to go."

"Miranda? On the lawyer . . . I wouldn't wait."

CHAPTER FORTY-SIX

3:10 P.M.

Miranda called the defense attorney every officer in the department—including her—despised because he walked so many perps. He was that good.

She met him at his Baton Rouge office. "Mr. Stanley," she greeted him, hand out.

"Dan," he corrected, shaking her hand, then grinning. "Let's go rap about why you're here."

She followed him into his office. Dan Stanley looked the antithesis of a shark in a suit. He was tall with thinning hair, Harry Potter spectacles, and penchant for Hawaiian shirts. In fact, she'd never seen him in anything else—even in court, forced to wear a sports coat and tie with it.

He motioned her toward one of the armchairs in front of his desk. When they were both seated, he said, "What can I do for you today, Detective?"

"I'm in a spot of trouble—" She bit the rest back with a self-deprecating laugh. "Of course I am, or I wouldn't have called you."

He didn't comment and she went on. "Yesterday, I was questioned in connection to the murders of former Harmony Police Department officer Clint Wheeler, and of Professor Richard Stark. Have you heard of either of the cases?"

"Stark's, obviously, because his father's such a prominent figure in Louisiana. But since you're here, I'll assume you were charged with neither crime?"

"That's correct. However, a source of mine within the department advised me that Chief Cadwell is considering charges and strongly recommended I contact an attorney."

"Strongly? So this source is a friend?"

"Yes."

"You cooperated with the HPD?"

"Absolutely."

"They recorded your interview?"

Miranda nodded. "I answered all Chief Cadwell's questions until his last couple. I requested representation, and he ended the interview."

"Just like that?" She nodded and he steepled his fingers. "What did he ask that changed your mind about representation?"

"When I realized he really did think I had something to do with the murders."

"Did you have something to do with them?"

She didn't blink. "No, absolutely not."

"My services don't come cheap. You're certain you want to move forward?"

Miranda nodded and leaned forward. "Before Chief Cadwell cut me loose, he told me he was sorry about what happened to me in the past, but he had a job to do. He wanted me to understand that."

Stanley's eyebrows shot up. "And that's on tape, as well?"

"No. He turned the recorder off first."

"Interesting." He tapped his pen on the desktop. "The past he referred to, what's that all about?"

Miranda told him, the story pouring out of her. About that night in June, then fast forwarding to Richard Stark's murder, the clipping at the scene, learning her prints had been found at there, and how Jake had backed up her story.

"I don't know how my prints ended up there. I'd never met Richard Stark, let alone been in his home."

"You had gloves on at the scene."

"Yes."

"But you said you didn't. Why, if not guilty?"

"Because I knew how it would look," she answered, tone and gaze steady. "And I knew I'd be taken off the case."

"Why would that have mattered to you?"

Her mouth went parchment dry. "Because I think I already knew."

"What's that?"

"That it was him."

"Him?"

"The guy who abducted me that night."

He looked unfazed by her revelation. "What happened next?"

Miranda shared the rest—her confrontation with Catherine and Ian Stark, her illegal search of the victim's home, finding the bag of roofies, and how they went missing. She explained about the key, then the lockbox and its contents and then being suspended from the force.

"From there, I went for a run and ended up at Clint Wheeler's place."

Stanley looked up. "Victim number two?"

"Yes. I found the body and called it in."

"This was the same Officer Wheeler as—"

"That night fourteen years ago, yes."

"Why'd you call it in?"

"Because it was the right thing to do."

"Not because you knew somebody like me could use it to argue your innocence?"

"No."

"Ladies and gentlemen of the jury, if my client was guilty, why would she call the police? Certainly, as a police officer, she knows that the person who finds the body is always a suspect."

Her cheeks heated. "What are you implying? That I killed him?"

"Not at all," he said, tone easy. "Is that it, the whole story?"

She nodded.

He nudged his glasses up his nose. "That was one hell of a lollapalooza."

"It's the truth."

"I believe it is."

"Because that's what I pay you for?" She didn't attempt to curtail the sarcasm.

"Yes." He smiled slightly. "But also because you're a cop."

"So? No love lost, right?"

He laughed. "If you were going to make up a story, Detective Rader, you'd keep it simple. You're smart enough to know there's too much in that story for a prosecutor to hang you on."

He was right. And there was nothing she could do about it because it was the truth.

Stanley had taken notes throughout and he took a moment to review them. "Best assessment right now, everything they have so far is circumstantial. Chief Cadwell may decide to charge you anyway, but I don't think it'll stick unless they have an ace up their sleeve—" He looked up. "Any aces I should be aware of?"

She shook her head. "Not that I can even imagine. But then, this whole thing has blown my mind."

"But as you probably already know, they have enough to make your life miserable. And every right to do it."

"You're right. I'm a cop so I'm quite familiar making a suspect's life miserable."

"I'll call Cadwell, have a little chat with him. See if I can take his temperature. Ask for the interview video."

"He's not going to be happy I hired you."

He smiled. "No, he is not."

She smiled back and stood. "You'll keep me posted?"

"I will. No more solo chats with the police, Miranda."

"Got it."

He followed her to her feet, walked her to the door. "May I make a suggestion?"

"You're my lawyer, it's sort of expected."

He laughed again, then sobered. "Unless you're lying to me, I think you need to figure out why this is happening to you."

CHAPTER FORTY-SEVEN

6:45 P.M.

Miranda couldn't get the attorney's words out of her head.

"You need to figure out why this is happening to you."

Up until now she'd been focusing on Stark, on proving he was a bad guy, the bad guy. All her energy had been directed to that task. All of it: her interviews, her illegal search of Stark's home, lifting the key—everything.

Stanley was right. If she figured out why this was happening, it would point to the who. After all, her prints hadn't gotten to Stark's on their own.

Her cell went off; it was Robby. "Is Mom okay?" she answered.

"She's good. She's asking for you, I just wondered—"

"I'm almost there. I had a meeting in Baton Rouge, and thought I'd swing by to say goodnight before I headed home."

"You've got a long drive, sis, I can just hand her the phone—"

"No, I want to do this. I want her to know she can count on me." Miranda paused and took a breath. "And I want you to know you can count on me, too."

Twenty minutes later, she sat beside her mother's bed, eating the Subway sandwich she'd picked up on her way in. Robby's wife and five-year-old daughter were visiting and she met the two for the first time.

Anna, his wife, was both lovely and gracious, giving Miranda a genuine-looking smile and a big hug. Little Chrissy was shy, so Miranda squatted down to introduce herself.

"I'm your Auntie Miranda, and I'm very happy to meet you."

She got a ghost of a smile in return and Miranda looked up at her brother. He had tears in his eyes and she felt as if her heart might explode with happiness.

Funny, but she'd never contemplated how their dysfunctional family affected her brothers. She'd always thought of them as part of the problem, not fellow casualties. And she'd certainly never considered that either of them would miss her or long to have her in their life.

She saw now how wrong she had been.

A short while later, after she said her good-byes, Robby offered to walk her to her car.

They stepped off the elevator and into the lobby before he spoke. "What's going on, Miranda?"

"What do you mean?"

"Remember my buddy Nate from high school?"

She nodded. He lived in Harmony and worked for the district attorney's office. "I saw him just the other day. Why?"

"He called me today. He said he'd heard you're in some sort of trouble. And that you were suspended from the force. Is it true?"

The small-town network never failed to shock and awe.

Miranda let out a resigned breath. "I wasn't going to

tell you. I figured you have enough to worry about. Yeah, it's true, and that's why I was in Baton Rouge. I was meeting with a defense attorney."

He stopped. Dragged a hand through his hair. "It's that bad?"

"It's all a mistake, suspicion based on a bucketful of circumstantial evidence. The lawyer said I don't need to worry."

Not the whole truth, but close enough.

"If you need anything, come to me. Character reference, bail, a file in a cake . . ."

She laughed, the sound tight. "I appreciate it, Robby. But I'm innocent so there's no way I'll be charged. No way."

They reached her car and stopped. He turned and looked her in the eyes. "I want you to know . . . I messed up last time, but I won't this time. I'm with you, Randi, one hundred percent. Anything you need, I'm here for you."

By the time Miranda got home, it was fully dark and the promised cold front had moved through. She pulled into her drive but didn't make a move to cut the engine. Her house was dark and she knew it'd be cold.

She didn't want to go in.

She didn't want to be alone.

Summer, Miranda thought. She wanted to check in on her, and even if she was too busy to talk, there'd be people and lights and conversations. And a cocktail or two tonight wouldn't be a bad thing.

Miranda shifted into reverse and backed out of the drive, heading toward the Toasted Cat. The bar was busy, but Summer looked up as she entered and greeted her with a smile. Miranda's spirits sank anyway—her friend didn't look good. It wasn't just her smile that was off, but her color as well. And the lines around her eyes and lips seemed more deeply etched than just the day before.

Miranda found an empty seat at the bar. It took Summer a minute to make her way over. "Hey, girlfriend," she said. "How're you tonight?"

"Hanging in there. How about you?"

Summer cocked an eyebrow in question. "About the same as you. What're you drinking tonight?"

"How about a cosmo?"

The eyebrow went up again. "Are we celebrating?"

Miranda thought of her mother and brother, of meeting his wife and the niece she hadn't realized she had. "Yeah," she said. "As crazy as that is considering the mess of my professional life, we're celebrating."

Summer brought her the cosmo, then had to move on. Miranda didn't mind being alone, and sipped her drink, letting the activity swirl around her.

The alcohol in the first drink caused just enough of a buzz for her to order a second. She made small talk with a Harmony old-timer, then fended off an octopus attempting to make a love connection.

Business finally slowed enough that Summer could stop and visit. She brought along another drink. Miranda eyed it. "You driving me home?"

"That could happen. Or we'll call an Uber."

"I can live with that." She exchanged her empty glass for the full one. "How are you feeling? You don't look so good."

Summer snorted. "Well, thank you very much. You don't look so good yourself."

"We agree on that." She lifted her glass. "So, how are you?"

"I'm feeling all right. No spells recently. That's a

good thing. What about you?" She motioned to the cosmos. "Last we talked, things weren't so rosy."

"They still aren't."

"But?"

"I went to see my mom in the hospital. And we talked. It was . . . good. Really good."

Summer leaned her chin on her fist. "Well, that's something I never thought I'd hear you say."

"I know, right? Me either."

Summer leaned forward, lowered her voice. "I heard some things today."

"About?" she asked, though she had a pretty good idea what her friend was about to say.

"Clint Wheeler. Somebody killed him."

Miranda realized she hadn't spoken to Summer since before Wheeler's death.

"I found him. Called it in."

"I heard that, too. Why didn't you tell me?"

The hurt in Summer's voice surprised her. "I didn't want to bother you with my problems. I wanted to come see you, but figured the last thing you needed was me whining to you."

"We're friends." Her cheeks turned red. "It's not whining when it's between friends."

Miranda was taken aback. "I'm so . . . sorry. I don't know what else to say."

Summer shook her head. "No, I'm sorry. I'm a little on edge. You were right—I haven't been feeling great and it's making me crabby."

"It's okay. You deserve a little crabby time."

She smiled slightly and went to serve one customer and close out the tab on another. The bar was nearly empty now, so she poured herself a glass of wine. "How'd you end up finding Wheeler?"

"I was running . . . trying to burn off some steam,

ended up by his place, and this need to talk to him about that night just . . . came over me. That's when I found him."

"And you called it in and are now an official suspect."

"That pretty much nails it." She fiddled with the edge of the cocktail napkin. "Why do you think this is all happening to me?"

"What do you mean?"

"Why? The clipping, my prints, all of it. Why?"

"Because shit happens to everybody. Look at me." Summer leaned toward her. "Tell you the truth, I've got no problem dying. If my big exit came tonight, I'd be okay with it."

"Don't say that, Summer."

"Why not? What's to hang around for? This is some screwed-up world."

"You don't mean it."

"The hell I don't." She finished her wine and poured more. "The system's jacked, Miranda. Justice is only for the rich, the powerful wield their might over the weak, and the world continues to turn. Nothing ever changes."

"That's not true. I'm a cop—"

"You were a cop."

That smarted, and Miranda flinched. "I'm suspended, not fired."

"Unjustly suspended. And why? Because Ian Stark wants somebody to hang for his kid's death?"

The bitterness in Summer's voice came from out of the blue, as did her angry worldview. "I'm not totally innocent here. I had a job to do, protocols to follow, and I didn't do either. So I was suspended."

"But look at your situation. You say Richard Stark was a scumbag, a sexual predator, but because of who his father is, nobody believes you. And that's not screwed up?"

It was, Miranda acknowledged, pushing her drink away, the pleasant fuzzy-headedness from earlier gone. "But it's the only system we have and it's a hell of a lot better than a lot of countries."

"I hate when people go there. We should be better than this. Everyone should."

"You're right," she said, "we should, and it's why I became a cop. Part of the reason anyway."

An awkward silence fell between them and Miranda wasn't certain how to break it—or if she even wanted to.

She scooted off the barstool. "I think I'm going to head out. It might be another big day tomorrow."

"Don't . . ." Summer caught her hand. "I'm sorry, I've ruined your night out." She grimaced. "Some bartender I am."

"You didn't." She squeezed, then released, Summer's hand. "You're a really good friend. And I'm really . . . thankful you're in my life."

Summer sent her a lopsided smile. "Back at you."

She paid her tab and crossed to the door. There, she glanced back to find Summer staring blankly past her, obviously someplace far, far away.

CHAPTER FORTY-EIGHT

11:00 P.M.

Jake was waiting in his truck for her when she got home. When Miranda pulled into her driveway, he climbed out and came to meet her.

Before she could speak, he cupped her face in his hands and kissed her. His hands were cold but his lips were warm and she melted into him, bringing her own hands from his chest to his neck.

He broke the kiss and rested his forehead against hers. "Hey."

She smiled. "Hey back."

"I missed you."

The simply stated words hit her like a wrecking ball. "I missed you, too."

"Can I come in?"

She replied by catching his hand and leading him into the house. They didn't bother with lights or flipping on the furnace—they had enough heat between them to burn the house down.

And start a fire they did, tugging at buttons and zippers, yanking away clinging fabric, cursing denim that resisted, impatient, greedy, and unashamed of it.

Naked, they toppled together to the bed. Miranda took the role of aggressor, then he did, anchoring her arms above her head, ravaging her mouth. And she allowed it until she didn't, flipping him onto his back, pinning him to the mattress.

This was angry need. Nothing tender or soft at the edges here. Sharp, white heat. Furious desire.

She felt it in him, too. Refusal to relinquish control. Anger. Or was that frustration?

With a primal sound he had her on her back and was atop her, thrusting into her. She cried out in both fury and pleasure, digging her fingers into his back, urging him to go deeper. Harder.

And then, with a joint cry of release, it was over. They lay panting, side by side but not touching. Seconds of silence became minutes.

He broke the silence first. "What was that?" he asked, voice raspy.

"You tell me."

They both knew. The investigation. Details shared. Trust broken.

"I had to tell him about us, Miranda. It was going to come out."

If she became a suspect, everything would be exposed. She could hear her nearest neighbor saying, "I saw Officer Billings leaving her place real early in the morning," and retired social-studies teacher Tula Guidry, who lived at the very end of the road, sharing that "Officer Billings used to come by and visit at night . . . didn't notice him leave until morning . . . figured it wasn't any of my business."

"And the button?" she asked, a pinch in her chest.

"It's evidence, Miranda. You know that."

She did. But it pissed her off anyway. It hurt. Because that was hers. Her truth. Her history.

"What about you, Jake? Who was that man just now?"

"Buddy suspended me. This afternoon."

"Oh." She processed the news a moment. "For how long?"

"One week, without pay. Pending further investigation."

"I'm sorry."

"I'm a big boy. I made my own decisions."

"But you're angry. You think I couldn't feel it?"

"I didn't try to hide it. Besides, ever consider maybe I'm angry at myself?"

She wanted to ask him why. But she didn't want to know the answer—she was afraid he would tell her he was angry at himself for wanting her.

Instead, she sat up, pushing her hair away from her face and tucking it behind her ears. "I'm hungry," she said. "How about you?"

He looked at her then, for the first time since they'd finished making love. "This doesn't resolve anything."

"Yeah it does." She grinned. "I won't be hungry anymore."

"True that."

He rolled out of bed. She watched as he crossed to his jeans, lying in a heap on the floor, watched the subtle play of his muscles as he bent to pick them up, as he slipped one leg in, then the other.

"Jake?" He glanced over his shoulder at her in question. "You're gorgeous."

Why hadn't she noticed before? Why hadn't she lingered over the place where his pecs met the ridge of his abs, or admired how his abs narrowed, leading her gaze lower. Tempting her to follow with her hands.

He flashed her a quick, surprised smile. "Thanks, Rader. Can't say I've ever thought of myself that way before."

"Maybe you should start? But don't let it go to your head."

He laughed, plucked up his T-shirt, and tossed it at her. And just like that, the mood between them changed, becoming light and easy.

They laughed and chatted, raiding the refrigerator and freezer. He downed a leftover slice of pizza; she attacked a pint of Rocky Road ice cream.

From there he rummaged in her pantry, coming out with a box of Captain Crunch cereal. "Seriously?" he asked, holding up the box in mock horror.

She snatched the box from him. "This happens to make a delicious topping."

"For what? An ice-cream sundae?"

"Yes, as a matter of fact. But it's even better on a peanut butter sandwich."

He grimaced. "That sounds . . . disgusting."

"You, sit." Miranda pointed to one of the chairs at the table, then marched across to the pantry for the peanut butter and bread. She slathered the nut butter on the bread, sprinkled on the cereal, then added the top slice of bread to both sandwiches. She poured them each a glass of milk—double checking the expiration date first—then brought it all to the table.

She took the chair across from him. "Take a bite of the sandwich, then a swallow of milk."

He didn't look convinced, but did it anyway. "Not bad," he said, munching, expression thoughtful. "You invent this?"

"Nope. My brother Robby did." As the words passed her lips, an image filled her head. She must have been five, maybe six, sitting around the table munching on the amazing delicacy her brother had whipped up.

"Mom had left Robby in charge," she said. "I think she had to go into work, and daddy hadn't come like he was supposed to. I remember being scared, and hungry. Real hungry." She smiled at the memory. "That sandwich made everything better. At least that afternoon."

Jake took his last bite, then chugged his milk.

"We made up," she said softly. "Robby and I did."

He reached across the table and she caught his hand. "I'm happy for you."

One corner of her mouth lifted. "Met his wife and little girl. Her name's Chrissy. She looks like me." Her throat closed and she cleared it. "I'm looking forward to getting to know them better. Hopefully it won't be through prison mail."

"Not funny."

She finished her sandwich and milk. "Not in the least."

He stood, collected their plates and glasses, rinsed them, and put them in the dishwasher.

"You get a lawyer?"

"I did. Daniel Stanley."

"Good choice."

"He said something to me, as I was leaving. That I needed to figure out why all this was happening to me."

He held out his hand. She took it and he helped her up. "I think that sounds like a good idea. But I have a better idea."

She frowned. "What's that?"

"Come here—" He tugged and she landed against his chest. "And I'll show you."

He lifted her and carried her back to the bed. They made love again, this time slowly, savoring each kiss, nip, and caress, each reveling in bringing the other pleasure.

How could everything change so quickly? Miranda wondered. How could it go from so wrong to so right or from so right to so wrong? Her and Jake, her feelings about her family, her job, reputation, and relationship with Buddy?

In the next moment, thoughts of anything but Jake and the waves of pleasure crashing over her fled her mind.

Afterward, they lay entwined, arms and legs, damp skin pressed to damp skin. This time in comfortable silence. Two people lost in their own thoughts, but connected by something deep and strong.

And totally unexpected.

"You awake?" he asked softly.

"Mmm hmm."

"He thinks you did it."

"What?" She tipped her head so she could see his face. "Who?"

"Buddy. He thinks you killed them both."

For a moment she wondered if she'd ever breathe again. When she did, it was with a terrible, choked sound. "He said that?"

"Not to me. To Ian Stark and his wife. I heard him."

She fought the urge to curl into a ball and sob. Buddy thought her a murderer. Her mentor and friend, a man she had believed in and trusted. She had thought he felt the same way about her.

"I'm sorry I told you."

"I'm glad you did." She drew in a deep, strengthening breath. "I need to know what I'm up against."

"I think Buddy suspended me yesterday because something's going down this week. Maybe even in the morning. And they don't want me involved or connected in any way."

"Afraid you're going to feed me information?"

"Probably. And they'd be right."

"You don't think—" She stopped, the words sticking

in her throat. But she had to ask, so she forced them out. "You don't think that do you? That I killed them?"

"I wouldn't be here if I did."

Miranda let out the breath she hadn't realized she was holding. Deep down she had known his answer, but she'd needed to hear it from his lips.

"Buddy's next move . . ." She thought a moment. "Search warrant, it's got to be."

"Or an arrest."

"Stanley didn't think they had enough."

"Yet."

"Exactly." She nodded. "Search warrant it is. Which means you have to go."

He started to argue; she cut him off. "I've gotten you in deep enough. And if Buddy is so obsessed to think I could do this, he might be crazy enough to try to tie you up in it."

"I'll leave in the morning," he promised. "Before it's light. But not now, not this way."

She could have argued, but the truth was, she didn't want to. She didn't know what tomorrow might bring, but she knew what she had tonight. And she wasn't ready to let go.

CHAPTER FORTY-NINE

At eight sharp, Miranda heard the slam of car doors. She was dressed and ready; she'd had breakfast and several cups of coffee, had called Stanley and shared what she learned from Jake.

Jake left at first light. After, she'd tried to grab another hour of shut-eye; instead, she'd tossed and turned, unable to fully let go and let her mind turn off. Her thoughts kept circling back to the same fact: Buddy Cadwell, her superior officer and friend, thought she was a killer. How did she wrap her head around *that*?

The several times she managed to drift off, she'd dreamt of running for her life from unknown assailants.

And now, they were here. Jones, she saw when she opened the door. Williams and Garcia as well. "Wow, I didn't know I was having a party this morning."

Jones looked uncomfortable. He held out the warrant. "Sorry about this, Rader."

"Just doing your job. I get it." She took the document from him and skimmed it. Her house and vehicle. A full search, every nook and cranny. Among other things, they were looking for a rhinestone button, a black Sharpie marker, and packing tape. The order had been signed by Judge Jay Clark.

Miranda handed it back. "It's your time to waste. Come on in." She stepped aside. "You don't mind if I tag along, do you?"

Obviously they did, but she was within her rights and they couldn't refuse her. She followed them from room to room, standing by while they picked through her drawers and rifled through her closets. The worst was her underwear drawer; she wasn't certain which was more embarrassing, watching them handle her unmentionables or wondering what they were thinking.

There were just some things your colleagues should never see.

Four hours later, they were gone. It was four of the longest hours of her life. They collected everything they'd come for, plus her running clothes and shoes from the day of Wheeler's murder, and a handful of other items she couldn't imagine could have any connection to the investigation.

And the rhinestone button.

She sank onto the couch, taking in her upended living room, feeling violated. How many times had she been part of a search team but never considered the subject's feelings?

But they'd all been guilty-as-hell perps.

Or so she had assumed.

Miranda dropped her head into her hands. *"Figure out why this is happening to you."*

She lifted her head. Of course. Stanley was right—it was her only option.

She stood, started to pace.

Why is this happening to you, Miranda? Figure it out. You're running out of time.

Start at the beginning. The first thing that had jumped out as not making sense.

The clipping. As far as she knew at the time, there was no reason for it to have been there.

But it had been.

Why?

She now knew that Richard Stark had been her abductor all those years ago, but at the time she'd thought it a bizarre coincidence.

Not a coincidence. A plant. Otherwise, it would have stopped there.

No prints. No box on her porch. No button.

She stopped pacing, took a deep breath, refocusing. *Don't get ahead of yourself, Miranda. Slow down, one step, one piece of the puzzle at a time.*

She moved on to the prints. They made no sense at all. She hadn't known Stark, had never been in his home before the night he was killed. And despite her claim to Buddy, she'd had her gloves on the whole time.

Yet, her fingerprints were found at the scene.

Also, obviously, planted.

Where were the prints found? On what? And how many times? She'd been so shocked and so busy covering her ass, she hadn't asked.

Stupid, Miranda. Careless.

She crossed to her front door, stepped out onto the porch. The lockbox and key. She looked at the spot where the bag containing the box had been. If not Catherine Stark, then who? And why?

Someone had left it for her to open. Not Jake or Buddy. Her. They had wanted her to find the contents and know what those items meant.

The button. Like the clipping, no reason it should have been there. Why, if a trophy, only one? That didn't fit with a serial offender's MO. The serial part meant they closely repeated a crime over and over. If taking a trophy was part of that ritual, the perp would take one from every victim.

Unless she was the only one who got away.

She shook her head. *You're not special, Miranda. That's not it. Keep searching.*

The clipping. The button.

Unique. Out of place.

Both planted. Like the prints, to tie her to the victim. And to make the investigation personal.

To her.

Of course. The killer wanted her to care. They wanted her to wonder—was Stark the one from fourteen years ago?

Now, she believed he was and had become obsessed with proving it.

She had played right into their hands.

The killer's hands.

Why is this happening to you, Miranda?

The realization hit her like a thunderbolt. She stopped pacing, audibly caught her breath.

Because it's about you. And the past. And the other girl.

The other girl.

All these years she had wondered what happened to her. Whether she was alive or dead.

She was alive.

And she was here, in Harmony. She killed Stark and Wheeler. She planted the clipping and took the lockbox. She was the one who'd found the rhinestone button— and kept it all these years. She put the button in the lockbox, creating another physical tie between Miranda and Stark.

The fingerprints, also planted. But how? If they'd been lifted from an object, the possibilities were many. A gum wrapper or water bottle. A paper coffee cup or a dozen other things one handled and tossed during the course of a day or week.

Why is this happening to you, Miranda?

She was being set up. Of course she was.

Someone she didn't know, following her, scooping up a discarded item or going through her trash. No. She shook her head. Someone in her sphere, a colleague, an acquaintance, or neighbor.

A friend.

No, not a friend. She crossed to the sliders that led to her back porch, stepped outside, and went to stand at the rail. The cold air stung her cheeks; she breathed it in, willing it to clear her thoughts. Clear away what she was thinking.

She curled her hands into fists. Did she know any Cathys? She searched her memory. None that fit—either too old, too young, or she'd known them all her life.

The university employed hundreds and hundreds of people, most of whom she'd never met. Her Cathy could be hiding in plain sight. She could even be an older student. Or she could have changed her name.

Start at the beginning. Again.

Why is this happening to you, Miranda?

Because both Stark and Wheeler's murders had nothing to do with the present and everything to do with that summer night fourteen years ago.

Summer.

Knight.

No. She shook her head again. God no, not her friend. Not Summer.

How much could she have changed, that she wouldn't recognize her? To not recognize Stark was one thing— he'd been driving that night, she sat in the back seat; he was wearing a ball cap, pulled down low on his face.

Miranda shut her eyes. Cathy in the front seat, next

to him. Turning back to her, talking and laughing, passing the joint to her. Cathy, whose image had haunted her for years.

Fourteen years. No way could she have changed so much she wouldn't recognize her. No way.

Miranda felt sick. Her hands shook. So what did she do now? Where did she look next?

Her phone went off.

Jake.

"I heard they were there this morning."

"Who from?"

"Jones. He thought I'd want to know." He paused. "He felt real bad about it."

"I could tell."

"How're you holding up?"

"As well as can be expected. Doing a lot of thinking."

"About what?"

"Why this is happening to me."

"And?"

"I've got a couple theories."

"Pass 'em by, maybe I can help."

"They're not that far along." She drew her eyebrows together in thought. "Do you recall my prints at the Stark scene—how many and what were they lifted from?"

He was silent a moment. "I don't. I could ask Jones to look it up?"

"Do you think he might do you another favor? I'm wondering if they got any prints off the clipping and who they belong to."

"Yeah, maybe. What's up?"

"I'll let you know when you find out."

"You're thinking the clipping was planted?"

"Yeah. Call me back. There's someplace I have to go."

She hung up before he could ask where. She couldn't voice what she was thinking, not yet. Not even to Jake.

CHAPTER FIFTY

1:00 P.M.

Miranda had a friend in the St. Tammany Parish Sheriff's Office. They'd met during a multi-jurisdiction case several years back, hit it off, and dated for a while. They'd mutually decided they were better friends than lovers and jointly ended the relationship.

The Sheriff's Office had state-of-the-art forensic imaging software, including photo-regression capabilities. If she had the time to wait for results, she could accomplish the same thing via the Internet. Or, if she still had a badge, at the HPD.

But she had neither, so she decided calling Shawn was her best, safest bet. She called him from her car and he met her in the STPSO lobby.

Tall, with sandy hair, hawkish features, and a devilish smile, he'd reminded her of a cross between Dennis the Menace and the Terminator. Go figure.

She smiled and held out her hand. "Shawn, thanks for making time to do this for me."

They shook hands. "Of course. How are you, Miranda?"

"Good. You?"

"Can't complain." He motioned toward the flight of stairs. "Which case are you working?"

"Cold case. Missing person." At least that wasn't a lie, she thought. She took the truth one step farther. "Actually, it's not official. I'm helping out a friend."

"Gotcha. Here we are."

She saw the plaque on the door and cocked an eyebrow. "Captain now? Congratulations."

"Thanks. Just happened. I've got to say, I'm pretty pleased with myself. Pull a chair around."

She did, then handed him a photo of Summer; he scanned it into his computer.

"How old is she here?"

"Thirty-two."

"And you want to go back fourteen years?"

"That's right."

He nodded. "That's pretty easy. Changes aren't going to be that big."

She watched as he manipulated the image via toolbar and keystrokes. A minute and a half later he stopped and turned the monitor her way. "There you go. Like I said, fourteen years isn't that much."

A younger Summer. Fuller cheeks, higher brow, no softening under the eyes, wrinkles nonexistent.

But not Cathy. Relief was like a huge weight lifted from her shoulders. She felt practically giddy.

"Is this what you needed?"

"Yes, thank you." She stood and tucked the photo back into her jacket pocket. "That's perfect."

"You want me to print it out?"

She opened her mouth to say, "Don't bother," but nodded instead and waited while he printed it. A moment later, the printout was also tucked into her pocket.

"Good seeing you, Miranda."

She smiled. "You, too, Shawn."

"Hey, Miranda?" She stopped in the doorway and looked back. "It probably doesn't affect what you're doing, considering the age of the subject, but one of the limitations of these programs is they can't take into account unknown factors."

"Such as?"

"Illnesses, drug or alcohol abuse, accidents. Just wanted you to be aware."

She smiled again. "Thanks, I appreciate that."

Miranda was in her car, engine running, before it hit her—Summer had been in a bad car wreck right before she moved to Harmony.

Summer was deep into a conversation with a customer when Miranda walked in. She looked up and smiled in greeting and the knot in Miranda's stomach tripled in size.

Miranda smiled back and headed to the bar. "Hey, Tara," she said to the young woman. "You have a soup today?"

She smiled. "Good, old-fashioned chicken noodle."

"Sounds perfect," she said, unzipping her jacket. "I'll take a bowl."

"Bring me one, too," Summer said from behind her. "We'll be in one of the booths."

They took the booth in the far corner. Miranda slipped off her jacket, tossed it on the seat, and slid in. "I'm sorry about last night," Summer said when they were seated. "I didn't mean to go all postal on you."

"You didn't. It was a long day, that's all."

"You're sure? I—" Summer bit back whatever she was going to say, and started again. "I don't know what I would do without our friendship."

The knot grew again. Miranda cleared her throat. "You don't need to worry about that, Summer."

Summer searched her gaze. "You're not going any-where, right?"

"Maybe to jail, but we can still be friends."

Summer laughed. "That's not funny."

She met her eyes. "I'm not trying to be."

Her smile faded. "What are you saying?"

"Apparently, Buddy's not just crossing t's and dotting i's. He really thinks I killed Richard Stark and Clint Wheeler."

"That's crazy!"

"A judge signed a search warrant. They came this morning."

"I'm so . . . sorry."

"What do you have to be sorry for?" Her words came out with an edge she hadn't intended, but she couldn't take it back. "It's not your doing, right?"

"Right. But you're my friend, so it matters to me." She leaned forward. "What are you going to do?"

"I got a lawyer, a good one. And I'm going to fight it."

"He . . . Buddy, is he going to arrest you?"

"That's his goal, I'm sure. That's what the search this morning was all about. I'm not scared. I've lived through worse."

"That night," Summer said softly.

"Yes. That night. And everything that came after." She dropped her hands to her lap and squeezed them into tight fists. "What about you?"

Summer shifted in her seat. "What about me?"

"What's the worst you've lived through? Your car wreck, I guess?"

Summer hesitated, cleared her throat, and nodded. "Yes."

"Tell me about it."

"My wreck?"

Tara came over with their setups and waters. "Anything else to drink?"

They both responded "No," then when Tara was out of earshot, Miranda continued. "You were about to tell me about your accident. What happened?"

"It was pretty straightforward." Summer fiddled with her soupspoon. "I lost control of my vehicle and crashed into a wall."

"That sounds horrible." Miranda lifted her water glass, glad to see her hand was as steady as a rock. "How fast were you going?"

"Very . . . eighty."

"My God." She took a sip, set the glass down. "What about your injuries?"

"What about them?"

"You said you were in the hospital a long time."

"I was pretty smashed up."

"Your face, too?"

She'd pushed too far, Miranda saw. Summer's expression changed, seemed to close.

"That's a weird question, Miranda."

"Is it?" She feigned surprise, then regret. "I'm sorry. You don't have scars, so I wondered."

"I have scars," she murmured. "Believe me, I have plenty of scars."

Invisible scars. Miranda reached across the table and caught her hand. "I understand. I have them, too."

Summer's eyes turned bright with tears; she looked away, blinking furiously.

"It's okay to cry."

But she didn't and in that moment, Tara arrived with the two steaming bowls of soup and a basket of crackers. As if picking up on the emotional tenor between them, she delivered the food and without a word, returned to the bar.

Miranda and Summer both dug into the soup. The broth was rich and tasty, and Miranda was half-finished with the bowl when Summer suddenly picked up where they had left off.

"I should be dead, but here I am."

The spoonful of soup seemed to lodge in her throat. Miranda washed it down with a sip of water and pushed the bowl away, appetite gone.

"I lived," Summer went on, lifting her gaze to Miranda's. "And now, I'm going to die."

Miranda struggled to come to grips with her suspicions and her affection for the Summer she knew. This was her friend. And she was in pain.

"We're all going to die," she said softly, voice thick.

"But some of us sooner than others." Summer paused. "But like I told you, I'm ready to go. I should have been dead, but was given a reprieve. How many folks get that? How many get a chance to close the book on the story of their life?"

Miranda's eyes stung and she blinked against the tears. "Not many."

"Exactly." Summer leaned forward. "There was something I wanted to talk to you about."

"What?"

"The bar. When I die—"

"Don't."

"When I die," she went on, voice shaking, "I want you to have it. And my condo, too. Everything really."

Miranda stared at her, at a total loss for words. She'd walked in here, suspecting Summer of being a killer and a false friend, plotting revenge. And instead, the only thing she was planning was her own death.

"I don't have anyone else, Miranda." Summer's eyes brimmed with tears, but she held them back. "It's hard to talk about, but it could happen anytime. I want to be . . . prepared. In every way."

Miranda reached her hands across the table. Summer grasped them, squeezing tightly. "Thank you for being my friend."

Her thanks was like a knife, twisting in her gut. "Don't, please—"

"Why not?" The bell over the door jangled and a few guys she recognized from the HPD strolled through, probably looking for a quick lunch.

Summer glanced at them, then back at Miranda. "I've got to go help Tara. By the way, it's done."

"What do you mean?" She drew her eyebrows together. "What's done?"

"I had an attorney draw up my will. You're my beneficiary, Miranda."

CHAPTER FIFTY-ONE

Miranda sat in her car, engine idling. Her hands shook and her thoughts raced. How could she have been so wrong? How could she have so unfairly judged her friend? She hadn't even been able to look her in the eyes when she left.

Summer wasn't the other girl. She wasn't a vengeful killer. Then who was setting her up?

"Miranda! Wait!"

She looked in the direction from which the voice had come. Tara hurrying across the parking lot with Miranda's jacket. She lowered the window and smiled. "Thank you, Tara! I sure would have missed this when the sun went down."

Tara laughed and handed it to her. "Glad I caught you. Have a great day!"

"You, too." She tossed it on the seat beside her and her cell phone tumbled to the floor. She scooped it up and checked the display. Jake had called twice.

She shifted into drive and dialed him back. "Hey," she said when he answered. "Sorry I missed your call."

"I have the information you asked for."

She rolled out of the parking lot. "Shoot."

"Your prints were found on a water bottle. Smart Water, by the way."

She didn't drink bottled water that much, but when she did, that was the brand. It was probably just brand hype, but drinking it made her feel like she was doing something good for herself. "Nowhere else?"

"Nope."

"What about the clipping?"

"Your prints weren't on it."

"So, they did check." She stopped at the four-way, then rolled through.

"Yup. And get this, neither were Stark's."

"Bingo."

"My thoughts exactly."

"Someone must have handled the clipping."

"They got a partial off it, ran it through the system but didn't get a hit."

"Whoever planted the water bottle, planted the clipping and the prints—"

"—to tie you to the scene."

"Exactly."

"What about you? You said you were following up a theory this morning. Any luck?"

"Dead end," she said. "I thought I knew who the killer was, but I was wrong." She recalled her suspicions and added under her breath, "And ashamed of myself, too."

"What's that?"

"Nothing."

"Look, I . . . got a call from my dad. My mom's not doing well and I need to hop over to Tuscaloosa to see her."

"I'm sorry. She's ill?"

"No." He paused. "I had a sister who died and tomorrow's her birthday. Mom always takes it hard, but this year she's particularly upset. Dad thought seeing me would help."

"You never told me you had a sister."

"It was a long time ago. She died . . . young."

She wasn't accustomed to evasions from him and she frowned. "Oh, wow, I'm sorry. How'd she . . . what happened?"

For a long moment he was silent. When he spoke, he sounded like someone she didn't know. "She killed herself."

Miranda couldn't have been more surprised if he'd announced himself an alien from a planet she'd never heard of. They'd been colleagues, then friends, and now lovers, and he'd never shared this?

She thought of his hurt the day she told him about her past—about that night fourteen years ago and going to juvie. She understood it now—because this time it was she who was hurt.

And more clearly than ever, she understood that people kept secrets, even from the people they were most intimate with.

"You there, Miranda?"

"Yeah, just . . . surprised, that's all."

"I don't talk about it much."

"I get that." She paused. "I guess I shouldn't have pried."

"You didn't. I should have told you before this. When this is all over, you'll know everything."

What an odd choice of words, she thought, hearing the sound of his truck starting. "You're heading to Alabama now?"

"Are you going to be okay if I go?"

She fought the sudden urge to beg him to stay, or ask if she could go along with him. "Of course I will. How much more trouble could I get into?"

He didn't laugh. "Be careful, okay?"

"I'll avoid Buddy at all costs."

"He's not who I'm afraid of. He'll just throw you in jail."

"Then who are you afraid of?"

"I don't know, maybe the person who's killed two people and implicated you in their murders."

The other girl.

"I don't think you have to worry. She needs me to take the fall for her." She said it lightly, but for the first time she wondered if her life could be in danger. "Drive safe. Call me later."

She ended the call fighting the nagging feeling that Jake was hiding more from her than the fact he'd had a sister.

CHAPTER FIFTY-TWO

4:35 P.M.

Miranda had never been good at inaction. So sitting around waiting for the other shoe to drop—or a hatchet to fall—was not working for her. Lawyer's advice be damned; she and Buddy were going to have a chat.

She parked in front of the station and climbed out. It felt strange walking in without a badge and knowing that everyone was staring at her, even if they were pretending otherwise.

She stopped at the information desk. "Hey, Gloria, how are you today?"

The woman's eyes widened. "Miranda, hey. I'm . . . okay." She glanced around her, then leaned closer. "How about you?"

"I'm okay."

"I'm glad, I . . ." She lowered her voice. "What's going around, I know it's not right."

Miranda smiled. "Thanks, Glo. And no, it's not right."

Jones appeared at the squad room door, saw her, and turned around and went back inside.

Gloria cleared her throat and straightened back up. "What can I do for you, Miranda?"

Her hands, Miranda noted, were shaking. The last

thing she wanted to do was get someone else suspended. "Is Buddy around?"

"He is. Let me see if he's available."

Two minutes later, Buddy waved her into his office. "C'mon in, girl. Close the door behind you."

She did and took a seat. "You seem in good spirits."

"Just surprised to see you."

"I thought you might be." She crossed her legs. "How're you doing, Buddy?"

"I've been better." He cocked his head. "I've lost my two most experienced detectives."

"And whose fault is that?"

He narrowed his eyes. "What are you doing here, Miranda?"

"I thought we could have nice little off-the-record chat."

"Your lawyer give you his blessing on that?"

"What do you think?"

"All right then." He folded his hands on the desk in front of him. "Let's chat."

"I hear you like me for these murders. What do you have?"

He laughed. "You're not serious."

"Dead serious. How about I tell you what you don't have? DNA, because there's none to be had."

"As you know very well, DNA's not back yet. Forgive me for doubting you, but I'll wait for the test results before I agree with you."

"You have the prints."

"Yes."

"One set on a water bottle."

"The kind of water everyone's seen you drink."

"A piece of evidence so easy to plant it's laughable."

"I'm not laughing." He leaned forward. "And I wouldn't if I were you."

"Is that so?"

"Why'd you lie, Miranda?"

"I'm not aware I did."

"You took off your gloves? To make that call to Jake?"

"I did."

"You have an Apple iPhone, correct?"

"I do."

"We tested it, Miranda. The keypad worked with the gloves."

"It didn't that day."

"Bullshit. And a jury won't buy it."

"You know what else a jury won't buy?" she asked. "Why my fingerprints weren't found anywhere else besides that so very portable piece of evidence. The bottle was planted."

"Says you."

"You're not the least bit worried about that possibility?"

"Not at all."

"I'd call you a liar, but considering our long relationship that'd be rude. But wait, you're sitting there calling me a murderer." She leaned forward slightly, eyes narrowed. "You're a liar, Buddy Cadwell. I never thought I'd say that. Not ever."

Something ugly moved across his expression. She'd struck a nerve, no doubt about it.

"Careful," he said softly. "Considering how we found Wheeler, you're building our case."

"Then there's the clipping," she went on. "It's a bit of a conundrum for you, considering it's a link between Stark and the crime I say he committed."

Cadwell shrugged. "I think that works in our favor."

"Interesting thing is," she went on, tone nonchalant, "my prints aren't on it. And neither were his." He didn't reply and she pressed on. "Which suggests, like the bottle, the clipping was planted."

He snorted. "To what end?"

"The killer, our unsub, wanted us, particularly me, to know who Stark was. And why she'd killed him."

"Again, to what end?"

"Justice. Pure and simple."

"And that's what you're looking for, isn't it?" He leaned back in his seat, the picture of confidence. "You wrongly fingered Richard Stark as the one who abducted you all those years ago—"

"Now you admit I was abducted? Wow, I am making progress here."

He ignored her and went on. "And now, their murders are your idea of justice."

"I'm not the one looking for justice—" She leaned forward, studying him. "She is. Does that frighten you at all?"

A dull red crawled up his cheeks. "Of course not."

"Maybe it should."

"Are you threatening me?"

She tilted her head. "Where were you that night?"

"What night?"

"C'mon, Buddy, what night are we talking about here? Fourteen years ago. Ms. Roxy called you. It was an hour before you arrived. Where were you?"

"I was home, sleeping."

She recognized he was lying and her heartbeat quickened. "You were winded when you got here. And sweating."

"It was summer."

"You told Roxy you needed a minute," she went on. "To pull yourself together."

"Of course I did. It was the middle of the night. I was

awakened from a dead sleep with a tenuous situation on my hands."

The more he talked, the deeper hole he dug. "Tenuous?"

"I needed to focus myself."

"Why? Because a fifteen-year-old had been picked up for pot?"

"Because she was spreading a very serious story that could have hurt a lot of people."

That was it. Her story. The people it could have hurt.

She had thought him her savior that night. Besides Ms. Roxy, the one person who had believed her and tried his best to help.

He believed her because he'd known it was true.

"You covered it up, Buddy."

"I don't know what you're . . . for God's sake, Miranda! You were making some pretty big accusations that night."

"No, I wasn't. Who was I making accusations against?"

"Claims," he corrected. "Abduction and rape? Come on, that's serious stuff."

"Yeah, it was." For a moment she wondered if she'd ever breathe again. And then she did. "That's why you needed to compose yourself, isn't it? Because you'd just covered up a crime and were going to have to look a fifteen-year-old victim in the eyes and lie? And pretend that you were such a good guy?"

"You've gone off the rails, Randi. Just like all those years ago."

A diversion instead of a denial. She felt sick to her stomach. "You were so kind to me that night. I remember being surprised by that kindness. Really . . . touched by it. But I get it now." She made a choked sound. "Why you've been kind to me all these years. Why you took me under your wing. Guilt."

"I think you should go, Miranda. For your own good."

She didn't make a move to stand. "Fourteen years ago you did exactly what you're doing now."

"I don't know what you're talking about."

"You covered up what happened. Because of whose son he was." She shook her head, disappointed to her core. "You're his puppet. That's what happened with the roofies, isn't it? Who'd you call? Wheeler?"

He didn't respond and she went on. "That night, that's why you kept stalling. You had to hear every detail of my story, you said. Truth is, you had to give Wheeler or whoever enough time to get rid of all the evidence of the crime."

At his silence, she stood, flattened her hands on his desk and leaned toward him. "Say something, dammit!"

"You'll never prove any of this."

She flinched, the words affecting her like a physical assault. "All the women Stark assaulted, all these years. You could have stopped him. And *that's* what it comes down to? I'll never be able to prove it?" She made a sound of disbelief. And of disgust. "I always thought Wheeler was a bad guy. A crooked cop. And now I see you're even worse."

"This chat is over, Miranda," he said, voice shaking. He stood and crossed to the door.

"Go ahead," she dared. "Open it. I think everybody should hear this."

As she had known he would, he stopped and turned back to her.

"Did you know about the lockbox? About Stark's escape papers? Maybe you even helped him pull all the documents together."

She pictured the contents, remembering the self-storage contract. "What was in the self-storage unit, Buddy?"

"I don't know what you're talking about."

Keys, she remembered. Of course. "It was a car, wasn't it? Registered to Michael Weisman."

"You're losing it."

"Tell me what happened, Buddy. Just between you and me. When I got away, young Mr. Stark freaked out, didn't he? He called his daddy and his daddy called you. Is that the way it went down?"

When he didn't respond, she went on, "What did he promise you? His undying loyalty and sponsorship for as long as you both shall live?"

"Do you have a recorder, Miranda? Is that what's going on here? You trying to trap me? That's never going to happen. *Never.*"

"It already has." He blanched and she smiled grimly. "You were trapped fourteen years ago, the minute you agreed to lie for him."

She stood and walked around him to the door. "You're not the man I thought you were. You're not even close."

CHAPTER FIFTY-THREE

5:20 P.M.

Miranda managed to make it to her car. She managed to unlock it and slip inside, start it up, and even buckle her safety belt. She shifted into gear and backed out of the parking space, her only thought leaving the HPD behind. She turned onto the first side street she came to, pulled to the side, and cut the engine.

And broke down sobbing. For herself. Betrayed by someone she trusted. All his kindness, the fatherly advice, the camaraderie she felt they shared all these years—it was all a lie, a sham. His kindness, all of it, had been an act of guilt.

She sobbed for all the women Stark had assaulted. Over the years, how many had there been? Their lives altered forever, some shattered beyond repair?

The overwhelming weight of it was crushing.

She brought her hands to her eyes, her shoulders shaking with the force of her sobs. Back then, had it seemed like nothing to Buddy? A little favor: help a rich, powerful man get his son out of hot water? After all, boys will be boys. She could hear Ian Stark, in that slightly nasal voice of is, saying, "He has his whole life ahead of him" and "Don't let this little mistake ruin his life."

Little mistake.

Fury replaced despair and she pounded her fists on the steering wheel. Bastards. Stark never should have gotten away with it. All the lives he ruined . . . her own life. The other girl's.

Cathy. Her name was Cathy.

Miranda stilled, picturing the young woman in the front seat of the car, looking back at her. Laughing, full of excitement for the night—and what the future held.

Miranda frowned. She hardly ever thought of her as Cathy, always as "the other girl." Why was that?

With the heels of her hands, Miranda wiped the tears from her cheeks. Because there had been two of them that night? Her and the other girl?

It seemed somehow disrespectful.

Is that the way Cathy had thought of her all these years—as the other girl? Or maybe she thought of her as "the girl who got away" or "the girl who left me behind."

Like they were numbers. Girl one, girl two. This girl and that girl.

If they thought of each other that way, how did men like Ian Stark and Buddy Cadwell think of them? As objects? Just another piece of ass?

And whose fault was that?

The other girl had a name.

Cathy.

Miranda expelled a shuddering breath. She would never refer to Cathy by anything but her given name. Never again.

The car had grown cold, the evening dark. She shivered and started the engine, cranking on the heat. But still she felt chilled to the bone. Would she ever be warm again?

Jake could warm her. His arms. His belief in her. Just hearing his voice would chase the cold away.

She retrieved her phone, dialed his number—and got his voice mail. "Jake, hey, it's me. I just wanted . . . I needed to . . . hear your voice. I just left Buddy. . . . I'll tell you everything when we talk. He covered everything up. Fourteen years ago and now. I feel so betrayed. I guess I better . . . Jake, I—"

The message clicked off; she finished her thought anyway.

"—love you."

For a moment she sat frozen in shock at her own words. She loved him? Where had that come from? The sentiment had sprung unbidden from her mouth, no forethought or planning. No . . . conscious recognition. Was it even true?

Yes. She loved him. It wasn't the situation or the drama of the day; she was in love with him. When had it happened? How?

Truth was, she didn't care when or how. The feeling was amazing, like a place inside her had just broken wide open and what was spilling out was bright and fresh, like a new day.

She had to tell him. Before she lost her nerve or rationalized herself out of it.

She hit redial. His voice mail kicked on. At his voice in her ear, his image filled her head. With it, sensory details—the way he smelled, crisp and clean, the feel of his skin beneath her palms, the way he always brushed his mouth lightly against hers before taking his kiss deeper.

"It's me again," she said, sounding breathless to her own ears, "I had to finish what I was about to say. . . . I love you, Jake. I'm in love with you. I just wanted . . . I needed you to know. Get home safe so I can show—"

Another call beeped through. Certain it was him, she clicked over. "Jake! I'm so glad you got my message—"

"It's Summer."

"Summer?" Miranda repeated, struggling to shift gears. "What's . . . are you okay?"

"I'm fine. Dizzy and nauseous, but what else is new? Where are you? Can you come over?"

She didn't sound right. Miranda frowned. "What's going on?"

"A woman confided in me about Stark assaulting her." She lowered her voice. "I got her to agree to talk to you."

Miranda could hardly believe her luck. "You think she might be willing to step forward?"

"I think so. She's really skittish, but I think I've convinced her she can trust you."

This could be the break she'd been waiting for. Miranda worked to tamp down her excitement, reminding herself it could be another disappointment. "You're at the bar?"

"No, home."

Miranda shifted into drive and pulled away from the curb. "Don't let her leave, Summer."

"I won't, I promise. But hurry, okay?"

Miranda made an illegal U-turn in the intersection, heading back toward Summer's place. "I'm on my way."

She made Summer's condo in five minutes, and her friend met her at the door. She looked anxious.

"Where is she?" Miranda asked.

"The back bedroom, lying down. She's pretty emotional."

Miranda started down the hall, Summer right behind her. "But she knows I'm coming and is ready to talk to me?"

"Absolutely."

The door to the bedroom stood open, the soft glow of a lamp spilling into the hall. "What's her name?" Miranda asked softly, glancing back just in time to see the butt of a gun coming for her head.

Pain mingled with Summer's voice as stars exploded in her head.

"Cathy," Summer said. "Her name's Cathy."

CHAPTER FIFTY-FOUR

7:10 P.M.

Miranda came to with a splitting headache. Disoriented, she looked around her. She was on the floor, propped against the wall of a small, plain bedroom. Bed turned down. Water and a plate of cookies on the night table. Lamp burning, nice and cozy.

Where was she? She brought a hand to her head; it came back sticky with blood. Miranda gazed at the red staining her fingers.

And remembered. Summer calling . . . a woman ready to step forward . . . turning to ask the woman's name—

Cathy.

Summer was Cathy from all those years ago. But having been right brought her no satisfaction.

She had to get out of here.

Miranda reached for her phone, only to find it wasn't in her pocket. Of course it wasn't; Summer had thought of that. Miranda got cautiously to her feet, head throbbing with every move. She crossed to the closed door, grabbed the knob, and twisted.

Locked. She was locked in.

She jiggled the knob, just to make sure, then heard

footsteps from the hallway beyond. "Help!" she called. "I'm hurt and can't get out!"

Silence. The sound of soft breathing.

Summer.

"I know it's you, Summer. Open the door. Let's talk about this."

"There's nothing to talk about." She sounded despondent. "How's your head?"

"It hurts. I think I need stitches."

"I'm sorry."

"Don't be sorry, just let me out." She jiggled the knob again. "Please Summer."

"I can't do that, Miranda. I'm really sorry, I didn't want to hit you."

"Then why did you?"

"You left me no choice. I saw the printout."

"The printout? What—"

The age regression of Summer. How had she . . . She'd forgotten her jacket in the booth at the bar. . . . It must have fallen out of her pocket.

Stupid, Miranda. Careless.

Miranda breathed deeply, willing her racing heart to slow, trying to clear her mind.

Think, Miranda. She has a plan. What is it? Figure a way out.

"I know you're angry at me. And I'm so sorry." She leaned her forehead on the door. "I tried to get help, I did. No one believed me."

"I know," Summer said softly. "I'm not angry with you. I was for a long time, but then I learned the truth . . ."

Her voice sounded muffled, as if she also had her face pressed close to the door.

"Now I know you're a victim, just like me."

A victim. She used to be. But not anymore. "Then why are you doing this? I thought we were friends."

"We are."

"Then why'd you hit me?"

"So you couldn't stop me."

Miranda's mouth went dry. "Stop you from what?"

"Don't you want to hear what happened that night, after you got away? Haven't you wondered all these years?"

She had. So often. But now, a part of her didn't want to know. "I was so afraid you were . . . that he'd killed you. I always hoped you were alive, Cathy."

A soft sob came from the other side of the door. "But he did kill me. They killed me. You understand, don't you, Randi?"

"Yes," she whispered, the word coming out a croak.

"Because he did the same to you."

She pressed her palm against the door. "That night . . . after I ran, what did he do?"

"Lost it . . . just went totally off the rails. I screamed and screamed, I couldn't stop . . . so he hit me until I did."

The screams she'd heard that night, the ones that echoed in her head for years. Goose bumps raced up her arms.

"When I woke up, I didn't know where we were but I learned it was his family's summer place. On Lake Pontchartrain. I was pretty messed up. . . . He was pacing . . . scared about what was going to happen to him."

Summer's voice dipped even lower; Miranda pressed closer to the door. "His dad showed up, slapped his face. I thought he was there to save me . . ."

She choked on the words; Miranda finished the thought for her. "But he was there to save his son."

"Yes," she whispered. "I was a problem to be taken care of."

"His dad, he wasn't alone, was he?"

"No. He had two cops with him."

"Chief Buddy Cadwell," Miranda said, heart hurting. "And Officer Clint Wheeler."

"Yes." She paused, as if collecting her thoughts. "His dad offered me money to keep quiet. He said no one would believe me, I was just a tramp. Trash, same as you were. Nobody was going to believe us making accusations against a fine young man like his son."

"How much money?" Miranda asked, voice tight. "What was your silence worth to them?"

"Five thousand dollars. It seemed like a fortune back then."

"So you took it."

"I convinced myself the money would make up for what he did to me. I convinced myself I'd forget, move on."

"But you couldn't?"

"Did you?"

No, Miranda acknowledged silently. That night, its aftermath, had colored every moment, every decision of the past fourteen years.

Anger swelled up in her. It tasted bitter against her tongue. She hated feeling this way—discounted and overlooked, betrayed in the most elemental way.

Let it go, Miranda. Help Cathy let it go, too.

"It's done," Miranda said. "It's over. We have to move on."

"I tried. I can't." Her voice cracked. "I'm finishing this."

She meant to kill Buddy. And Ian Stark. "Listen to me, Summer . . . Cathy," she corrected, "we can beat them. You and me, together."

"No, nothing's changed. They have the money and the power and we don't."

"We're not naive girls anymore. We're strong, smart women. People will listen."

Summer was crying. Miranda's heart wrenched at the broken sound. "We need to let it go, Summer. Both of us."

"That accident you asked me about, the one that took my face? That was no accident, Miranda. I wanted to die. Every day, I'd drive past that wall and imagine driving into it . . . pressing down the accelerator and pointing my car at it."

She paused and cleared her throat, then went on. "But I didn't die. Instead I woke up in the hospital a mangled mess. That's when I realized that *I* wasn't the one who was supposed to be dead. They were."

Miranda brought a hand to her mouth to hold back a cry. It hurt. To know the pain this woman she'd grown to care about had suffered, how she still suffered.

"What justice would there be in me dying?" she continued. "I was the victim, they were the monsters."

"Let me help you, Summer."

Summer went on as if she hadn't heard her. "That's how I fought my way back, through brutal surgeries and physical therapies. Every minute was torture, but I made it through by focusing on my goal. Justice, Miranda. For me and you and every girl they hurt."

"You were a victim. But you don't have to be anymore. Don't let them make you a murderer."

"That's already done. I have two left, that's all."

She had to stop her. But how?

"I've got to go now, Miranda. You'll be okay. I'll make sure they know where you are."

"Wait!" Miranda cried, grasping for a way to stall her. "I have to know—were you trying to set me up? Is that why you planted the news clipping and the water bottle?"

"No!" Her voice shook. "My plan was never to have you take the fall for this. I wanted you personally involved, because I wanted you to be on my side. I needed your help bringing the truth to light. I knew you wouldn't back down until that happened. Even if I was caught or died before I made them all pay . . . you would keep on until everyone knew the whole truth."

She paused a moment. When she went on, her voice vibrated with emotion. "And you didn't know about Stark, that it was him. . . . You deserved to know."

"You're the one who put his strongbox on my porch."

"Yes. I saw it in his closet."

"How did you know what was in it? It must have been locked."

"It was. I didn't know but I suspected . . . no, I hoped, so I took it. And when the time was right, I got it to you."

She fell silent a moment before continuing. "What was in it, Miranda? I was right, wasn't I?"

"Yes, you were right. Everything he needed to escape and start a new life."

"And Cadwell did nothing? That son of a bitch."

Summer never opened the box. That meant Miranda had been wrong about one thing. "You didn't plant the button."

"What button?"

"The one from the shirt I was wearing that night." Her voice shook. "It was in the strongbox. He saved it all those years."

Why'd he keep it? Miranda felt sick to her stomach. Did he look at it, touch it? In those moments, did he wonder what his life would have been like if she hadn't escaped? Did he regret going for food and leaving them alone? Did he long to finish what he'd begun?

Summer broke into her thoughts. "At the bar today,

I heard that Ian Stark's planning a memorial garden for his fallen son, with a statue and everything. And what do we get?" Her voice hardened. "You know what, that's just not going to happen. I'm going to make sure it doesn't."

"Wheeler," Miranda said quickly. "How did you manage to surprise him that way?"

"That was no surprise. Old Clint used to come around the bar. I befriended him. In fact, I took to bringing him by a cold six-pack now and then."

Delivery day, Miranda remembered. When she talked to Summer the day Wheeler died, that's what she had called it.

"You brought him the beer, then shot him in the back of the head."

"Yup. I'm not going to be as subtle with *President* Stark and *Chief* Cadwell. They need to know how much we suffered."

"Don't do this, Summer! We'll go together . . . to the Sheriff's Office, we'll tell them everything and this time they'll believe us!"

"We already talked about this. No. I have other plans."

"It's different now. We're different. Please . . . Cathy, listen to me! They'll lose everything!"

"The way we lost everything?" Her voice turned cold and hard. "I listened then, I'm not going to now. Good-bye, Miranda."

"No! Wait . . . Summer!" She pounded on the door. "If we step forward other women will, too! They'll know they're not alone!" She pounded again. "There's power in the truth! I believe that. . . . Please . . . please, don't do this!"

But Summer was already gone.

CHAPTER FIFTY-FIVE

7:40 P.M.

She had to find a way out, and she had to do it quickly. Miranda tried the door again, jiggling the knob, assessing the strength of the lock. Deadbolt, newly installed by the look of the hardware.

She moved her gaze over the door. Four panel. She thumped her fist on the wood. Solid, not hollow core.

Still, she had to try. She reared back and in the way she was trained to do, kicked it. She landed a good blow; pain shot up her leg. The wood didn't give. She tried again, same place. Again, nothing but pain.

Her legs would give out before the door did.

She turned to the room's single window. Break it and climb out. Miranda crossed to it, knowing it wouldn't be that simple. She lifted the shade. Overgrown shrubbery blocking the view out—and in. Window nailed shut, burglar bars. Dammit.

She wasn't getting out, but she could call for help.

She crossed to the dresser, removed a drawer, dumping its few contents on the bed, then returned with it to the window. She hoisted the drawer and with a mighty swing, connected with the glass. It cracked but didn't give. She swung again and this time the window exploded, pieces of glass flying in every direction.

The night air wafted in, with it the pungent smell of weed. Miranda froze, her mind tumbling back in time.

Headlights slicing across the road. Her, jumping up and down, waving her arms, praying the driver would stop.

He did, pulling to a stop at the side of the road. He lowered his window; the smell of pot rushed over her in a cloud.

She saw his face clearly now, a young Richard Stark.

"Need a ride?" he asked.

She shook her head, forcing back the memory, holding on to the here and now and her predicament. Someone—or several someones, were out there, having themselves a little party. She had to get them to come to the window.

"Help!" she called. "Please, somebody . . . I need help!"

A moment ticked past, then several more. She tried again. "Please, I just need your help. I'm trapped in here and can't get out!"

Miranda waited. Nothing, absolute quiet. Even the smell of the marijuana seemed to evaporate. She wanted to cry. She was too late, too far behind Summer to hope to stop her.

Then a rustling came from the bushes, a mumbled curse followed by a face peering through branches. A young man with unruly hair and bloodshot eyes. He looked to be about twenty and wore a Pink Floyd T-shirt.

"Thank God you heard me."

He shimmied free of the branches. "Yo," he said. "What's up?"

Miranda wanted to laugh; she wanted to cry. "I'm locked in here and can't get out. Can you help me? It's an emergency."

He stared at her a moment as if looking at some form of alien life. This is your brain on drugs, she thought. "Go around to the front door. My friend Summer, she's sure to have a key hidden somewhere."

He cocked his head, eyes drooping. "That's messed up."

"No . . . no, it's not. It's—"

He grabbed the burglar bars and tugged. They popped right out of the masonry, obviously rusted out.

Miranda stared in disbelief. Leave it to a stoner to find the no-brainer solution. "Oh, my God, thank you! You saved my life!"

"Cool." He wobbled slightly. "Gotta bounce."

"Wait! Can I borrow your phone real quick?"

In a different situation, his perplexed expression would have made her laugh out loud.

He dug in his pocket, then held it out. "FYI, it's out of juice."

"What?"

"Juice," he repeated slowly, as if she was the one operating on a different plane. "You can still borrow it, if you want."

"That's okay. Thanks, man, I appreciate all the help."

She watched him fight his way back through the shrubbery, then hoisted herself onto the window ledge and hopped to the ground. As she did a branch caught in her hair, throwing her off balance. She landed sideways in a holly bush. She righted herself, recalling another night, another desperate race for help. The memory filled her head.

Cathy's screams sounded in her head.

Sobbing, she stumbled through the underbrush, branches and thorns tearing at her bare legs. She tripped on a root and went skidding forward, landing on her hands and knees, pain shooting up her arms . . .

Miranda righted herself, picked her way free, and ran for her car. Crazily, she could still hear Cathy's screams. All these years later and she was still screaming.

She had to save her. This time she wouldn't fail.

Summer hadn't confiscated her car keys; no doubt she hadn't expected her to get this far. Miranda unlocked the vehicle and slid in. This wasn't about saving Ian Stark's life or even Buddy's, it was about saving her friend's. Summer . . . Cathy, deserved peace. And killing two more people in an act of vengeance wasn't going to give it to her.

Miranda unlocked her console and checked for her backup weapon. She stared it a moment, heart thundering. Could she use it against Summer? To save two corrupt men that in every way but one, had killed her first?

Yes. If she had to. Because it was the right thing to do and if she took the lesser path, she'd be no better than they.

She cranked the engine and tore away from the curb. Buddy? Or Ian? Who would Summer have gone after first?

Buddy, she decided. Praying she was making the right choice, she affixed her beacon light to her roof and flew.

CHAPTER FIFTY-SIX

8:25 P.M.

Miranda reached Buddy's ranch-style home in less than five minutes. No vehicle in the drive; home was dark, shades were drawn. She pulled into the drive, her blue and red light rotating crazily, turning the quiet night into a carnival.

And just like that, she was fifteen again, Clint Wheeler behind the wheel of his HPD cruiser, her in the back, craning her neck to see the spot where she'd stumbled out of the woods, trying to memorize it as it disappeared from sight, praying she didn't puke.

Wheeler met her eyes in the rearview mirror. "Back there, you asked me why I wouldn't listen to you. It's because you're a liar, Randi Rader. You've proved that a hundred times over. And some cats don't change their spots."

Not anymore, she wasn't. Miranda retrieved the gun from the glove box and checked it—full magazine, bullet chambered—and climbed out of her car. Not a liar, a victim, or a scared teenage girl.

She moved her gaze up and down the street. Summer's car was nowhere in sight but that didn't mean she wasn't here.

But neither was Buddy's. Could be in the garage.

Could be he was at work, called in for one thing or another. Maybe on an emergency call to President Stark's residence.

She started up the front walk. A real possibility. Summer went to Stark's and had him call Buddy and lure him over. Take care of both men at the same time. She hoped to God she was wrong.

She had to make sure.

Miranda peered through the sidelight. A faint glow, coming from the kitchen. No sign of life. She tried the door; the knob turned and her heart sank. Buddy would never leave his door open.

She nudged it the rest of the way and entered, gun out, swinging left then right. "Summer," she called, "it's Miranda. Let's talk about this."

A muffled moan came from the kitchen.

Buddy.

She found him bound to a chair at the table, shirt and pants soaked with blood. His mouth was taped with a single strip of plastic tape, LIAR written in bold black. On the blood-smeared table lay a notebook and pen, also bloodied.

"Buddy!" Miranda cried and ran to him. He'd been shot once in the chest. She checked the wound, saw it didn't look life threatening, and grabbed a dishtowel. She pressed it to the wound to stem the flow of blood, then turned her attention to the next most urgent thing.

"This is going to hurt," she said. She loosened an edge of the tape and pulled.

Buddy gasped, then sucked in a lungful of air.

"Sorry," she said, working on the sailor's knot. "You'll be free in a moment." Miranda peeled away the rope, then grabbed him as he started to slide off the chair. As carefully as possible, she eased him onto his back on the floor.

"Hold this." She took his hand and placed it on the towel. "Keep pressure on—"

"St . . . ar . . . star . . ."

"Pressure," she repeated, holding his hand in place. "I want to feel you try. C'mon, Buddy, you know the drill."

He finally responded and she shifted her focus. "Your phone, Buddy. Where's your phone?"

"Star . . . k. She's . . . gone . . . to—"

"I know, but I'm not leaving you. Not until I know help's on the way. Where's your phone?"

She followed the direction of his eyes. She saw it, on the floor, by the refrigerator. She snatched it up; called emergency dispatch. "This is HPD Detective Miranda Rader. Officer down, I repeat, officer down at four-sixteen Hollygrove. Chief Buddy Cadwell."

She turned and found him gazing at her, face etched with pain and eyes filled with regret. "Don't, Buddy. Save your strength. You're not going anywhere. We'll have plenty of time to catch up."

Tears filled his eyes and Miranda wondered if he was just now realizing his life was never going to be the same.

She heard the sound of sirens and tucked his phone into her pocket. "You'll be okay. Paramedics will be here any minute."

"Go," he managed. "Save . . . him."

"I will," she said. "But first, I've got to save her."

CHAPTER FIFTY-SEVEN

9:10 P.M.

Miranda had called for backup on her way to Catherine and Ian Stark's home; she half-expected to find it surrounded by police already. Instead, light glowed reassuringly from the curtained windows as if it was any other night at the president's home; Summer's blue Ford Focus sat in the drive, looking for all the world like nothing more than a friend had stopped by for a visit.

Miranda parked directly behind the Focus and climbed out of her vehicle. A squad car would be here any minute. That gave her precious little time to save Summer from more blood on her hands.

If Stark wasn't dead already.

He wasn't, Miranda told herself. That would be too easy. Just as Summer had wanted more from Buddy, she wanted something more from Stark, as well.

If history held, Summer had gone right to the front door. She was a local business owner; perhaps she had portrayed herself to Stark and his wife as a friend? One who had come with information about their son's killer?

Stark would have invited her right in, practically rolling out the red carpet for her.

Would the door be unlocked? Probably not. Unless

Summer had taken control of the situation right away, pulling her gun, herding them to the kitchen.

Miranda made her way up the front walk. It wasn't so late that the streets were quiet—cars rolled regularly past, students on their way to and from, some in a group, others alone, weighted down by their loaded backpacks. No one would look twice at the woman casually approaching President Stark's front door.

She reached it and peered through the sidelight at the empty entryway. She tried the door, found it locked, and swore softly. With a quick glance over her shoulder, she broke the glass with her elbow.

She reached inside, unlocked the door, and slipped inside. Summer's voice, coming from deeper in the house. Stark was alive; she wasn't too late.

Miranda eased the gun from her waistband, praying she didn't have to use it. She followed her friend's voice, moving as quietly as she could, not wanting to propel Summer to action.

Summer's voice grew louder. Light spilling out of a doorway dead ahead. Miranda pressed herself against the wall and listened.

"The pen, you son of a bitch. Pick it back up. Now."

Miranda reached the doorway, peered around the jamb. Stark, like Buddy, tied to a kitchen chair, the taped proclamation across his mouth, eyes wide and terrified. Unlike Buddy, Stark had only one arm tied behind his back.

Summer stood beside him, a gun aimed at his head. "Sign it."

A confession, Miranda realized. That's why there'd been a spiral notebook and pen on Buddy's kitchen table as well.

She'd had both men write a confession.

Unfortunately, it appeared Ian Stark didn't want to sign his.

"You're the worst, you know that?" Summer all but spat. "Because you allowed it. You supported it. You created the monster."

Stark looked up at her, silently pleading. Summer's cheeks turned an angry red. "You think that's going to make a difference? Did it make a difference when I pleaded with you? You didn't care about me, about what your son did to me. Pick up the damn pen, sign your name, or I'm going to blow your brains out."

He whimpered and shook his head, making a sound, deep in his throat.

Summer's eyes narrowed, and Miranda firmed her grip on the weapon, recognizing that Summer meant what she said. Miranda didn't want to shoot her friend, but she would if she had to.

Summer clucked her tongue. "What are you trying to tell me, President Stark? That your wife created the monster? And here I thought she was like me, just another victim. That's why I chose tonight, Catherine's regular Guild night with the girls, so she wouldn't have to see this. I thought she'd suffered enough." She nudged him with the gun. "Was I wrong? Should I wait for Catherine to arrive home? Include her in our little party? Just like your son, I came prepared. I have plenty of tape and bullets."

He shook his head again, this time violently.

"Okay then, last chance, Dr. Frankenstein—" She pressed the barrel to his temple. "Sign it."

Miranda held her breath, gripping the butt of her gun, hands as steady as a rock. Five seconds, she thought, and counted down—four . . . three . . . two—

Stark went for the pen, hand shaking so badly

Miranda wondered if his signature would even be legible. He scrawled his name and as the pen slipped from his fingers, Miranda swung into the doorway. "Drop your weapon, Summer. Step away from President Stark."

Summer glanced over, looking unperturbed. "You got free. Considering past experience, I guess I should have planned on that."

"I need you to lower your weapon and step away from President Stark. I don't want to hurt you, but I will if I have to."

Summer snorted. "You'd shoot me to save this piece of garbage? C'mon, Randi, the world would be a better place without him."

Miranda didn't blink. "That's not for either of us to decide."

"So who will? The courts? The police? People in power, ones like Stark here and Cadwell?" She shook her head. "Nope, no more. They don't get away with this. Maybe if enough women get the guts to take the law into their own—"

"No," Miranda said, cutting her off. "Violence to combat violence doesn't work. Stand up for themselves, yes. Things can change. And they will." Miranda lowered her voice, coaxing. "But not this way." She took a step forward. "Please, Summer, it's not too late."

"You have no idea what I'm doing."

"I think I do. You had them write confessions, didn't you?"

"Yes." She smiled slightly, pleased. "It made so much more sense than just killing them. Every detail of how they covered up the truth. It's all there, Randi. All of it!"

"Good," Miranda said soothingly. "It's done, then. You've won. Give me the gun."

A cell phone sounded from Summer's pocket. "That

one's yours," she said. "Probably Jake again. He's been trying to reach you. He's called three times. Maybe you better talk to him?"

Gun still trained on Stark, Summer took the device from her pocket and tossed it to Miranda. "But be careful, my friend. Don't say the wrong thing."

Miranda caught it, brought it to her ear. "Jake," she said, sounding out of breath. "What's up?"

"Miranda?" She heard the frown in his voice. "Are you okay?"

"I'm good. Why?"

"I've been trying to reach you. Where've you been?"

"Tied up. I'm with Summer now."

A moment of dead silence. "Miranda, she's the one. Get away from her as quickly as—"

"Yes, I know. You had a good day?"

Again, a moment of silence. "With Jones's help I took a look at the print evidence again. The partial from the clipping was a match to one taken from the water bottle. Nobody cross-referenced the two."

"Interesting." She glanced at Summer from the corner of her eyes.

"Going on your theory it was the other girl from that night, I narrowed the ages—"

Summer was looking at her strangely, so she cut him off. "Your mom's okay?" Conversational tone. Like she didn't have a care in the world.

"I went to Baton Rouge instead, to the office of Alcohol and Tobacco Control. To acquire a permit for a liquor license, you have to be fingerprinted. And bingo, we got a—"

The sound of sirens from outside, growing closer. "Give me the phone, Miranda. Time to say good-bye."

Jake obviously heard the command, because he sounded panicked. "Call nine-one-one, now."

"Done already. Gotta go. Summer's anxious to finish our chat."

"Miranda, don't—"

"Hang up," Summer interjected. "Now."

"Good-bye, Jake."

She ended the call, held out the phone for Summer.

"Keep it."

Miranda frowned. "I don't understand—"

"I didn't think so." She smiled slightly. "Jake's one of the good guys, isn't he?"

"This is over, Summer." The sirens screaming, right out front. "Let me have the gun, Summer. It'll be better if I have it."

Summer didn't move. "You know what you said earlier? About letting it go? To just let it go and forgive?"

"Please! Give me the—"

"You were right. I'm tired of hating. I'm tired of hurting."

"I know. You helped me let go." The sound of the front door crashing open; the thunder of footfalls. Miranda held out her free hand. "You saved me. Now, please, let me save you."

"I think you already have. Thank you, Randi."

As a half dozen officers stormed the room, Summer turned the gun on herself and fired.

EPILOGUE

One night in June

Spring became summer. In the weeks and months that had passed since that night at Ian Stark's, the wheels of justice had turned. Once Summer's story became public, women who had been victimized by Richard Stark had begun to come forward. A lot of women. Some—like Jessie Lund—students who had put their trust in the university and a man they looked up to as a mentor; others—like Paula Gleason—who had been fooled by appearances but decided to cut their losses for fear of being stigmatized; and still others—like Miranda and Summer—who had simply been young, foolish, and in the wrong place at the wrong time.

Miranda had spent many a night crying for them—and for the friend she had lost. Through it all, she'd had Jake to hold onto and her brother to lean on. And Summer's final words—that Miranda had saved her—to cherish.

Miranda stepped out into the hot, still night. The screen door slapped shut behind her. Muggy and as close as a tick on a retriever, she thought, lifting her hair off her neck, hoping to catch a stirring of breeze.

It turned out Summer wasn't the only victim Ian

Stark had paid off for her silence. And not the only one
Buddy had used his position to intimidate. Miranda
had gone straight to the Sheriff's Department with the
signed confessions. Buddy had resigned and Ian Stark
had been stripped of his position. Both would be going to jail, although Buddy, as a public servant, sworn
to uphold the law, would serve a much bigger sentence
than Stark. Ironic, considering—as Summer said—that
Stark fed the monster he could have stopped at any
time.

She turned her gaze to the U-Haul trailer parked in
her drive, ready to be packed in the morning. She'd
always promised herself she would leave this place and
head to the west coast, start a new life there.

Then why did fulfilling that promise feel so wrong?

"Couldn't sleep?"

She glanced over her shoulder at Jake, wearing
nothing but gym shorts, his hair mussed from sleep.
"Nope."

He came up behind her and drew her back against
his chest, arms encircling her. As the officer with the
most seniority on the force, he'd been offered the position of temporary chief of the HPD. He'd accepted but
with no promise of running for the permanent gig.

It depended on her, he'd said. On whether she had
room for him in her life out in California.

"You've got a big day tomorrow. Maybe give it another try?"

A lump formed in her throat, a realization with it. The
reason she hadn't been able to sleep for nights running,
the reason she'd felt more dread than excitement about
this day coming. She pictured Robby and his wife waving good-bye the night before, remembered little Chrissy's arms around her neck, and her mother's tears.

Miranda turned in his arms and met his eyes. "I'm not going."

"To bed?"

"Tomorrow. To California. I'm returning the trailer first thing in the morning."

He searched her gaze. "It kills me to say it, but I'm not going to let you stay. I don't want you to always look back and wonder what could have been. It's your dream, Miranda."

"Was my dream," she corrected. "It's not anymore."

"Don't do this because of us."

"I'm not." A smile touched her mouth. "I just realized . . . I always wanted to leave this place because I wanted to change me. Start fresh, be someone else. But I've done that, Jake. I moved on without running away."

She thought of Robby, of how she was enjoying getting to know him and his family. Of her mother's continued path back to health, both emotional and physical—and how rewarding it had been to be by her side, helping her.

"You're sure?"

"I am."

"You quit your job."

"I did."

"I'm pretty tight with the chief. I could see about having you reinstated."

"I have another idea." She looked up at him. "I was thinking about turning the Toasted Cat into a coffeehouse. Serve a little food and wine, too. I'd call it Summer's Place."

He rested his forehead against hers. "She would've liked that."

Miranda pictured her friend, not as she'd been

that last night, but on that first night, smiling back at Miranda, excited to be alive and about the future.

Excited about the future. The way Miranda felt right now. "I think so, too. I think she'd like it a lot."

Miranda caught Jake's hand, laced their fingers. "How about we go back to bed? I've got a big day tomorrow."